KILLER
KNOTS

A Bad Hair Day Mystery

KILLER KNOTS

NANCY J. COHEN

Kensington Publishing Corp.
http://www.kensingtonbooks.com

ISBN-13: 978-0-7582-1227-6
ISBN-10: 0-7582-1227-5

First hardcover printing: December 2007
First mass market printing: November 2008

10 9 8 7 6 5 4 3 2 1

Printed in the United States of America

Dedication

*To my friends and family, for the memories of all the
good times we've shared.*

*And to the hard working crews on cruise ships everywhere,
who make our voyages seem like paradise.*

Acknowledgments

There are always people to thank for inspiration, encouragement, and research in writing a book. Besides gratitude to my family for putting up with my writer's angst, my editor and agent for allowing me to continue Marla's adventures, and my critique group whose advice is always accurate, I'd also like to thank the following individuals:

Nancy Ann Gazo, an avid reader and aspiring writer, for the original book title.

Cynthia Thomason, multipublished author and critique partner, for the plot premise.

Barbara Dion, art auctioneer, Fort Lauderdale, Florida, for sharing her experiences aboard cruise ships. The information she offered was invaluable in giving me the necessary background to create the story.

Roxanne Hedlund, hairstylist at Who Does Your Hair Salon in Plantation, Florida, for the stingray adventure details.

Christine Jackson, Ph.D., Professor, Division of Humanities, Nova Southeastern University, for suggesting a triptych and for her expert critiques that continue to make my books stronger.

10-Night Caribbean Cruise Itinerary
Tropical Sun

Day	Ports of Call	Arrive	Depart	Excursion
Saturday	Miami, Florida		5:00 P.M.	
Sunday	At Sea			
Monday	San Juan, Puerto Rico	2:00 P.M	10:00 P.M.	
Tuesday	St. Thomas, U.S.V.I.	8:00 A.M.	6:00 P.M.	
Wednesday	Philipsburg, St. Maarten	8:00 A.M.	5:00 P.M.	
Thursday	At Sea			
Friday	George Town, Grand Cayman	7:00 A.M.	5:00 P.M.	
Saturday	Roatan, Honduras	9:00 A.M.	5:00 P.M.	
Sunday	Cozumel, Mexico	8:00 A.M.	7:00 P.M.	
Monday	At Sea			
Tuesday	Miami, Florida	7:00 A.M.		

Tropical Sun Deck Plan

Deck 1   Medical center, gangway

Deck 2   Movie theater, conference center

Deck 3   Pirate's Grotto, lower level; photo gallery; Mariner's Martini Bar; Balboa dining room; Meridian showroom, lower level

Deck 4   Pirate's Grotto, upper level; casino; salsa bar; Nautilus Lounge; Magellan dining room; Meridian showroom, upper level

Deck 5   Promenade Mall, Hook's Champagne Bar, Coronado dining room, Deadeye Dick's Pub, Guest Relations, Sailaway Lounge, Cargo Café

Deck 6   Cabins, business services

Deck 7   Cabins, library, art gallery

Deck 8   Marla and Vail's cabin, Internet Café

Deck 9   Kate and John's cabin

Deck 10 Cabins

Tropical Sun Deck Plan (cont.)

Deck 11 Outrigger Café, fitness center and spa, pools, solarium, Scuppers Steak House, Shanghai Chen's, Bridge view, ice cream bar

Deck 12 Teen and children's centers with disco and video arcade, sun deck, cigar room, card room, jogging, Ballast Beer Garden

Deck 13 Sports court, golf

Deck 14 Starlight Lounge

Deck 15 Galaxy chapel

CHAPTER 1

"**A**re you sure I won't get seasick?" Marla Shore asked her fiancé as they approached the Port of Miami via a bridge over the Intracoastal. Squinting at the white ships lining the pier like ducks on parade, she felt a twinge of queasiness in her stomach. Hopefully, her first Caribbean cruise wouldn't be her last.

"These big ships have stabilizers," Dalton Vail replied, focused on his driving. "It'll probably be so smooth you won't even notice we're on the water."

The handsome detective spared her a glance. He wouldn't admit to being excited, but she saw the spark in his gray eyes. She looked forward to sharing this experience with him and his fourteen-year-old daughter.

From the backseat, Brianna tapped Marla on the shoulder. "Look, there's the *Tropical Sun*! Can you see it?" The teen had talked about nothing but their trip for the past few weeks.

"It has their signature lounge on top," Marla pointed out, admiring the massive vessel's sleek lines. Her attention shifted. "Do you have enough cash for parking?" she asked Dalton as he followed signs to the garage. "It's twelve dollars a day."

"They take credit cards. Why don't you and Brie get off here with the luggage? The cruise terminal is straight ahead. I'll meet you at the entrance." After he pulled up to the curb, he helped them unload before jumping back behind the wheel and zooming away.

Marla grimaced as a stiff sea breeze blew wisps of her carefully coiffed hair about her face. Her hairstylist skills would come in handy on this voyage. Rummaging in her purse, she withdrew a few bills for the porter, who checked their bags.

"Where do we go now?" Brianna said, confusion muddling her brown eyes. She wore her toffee hair in a ponytail along with the standard teenage garb of jeans and a camisole top.

"Let's wait for your father."

Charter buses pulled up to the curb along with yellow taxicabs and a shiny metal Sysco supply truck. Cops wearing neon green vests directed the traffic that added to the noise level. Seagulls squawked. Engines idled. Porters shouted. Airplanes roaring overhead made Marla's blood pound in her ears.

Who said cruises were restful vacations? Mingling with three thousand other passengers doesn't fit my dream of a tropical getaway.

Diesel fumes warmed by the summer sun mixed with the aroma of hot dogs from a nearby vendor. A passenger next to her crunched on a potato chip, his ample belly filling his shorts and flowered shirt.

Oh joy. Eleven days to gain weight at endless buffets. It's a good thing my new salon will offer spa services in addition to the usual hair treatments. I'll be their first customer.

Marla knew Dalton was looking forward to the meals. He'd pored over the dining-room pictures in the brochure. Same for Brianna, whose growing stage made her continually hungry. Marla was more interested in checking out the shops and lounging by the pool. Forget the onboard salon. She'd take a peek, but that was one place she wanted to avoid on her vacation.

As Vail hustled across the street, she watched him with pride. His broad shoulders filled the Tommy Bahama black shirt she'd given him for Father's Day. Even with the silver peppering his ebony hair, his distinguished appearance made female heads turn in appreciation. She hoped this cruise would bring them closer together as a family.

"Let's go inside," he said, taking charge.

At the door, a uniformed official checked their passports and ushered them into the terminal. They entered the line for U.S. citizens and shuffled along like sheep in a herd until they reached the counter. Vail collected their papers and submitted their passports, cruise tickets, and credit cards for their onboard credit accounts.

"How does my hair look?" Marla asked before she grinned in front of a mini camera that snapped her photo. Just getting to the ship was an ordeal. She couldn't wait to get settled.

In the next room, another attendant handed them each a room-key card, which they signed on the back. Brianna's eyes bulged when she realized she'd be able to charge her own purchases.

"All right! I hope I meet kids my age to hang out with on the ship." Brianna stuffed the card into her Nine West purse.

"You will, honey," Marla said, giving her an indulgent smile. "They have an excellent teen program. You'll have your own activities and even your own newsletter every day."

"Over here," Vail said, directing them to the security detail. Like at the airport, they had to pass their carry-on bags through an X-ray machine while they walked through the gates. After they cleared, a guard waved them toward an up escalator. A long metal walkway open to the breeze awaited them at the top. Shaded by a blue awning, it led to the gangway onto the ship itself. But first they had to get past the pair of photographers who captured a quick picture of them in front of a *Tropical Sun* welcome aboard poster.

"I wonder how much that photo will cost," Marla remarked. She shivered with excitement as they crossed a plank over a short expanse of water. Once on the ship, they had to present their key cards. A crew member swept each card through a machine that brought up their photo ID. Marla noticed a dispenser of liquid hand sanitizer just beyond. Great; they'd need it to prevent norovirus.

"At last," she said, once they were free to find their room. She glanced at the bank of elevators, the wide carpeted stairway, and two long corridors flanking either side of the ship. "Where is our cabin, port or starboard?" she asked Vail, relying on his sense of direction.

"We're starboard on deck eight," he replied. "That's on the right side of the ship facing forward. I usually remember because port has four letters same as left." He nodded at the crowd waiting in front of the elevators. "It'll be a few minutes before the mob clears."

"We can take the stairs." Wondering why he peered around as though expecting someone, Marla put her foot forward just as she spotted an auburn-haired woman waving at them. She'd come off the down elevator, accompanied by a tall man with receding hair, eyeglasses, and a broad grin.

"Dalton! Brianna!" The lady descended upon them, spreading her arms wide.

"Grandma," Brie responded, rushing into the older woman's embrace while Marla stared.

Grandma? Don't tell me Dalton's parents are here. Her vision wavered. She felt as though the floor had opened beneath her, and she'd dropped into Wonderland. Why did no one else act surprised? Dumbfounded, she stood there like a statue.

"You think we'd pay for your cruise and not come along for the ride?" Brianna's grandmother said. "Besides, we wanted to meet Marla. At the rate your father is dragging his feet regarding a wedding date, this may be our only chance."

She grasped Marla's stiff hand. "We're delighted to meet you. I'm Kate, and this is John. Or call us Mom and Dad."

Vail hugged his father. "Dad, I figured you'd be looking for us down here."

Marla stood back, struggling to comprehend. Dalton had known his folks would be on the cruise, and he hadn't said a word? True, Kate and John had treated them to the vacation. Presumably the elder couple meant to smooth things over after Dalton's former in-laws created a strain between them. But if Dalton's folks were anything like Pam's parents, she'd plotz!

Not to worry. Kate and John flew in from Maine. They'll have plenty to do on the cruise.

And she really should forgive Justine and Larry, who still mourned Pam's death. It wasn't easy for them to accept Marla as a potential stepmother for their granddaughter.

Kate linked her arm with Marla's. "You're prettier in person than in your picture," Kate said with a warm smile. "I can't wait to get to know you, but I'm sure you and Dalton would like to unpack. We'll take Brie to our cabin. Her suitcase is already there."

Vail frowned. "Huh? Why would it have been sent to your stateroom?"

"I guess you didn't notice that her room number is different from yours. She's staying with us so you and Marla can have some privacy. I hope that's okay with you, sweetheart."

Brianna's expression took on a devilish gleam. "Sure, I have my own key anyway. As long as you agree that I don't have a curfew." She cast her father a smug grin.

"Now just a minute," he began.

Vail's dad made a dismissive gesture. "Let it go, son. Brie can't get lost on the ship, and she'll have a better time if she hooks up with some young people." He exchanged a knowing look with Marla that made her like him already.

"We'll catch up to you guys later," Kate told Marla, then squeezed her elbow.

Kate was certainly a touchy-feely person, Marla thought, appreciating how she appeared totally different from Justine, Pam's mother. It might not be so bad having her future in-laws on board after all. Wanting to accommodate Brianna, she turned her attention to the teen.

"Are you certain you're all right with this, honey? You know you're welcome to stay with us. We want to spend time with you, and—"

"She'll be fine." Kate wrapped an arm around the girl's shoulder. "Take your time exploring the ship. We sail at five; then we have the lifeboat drill before dinner. We'll meet up with you in the dining room."

After trudging up the stairs, Marla and Vail sought their cabin. Feeling like a conditioned laboratory rat, she followed the coral carpet down a brightly lit corridor that seemed to stretch to infinity. Brass plates displayed room numbers, and when they reached theirs, Marla noticed an envelope tucked into a seashell decoration by the door.

"Look at this," she said, showing Dalton the scrawl that addressed the message to Martha Shore. "Someone must've spelled my name wrong." After sticking it inside her purse, she unlocked the door to their cabin. "Yikes, my closet at home is bigger than this place!" Plopping her bags on the floor, she surveyed their home for the next week. There was barely enough space for their suitcases, let alone her and Dalton.

A queen-sized bed stood against the opposite wall, where a wide picture window showed a view of the pier. Other furnishings included a small nightstand, a desk that served as a dresser with drawers, a desk chair, and a small love seat facing a television mounted on a ledge.

She noticed Dalton eyeing the TV and said, "If I'm going to lose you to sports games, you can find me on the pool deck." Upon peering in the bathroom, she added, "Hey, look in here. If you turn around when you brush your teeth, you'll be taking a shower."

Vail excused himself to use the facilities while she examined a pile of papers on their bed: the *Tropical Tattler* newsletter, announcements about a preview art auction, gift shop flyers, and spa treatment specials. Always on the lookout for bargains, she stuffed them in her purse to read later and turned to her carry-on bag to remove her cosmetics.

From the bathroom, she heard a thump, followed by an explosive whoosh and a loud curse. The detective emerged looking shaken. "Jeez, if you sit on that thing when you flush, you risk losing some vital body parts. They aren't kidding when they say to close the lid first."

Marla laughed, then put her things down on the bed and walked over to kiss him soundly. "I can see one benefit to this cabin. We'll have to snuggle closer." They spent a few minutes doing just that until a knock sounded outside the door.

"Hello, my name is Jovanny," said their cabin steward, a short young man with a swarthy complexion. "May I assist you with luggage?" Their suitcases had arrived. Marla and Vail stood by while Jovanny dragged the luggage inside. "Your cruise guide will tell you what goes on each day," Jovanny said, with a flashy grin, while Marla strained to understand him. He spoke as though he had a wad of cotton in his mouth. "Today we have lifeboat drill at five-thirty. Life jackets are in closet. Your station is deck seven, C-4. Okay, lady and gentleman? If you need anything else, please call me on telephone."

As soon as he left, she returned to unpacking her bag. A loudspeaker blared, making her jump.

Ding dong, ding dong.

"Attention, all passengers," announced a deep male voice from a console on the desk. "According to SOLAS, International Convention for the Safety of Life at Sea, we are required to hold a lifeboat drill within twenty-four hours of sailing. When you hear seven short blasts and one long blast, this is the signal to proceed to your lifeboat assembly station. There will be no eating or drinking during this exercise. This is a mandatory drill even if you have cruised with us before."

The man's voice droned on, issuing further instructions, but Marla closed him out. She'd opened the envelope addressed to Martha Shore and pulled out a piece of paper inside. Narrowing her eyes, she stared at the typewritten words:

I know what you did and I have what you want.

Her blood chilled. Who would send this weird message?

She'd done a few bad things in her life, but mostly they'd been resolved. No one on board could possibly know about the erotic pictures she'd posed for when she was nineteen. That hadn't been the best moment in her life, but she'd needed the money to pay for an attorney after Tammy had drowned in a backyard pool. As her babysitter, Marla had been held accountable by the toddler's parents. She'd finally put the tragedy to rest, so why would it rear its ugly head now? Nah, this had to be a mistake.

"What's wrong?" Vail asked, giving her a curious glance. He'd started hanging up his suit jackets.

"Look at this note." She thrust it at him.

Scanning the words, he scowled. "Gotta be some sort of joke."

"Or it's been sent to the wrong person." Flushing with guilt, she grabbed the paper and tossed it into a drawer. Nothing would ruin her vacation. "Forget about it," she said. "Let's explore the ship. I'd like to make sure Brie is happy with her arrangements."

Vail opted for a snack, so they headed for the Outrigger Café on deck eleven. Unsure of where to go, Marla suggested they follow the trail of people holding drink cups. They found the dining room with several buffet lines, and Vail filled his plate with a juicy hamburger, French fries, pasta salad, and herb-roasted chicken, while Marla allowed herself coffee and fruit.

"How can you eat so much? It's nearly time for dinner," she said, sipping the brew.

"Don't worry, I'll be hungry again," Vail answered, his mouth full. "How's the coffee?"

"Rich and robust, with no bitter aftertaste. I saw a notice alongside the dispenser that says the brand is Hair Raiser. They must have the concession throughout the ship."

His eyebrows lifted. "I hope that isn't a portent since you do hair for a living."

You and me both, pal. This is one week where I want to lie out and catch the sun, not help you catch killers. "Maybe I should serve the stuff in my salon. I'll look it up on the Internet when I get a chance."

After bolstering their energy, they strolled outside to preview the pool, Jacuzzis, and solarium. Then they went indoors to ride the glass elevator down and ended up by Hook's Champagne Bar on deck five. Marla stared at the nine-story central atrium in confusion.

"How did we miss the salon, spa, and fitness center?" she asked. "Weren't they on the same deck as the pool?"

"I don't know. They could be at the other end. We need to look at a diagram." A couple of long blasts on the ship's horn sounded. "Forget it, we're about to cast off. Let's take the elevator back up."

Completely disoriented, Marla pointed to the carpet on their way aloft. "It's a good thing the design tells you what day it is. I could easily lose track of time here."

"I wonder if they change the carpet at midnight."

"You can stay and watch. I'll be too tired tonight."

As soon as she stepped outdoors into the afternoon July sun, she felt the vibration increase and realized the ship had begun moving. Jostling for a position by the rail, she felt a rush of excitement. She watched the pier recede before they entered the outlet leading to open sea.

Strains of "Hot Hot Hot," played from a steel band by the pool, where a costumed man on stilts led a line dance. Waiters hawked strawberry piña coladas as the drink of the day while the ship glided past Parrot Jungle Island, a fleet of anchored sailboats, cars racing by on the causeway, and mansions fronting the Intracoastal. A Jet Ski skipped along the water as the *Tropical Sun* neared the last strip of sand.

Marla tilted her head back, enjoying the fresh air and the warm sun that kissed her skin. They were embarking on a grand adventure, and her final view of the shoreline came with the realization that they'd have more than a week free from phone calls, work hassles, and chores.

Ding dong, ding dong.

"Good afternoon, ladies and gentlemen," boomed a male voice on the public address system. "This is Captain Rick Larsen speaking to you from the bridge. Our mandatory assembly drill begins shortly. When you hear the emergency signal, please proceed to your assembly stations with your life jackets. Staterooms and public areas will be checked to ensure that all guests have exited these locations. Smoking, drinking, eating, and the use of cellular phones is prohibited during the drill. Thank you for your attention and cooperation."

"Come on," Vail said, signaling. "We have to go below."

"Let's take the stairs. I need to work off all the calories I'm going to consume."

She gave a last glance at the late sun reflecting off the tall buildings of the Miami skyline. Forced activities might be the only cloud on the horizon, but she could tolerate even those if they took away the decision-making process. She'd dreamed of lying on a tropical beach with no decisions to make except which rum drink to try. That being her only goal for the cruise, she could be flexible otherwise.

Then again, she felt like a sailor at military inspection when they reported to their lifeboat assembly station. Upon their arrival on deck, a uniformed officer recorded the cabin number emblazoned on their vest fronts and directed them to join a group of passengers lined up in jagged rows. Squashed between an overweight fellow who sweated profusely and a mother of two whose youngest child wailed at loud decibels, she struggled to fasten her life vest. The bulky jacket forced her neck up at an uncomfortable angle.

Vail cursed beside her. He'd gotten himself tangled in the straps and flailed helplessly while attempting to snag the buckle. Knocking into a muscular guy in the row behind, he mumbled an apology. The fellow must have been easily over six feet tall. He wore a bandanna and tattoos like a biker dude.

"No problem, buddy," the tattooed man said with a grin.

"You have it on backward," Marla said to Vail. She bit her lip to suppress a smile. It wasn't often that she saw her fiancé at a disadvantage, and when she did, she just wanted to take care of him. She assisted him in putting the vest on correctly.

A female staff member wearing all white—blouse, skirt, shoes, and visored cap—glared at her charges. "Listen up, people." Everyone snapped to attention while she strode back and forth. "Make sure those straps are tight. Otherwise, if we have to pull you out of the water fast, we'll yank on the vest and you'll be left behind to sink like a stone. Come on, squeeze closer. This is how crowded it gets in the boat." She pointed to the vessel suspended overhead.

"Do we get to sit in the lifeboat?!" hollered one passenger.

"Sit, stand, or lie, you'll be crammed in there. Oh, and another thing, if you have to jump overboard, cross your arms in front like this. Otherwise, the jacket may hit your head upon impact."

"Oh joy. Something else to worry about," Marla murmured.

"Your automated light will flash when you enter the water," the officer continued. "It serves as a beacon. You can use the whistle to draw attention to yourself. Now, are there any questions?"

At Marla's side, Vail blew the whistle attached to his vest.

"Nice move," Marla crooned, "especially when you don't know whose mouth it touched last." She shifted her feet as she heard the familiar *ding dong, ding dong* from the loudspeaker.

"May I have your attention, please?" said a disembodied voice. "The general emergency signal that began the drill consists of seven short blasts followed by one long blast through the ship's whistle and internal alarm system. If you are in your stateroom when you hear this signal, grab some warm clothing, gather any medications you may require along with your life jacket, and proceed to your muster station. If you are not in your stateroom, go directly to your station, where in a real emergency, a life jacket will be issued to you. Do not use the elevators, as they will not work in a power failure. Lighting along the floors and stairways will show the route to the assembly stations."

Marla tuned him out, preferring not to dwell on the unpleasant possibilities. Instead, she contemplated how many times during the day these announcements would disrupt them.

Sweat dribbled between her breasts while she listened to the speaker repeat his message in several languages. "How long is this going to last?" she groused. "I'm dying from the heat."

Vail regarded her from under his thick brows. "You'll build up a good appetite for dinner. I wonder where Brie and my folks are. You don't see them, do you?" He stood on his toes to peer over the heads of taller figures.

Marla's gaze caught on a handsome older man who murmured something into his companion's ear. The woman, a blonde who looked about half his age, shrugged away. Not that it was any of her business, but she wondered if that was his wife or his daughter. She caught another person staring at the couple, a fellow with tousled dark hair, a shifty expression, and a camera with which he shot a quick photo of their profiles.

You're imagining things, she told herself. *He's probably just snapping a picture of the lifeboat beyond. People are here to have fun, and so are you.*

As soon as the ship's horn blasted the all-clear signal, she unstrapped her vest and yanked it over her head, mussing her hair. Jostled by other sweaty bodies, she proceeded indoors and followed the mob down the staircase to deck eight.

With a sigh of relief, she opened the door to their cabin and bounded inside to air-cooled comfort. "Man, is that thing bulky," she said to Vail, as they tossed their life jackets onto the bed. "We'll let the cabin steward put them away."

"I need a shower, but it's time for dinner already," Vail replied, raking a hand through his hair. He gave her a rueful glance, as though he would have liked to linger.

Hustling to the dining room, Marla despaired of having a minute free. She could end up being busier on this trip than in her salon at home. *At least you don't have to cook or wait on customers*, she thought gleefully as they were ushered to their table by the restaurant manager. Elegant white linens, vases with fresh orchids, subdued jazz music, and scores of uniformed waiters soothed her nerves as she took a seat.

"Typical of Brie to be late," Vail said in an indulgent tone. He grabbed a bread stick from a basket on the table.

"You're just eager to stuff yourself. We're the first ones here." Marla nodded at the other empty chairs. "I'm glad we have a table for ten, so we'll meet new people. Do you suppose the waiter will wait until everyone arrives to take our orders?" She glanced around the room, decorated with crystal chandeliers and floor-to-ceiling windows. "Some passengers may choose to eat in the café upstairs."

"Who knows? Can you pass the butter, please?"

As Marla complied, some of their other table companions appeared. She was startled to recognize the older couple from the lifeboat drill. Even though the newsletter indicated this evening's dress code was casual, they'd changed into fancier outfits than they'd worn on deck.

"I'm Oliver Smernoff, and this is my wife, Irene," the man said in a baritone voice. He wore a black suit that contrasted sharply with his graying temples. Most of the hair on top of his head had receded, leaving him partly bald, but his even features and tall stature made him attractive for a man in his fifties. His wife wasn't as young as she'd seemed at a distance, judging from her hands more than her face. The veins stood out on her overly tanned skin, making Marla rub her own hands and wish for lotion.

Irene attempted to smile, but her stiff facial muscles turned it into a grimace. She wore an elegant blue sheath dress and a necklace that shimmered with diamonds.

The newest arrivals, on the other hand, boasted a distinct age difference. "Thurston Stark at your service, and this is my wife, Heidi," the man boomed to Marla and Vail. He was a big guy with a confident smile, hazel eyes, and wheat-brown hair. With his broad shoulders, he might have been a football player in his earlier days. Heidi looked about thirty years younger, a typical blond trophy wife with a vapid expression. She wore a black dress so revealing that if the ship rocked, her boobs would risk tumbling out.

While Thurston and Oliver exchanged hearty greetings, their wives acknowledged each other with tepid nods. It appeared they already knew one another. Before Marla could inquire as to the nature of their acquaintance, more of their tablemates arrived.

"We're out of seats," Marla noted to Vail in an undertone. "What happened to Brie and your parents?"

"You're right." Half rising, he scanned the dining room. "I don't see them anywhere."

Marla's stomach sank. "Great, and I figured nothing could go wrong this week."

Vail gave a snort of disbelief. "The way you're a magnet for trouble, sweetcakes, we'll be lucky to get off this ship alive."

CHAPTER 2

"We're missing our companions," Vail said to the restaurant manager, a mustached fellow wearing a tuxedo. "We need to change seats so that we're at the same table with my parents and daughter." He gave their names and cabin numbers.

"I'll check my charts," the man said in a foreign accent, "but be aware the ship is fully booked, and any changes had to be made this afternoon upon arrival."

"I didn't realize there would be a problem. We reserved our cruise together. How could we have been separated?"

"Let me see what I can do, sir." Flashing a conciliatory grin, the man scampered off.

Marla touched Vail's arm. "Maybe we can find where your folks are sitting and ask someone at their table to change places. I don't understand how this could have happened."

Vail scowled. "Neither do I. Hold the fort while I go look for them, will you?"

After he left, Marla smiled at the strangers surrounding her. "There's been a mistake," she explained. "I don't think we're supposed to be at this table."

Nonetheless, she and Vail were stuck there, according to what he said when he returned. "I found Mom and Dad, but their table is full, and no one wants to move. This is ridiculous."

"Another table might free some spaces. Let the maître d' work on it." Their waiter arrived to take orders. "In the meantime, I'm starved."

Vail plopped down beside her and picked up his menu. "So am I. What are you having?"

She studied the Welcome Aboard dinner choices. "I'll start with shrimp cocktail, skip the soup course, and have the Boston lettuce salad. Then I can't decide between the sole supreme, roast duckling, or sirloin steak. Maybe I'll go with the duck since it's served with blueberry sauce. Oh gosh, look at that bread. I can't resist."

Throwing calorie counting to the winds, she gave the waiter her selections, then plucked a roll from the basket. If she walked up and down the fourteen decks enough times, maybe she'd wear off the extra pounds she was sure to gain.

"Bob, why don't you introduce us?" said a tired-looking matron from across the table. She nudged her companion, who wore a sports jacket and tie in an outdated style. His slick black hair, wire-rimmed glasses, and squinting mocha eyes gave him a nerdy look. "Fine, leave it to me," the woman snapped when he merely glanced at her. "I'm Sandy Wolfson," she told Marla, "and this is my husband, Bob."

They made a good pair, Marla thought, observing Sandy's mud-brown hair cut in limp, short layers; make-up that barely provided enough color; and dowdy pantsuit. Bulging bellies set the couple well into middle age. Oh joy, she and Dalton were seated with people who qualified for the condo crowd.

Well, not exactly. A pretty brunette occupied the

seat next to her. "Hi, my name is Betsy Marsh," the young woman said to Marla and Vail after acknowledging the others. "I'm so excited. This is my first cruise," Betsy added, with an infectious grin.

"Mine, too." Marla shot a questioning glance at the rumpled fellow sitting next to Betsy. He sat quietly, darting his eyes back and forth between them. The man's unruly black hair matched his thick eyebrows and seemed to shout defiance, same as his polka-dotted bow tie.

"Kent Harwood," he grunted as Marla realized she was staring. Was she imagining things, or had he been the man taking the photo at the lifeboat drill? No way; she must be suffering from the heat.

Take a few more olives from that relish dish. All this sea air is affecting your brain. You need to replenish your salt intake.

"I'm Marla Shore," she offered. Her table companions exchanged startled glances, as though her name meant something. "This is my fiancé, Dalton Vail."

"How interesting," Irene drawled, with a raised eyebrow. Oliver poked her, and she fell silent.

Betsy cleared her throat. "Have you ever been on a ship this size before, *Marla?*" she said, emphasizing her name. "Hello, I got lost finding the Coronado dining room."

"Tell me about it," Marla said, puzzled by their odd reactions. "We'll need at least another day to get oriented."

"You'll get used to it," Thurston replied, swiping a bread stick. "We've been on tons of cruises, so it gets to be routine. Our last trip took us down the Amazon. You haven't seen anything until you've gotten a glimpse of those piranha. And the snakes are even meaner!"

"You think? I was more impressed by the Nile," his wife, Heidi, said, pouting her ruby lips. She spoke in a little-girl voice that irritated Marla's ears.

Irene sniffed, lifting her nose. Unlike Heidi, whose copper highlights blended well with her hair, Irene's lighter tint shouted overprocessing. "With all the trips you've taken, I imagine you've been to some Caribbean ports before, darling. After all, the islands are practically in our backyard." Signaling for the wine steward who circulated among the tables, she placed an order for two bottles. "I hope you'll join us," Irene told everybody.

"Ladies and gents, can we get your photo, please?" said the ship's photographer before anyone could reply.

A costumed pirate stuck his scurvy face beside Marla's and grinned into the lens. The photographer snapped rapidly as the pirate hopped from person to person, then over to the next table. *What's next?* Marla thought. *A group picture?*

She leaned back when the waiter delivered their starter courses. As soon as they'd all been served, she tasted a morsel of shrimp cocktail, savoring the tangy sauce. "This cruise could be one of the best gifts I've ever gotten," she told Vail between bites, "except that I'll need a membership at the sports club to lose weight afterward."

"Not the Perfect Fit Sports Club, where Jolene got murdered, I hope."

His wry tone made her smile. She'd helped solve that case, to the detriment of her exercise plan. Maybe she should check out the ship's gym while on board.

Betsy jabbed her arm. "You got this cruise as a gift, too? Hello, so did I. I couldn't believe it when I opened my mail one day. Inside was the ticket along with a note of thanks for my work at the art museum. When I called the cruise line, they said it was legit."

"Tell us something we don't know," Oliver Smernoff's deep voice rumbled. "We got the same thing in the mail," he explained to Marla, wrapping an arm around his wife's chair. Irene leaned away from his dangling hand. "There wasn't any receipt or return address."

"I was blown away," chimed in Heidi, with a giggle. "Like, who would be so generous? Dearest Thurston makes such large donations to the museum, but this was totally off-the-wall."

"We all work together at the Camden Palms Museum of Art," Bob Wolfson pitched in, which made his mousy wife sit up straight. "It's a privately owned institution in Tampa. I have no clue about our unknown benefactor, despite being the museum's business manager." He spoke in a solemn tone that suited his stern countenance. You'd think he was at a meeting instead of on vacation, Marla thought, but maybe being with his colleagues wasn't his idea of fun.

Their desultory conversation was interrupted by the wine steward, who uncorked the bottles Irene had ordered. When she nodded her approval, he poured for those in their group who'd accepted a glass. Marla noted that Irene quickly downed a few gulps of cabernet sauvignon. For herself, she'd chosen chardonnay. Its cool, fruity flavor slid down her throat.

Kent Harwood spoke after the sommelier departed. His hangdog features and scruffy mien put him a slouch below the others, or maybe it was the way he glowered at them. "Beats me why I was invited on this trip, when I only work at the museum part-time," he said in a low growl. "Mr. Stark, you've been on lots of cruises. How come you tagged along?"

Thurston shrugged. "Why not? Didn't you ever hear the proverb 'Don't look a gift horse in the mouth?' Besides, we haven't been on this ship before, and we'll enjoy the art auctions." He blinked a couple of times in rapid succession, as though he had a facial tic.

"I can't wait to check out the music. How many bands do you think they have on board?" Oliver asked, looking at no one in particular.

"Shipboard music doesn't compare to your classical collection at home, Olly," Irene said with a sniff.

"So? That doesn't mean I can't enjoy it," he replied, with a quelling look in her direction.

"What about you?" Kent Harwood asked Bob Wolfson. "How did you get the week off?" Taking a toothpick from his shirt pocket, he picked his teeth, impervious to the opinions of others.

Bob scratched his jaw. "I had the hours coming to me. If I got as much time off from work as I deserve, I'd take more vacations. With my luck, it'll rain when we're in port."

Dalton and I are the only ones who don't belong here. Marla glanced at Vail, busy digging into his salad, and a wave of affection swept through her. Rarely did he have the luxury of relaxing and enjoying himself. But what a shame about his family. They'd have to catch up with Brianna and his folks later.

"What do you do at the museum?" Thurston asked Kent. "I don't recall running into you, not that I'm there that often. I'm involved with the foundation, you understand, not the day-to-day affairs." *Blink, blink.*

Kent gave him a sly glance. "I run an extermination business." Finished with his toothpick, he dropped it in his bread plate.

"Is that so? I respect that," Thurston said in a snotty tone.

"You should. I was called to flush out some palmetto bugs in the café. Did a mold inspection while I was there, too. You don't want any problems to develop because of leaks, especially where humidity control is so important."

The waiter delivered their entrées and then offered to debone Marla's duckling. She acquiesced, wishing she had the same service at home.

"Where are you from?" Betsy asked Marla, smacking her lips as she bit into a piece of steaming sole. "I am so going to have a great time this week. Gotta meet some guys, though. You two getting married soon?"

Marla nearly choked on a piece of broccoli. "W-we haven't set a date. As for where we're from, we live in Palm Haven. It's just west of Fort Lauderdale."

"No shit? I'm from Clearwater. So what's it like having a live-in? My last boyfriend ditched me before we shacked up together."

"I have my own town house," Marla replied. "This will be a second marriage for both of us. We're getting ready to move into a new home together, but Dalton has a teenage daughter, so we've been taking things slowly."

"You're from Palm Haven, eh?" Kent piped in. "What do you do there?" he asked Vail.

"I'm in the law field," Vail responded, meeting the man's appraising glance. Marla knew he didn't care to elaborate that he was a police officer.

"You didn't tell me you called an exterminator to the museum," Sandy Wolfson chided her husband. "I could have used him at home. We still have that raccoon in the attic."

"Critter Control handles that type of problem," Bob said, shoveling a piece of steak into his mouth.

"Don't give me that crap. It's typical of you to put

all your energy into work instead of our house maintenance." Sandy's eyes narrowed into slits. "How long ago did you hire this man?"

"He's been coming on a routine basis for a few months."

Thurston half rose from his chair. "Not since the, you know, that night—" He stopped when Heidi put a hand on his arm.

"The waiter is coming around, dearest. Could you please ask him to refill our bread basket?" she said in her childlike tone, batting her eyelashes.

The big man either fell for her ploy or decided to drop the subject. He complied as though accustomed to fulfilling his wife's wishes.

Marla gazed at Kent curiously. "How can you tell if there's a mold problem? I'm a hairdresser, and I'm about to move my salon to larger quarters. I never thought to check the new building for anything other than termites."

"Call in a certified inspector," Kent replied. "Molds produce toxins that can be hazardous to people exposed to them. Sometimes you'll see threadlike white substances or black circles accompanied by a musty odor. The spores themselves are invisible and will land on any moist surface. They can make you pretty sick if you're allergic."

"So what do you do during an inspection?"

He chugged down a gulp of water. "I'll take air samples and swabs. Mold is a living organism that needs moisture to survive. You have to be especially careful where you have leaks, flooding, and condensation."

Marla noticed how Bob Wolfson kept shooting furtive glances at Oliver Smernoff. Was she sensing an undercurrent of animosity there? And why did Kent strike her as being more educated than the average exterminator? Had he majored in entomology in college before opening his own company?

"So Marla," Oliver said, pointing at her like a teacher calling on a pupil—she noticed that he'd done a good job of cleaning his plate—"is this a vacation for you, or will you check out the salon while you're on board?"

"No way; I'm not going near the place. Dalton and I are just here to relax." She leaned back while the busboy, a young lad whose name tag said he came from Romania, refilled their water glasses.

"Hey listen, they're playing Mozart's string quartet number fourteen in the background," Oliver told them.

"We heard the greatest concert in Vienna," Thurston boasted in his loud voice. "You'd have appreciated it, Olly. Europe has the most amazing opera houses. You should go to the Baths of Caracalla to see *Aida*. Fabulous experience."

Marla, feeling adrift, exchanged smiles with Betsy, who cracked her knuckles under the table. "I've been lucky to get this far, never mind to Europe. If I ever cut back my hours at the salon, I'll do more traveling," she told her new friend.

As soon as she and Dalton finished dessert—he had Black Forest cake, and she'd ordered crème brûlée— Marla scraped her chair back. The waiters hovered, whisking dishes off the table so as to reset the dining room before the next horde arrived.

Maybe on another cruise, they'd ask for later seating so they wouldn't be rushed. In this instance, though, she was glad to escape from her tablemates.

"I need to go back to the cabin," she told Dalton as she rose. "If you'll excuse us," she said to the others.

"Mom said she'd save us seats at the show tonight if you don't mind waiting for the ten-thirty performance. She wants to check out the casino first," Vail said on their way upstairs.

"That suits me fine. All the shops are open now, so we can take a look. I just need to freshen up." The ship rocked underfoot, and she stumbled. Clutching the staircase railing, she realized they must be moving at a good clip. The swaying motion made her unsteady. She hadn't noticed it in the dining room, possibly because they'd been closer to the water level.

"I feel like I'm drunk," Vail said, grinning as a swell made them fumble to the left.

"It won't be like this the entire trip, will it?" Her full stomach clenched as the next dip drove them starboard. "Maybe I should take one of those Bonine capsules."

Vail slapped her on the back. "Have a few more drinks; then you won't notice."

Stopping on the next landing to catch her breath, she considered getting an exercise machine for their new home. "Did you think our dinner conversation was strange?" she asked.

"I wasn't listening."

"You were busy eating. I'm sorry about the mix-up in seating arrangements. Maybe the restaurant manager will straighten things out by tomorrow night."

"I hope so. He wasn't much help this evening."

"Betsy seems nice. I don't think we have much in common with the other people," Marla offered.

"They were fortunate to receive a free cruise ticket

from an unknown donor." He gave her an indulgent grin.

The sexy curve of his mouth and the tenderness in his eyes turned her thoughts in another direction. Hmm . . . making love while the ship swayed could be rather erotic.

Placing one foot above the other on the carpeted stairway, she resumed the climb. Her thigh muscles felt the strain. She did too much standing in place at work and not enough aerobics.

"They must have a rich patron who wants to remain anonymous. Art museums always get wealthy contributors."

"So what's bothering you?" He ran a finger inside his neck collar, making her want to loosen his shirt for him.

"For colleagues who work together, they seemed awfully uncomfortable with each other. If I didn't know better, I'd say things were tense among them."

"Well, sweetcakes, you don't know better, and if we're lucky, we'll be seated with my parents tomorrow evening."

When they reached deck eight, she couldn't remember if their room was port or starboard. Glancing at the corridors branching on either side of the elevators facing them, she hesitated. "Which way?"

"We're on that side." Vail let her cross in front of him.

Marla brushed against his torso and figured they might have a good time in the cabin until they met his parents. But when she saw another envelope tucked into the seashell decoration by their door, she dismissed that notion. "It's another message for Martha Shore," she told Vail, her stomach sinking.

"Open it," he commanded.

Inside their room, Marla ripped open the envelope and drew out a folded paper. Relief swept through her as she read the contents aloud while Vail shrugged out of his sports coat.

Please join us at the Fine Art Preview and Champagne Reception this evening at 9:00 P.M. in the Gallery, Deck 7, Forward. Don't miss this unique opportunity to preview some of the works we will have for sale and enjoy a glass of complimentary champagne. Meet Eric, your lively Auctioneer, who will explain the auction process and tell you about our artists featured during the cruise. Bring this invitation, and collect two free raffle tickets for a chance to win a five-hundred-dollar framed work of art.

"Sounds like fun," she said. "Maybe we should go. We don't have to meet your folks until after ten."

"I didn't know you were an art enthusiast." Loosening his tie, Vail approached her, his eyes gleaming with desire.

"I'm not, but it's a good chance to learn something new. Plus we might find a piece we like for our new house."

"That's true, but wouldn't you rather play a bit?" Rubbing his body against hers, he made his arousal known.

She cast a surreptitious glance at her watch. They could either make it quick, or savor each other later. Despite her wish not to get caught up in planned activities, she couldn't deny the feeling that they'd be missing an important event if they didn't attend the auction.

"We can relax after the show tonight. I didn't notice invitations on anyone else's door, although other guests probably received the flyer that was on our bed when we arrived. Maybe we received this special offer for a reason."

Speculation lit his gaze. "It's possible," he admitted. "All right, we'll stop by and see what's going on. Perhaps someone there can tell us why your name keeps being misspelled."

Her heart swelled with love. "Good idea. I knew I brought you along for a reason," she said, giving him a brief kiss.

Fifteen minutes later, Marla pushed open the door to the art gallery and entered a foyer that took her breath away. *This looks like one of those European opera houses that Thurston mentioned.* The plush red carpet, framed oil paintings, crystal chandelier, and curved staircase made her jaw drop in awe.

"Sweet," Vail remarked, with a cynical twist to his lips. *He's probably wondering how much they mark up the items for sale,* Marla thought. Certainly no expenses were spared in decorating.

Compelled to climb the stairs, she held on to a polished wood banister. At the top was a set of double mahogany doors. She entered the gallery proper, where rows of cushioned seats upholstered in red and gold faced forward. A bar took up a rear corner, with filled champagne glasses on its counter. Her nose detected a citrus fragrance while her mouth salivated for a glass of bubbly. Passengers milled about, chatting and sipping from fluted glassware. Paintings on easels lined the room, and more canvases were stacked against the walls.

Someone bumped her elbow. "Marla, I'm so glad you came. Now I'll have someone else here I know." Betsy, the brunette from dinner, gave her a wide grin.

"Oh, hi, Betsy. We got an invitation to the preview in our room, so we decided to attend. We've never been to an art auction before." Vail meandered toward the bar, leaving them alone. She hadn't thought about it, but if Betsy had received a free cruise ticket, she still could have come with a companion. "Pardon me for asking, but did you come on the cruise by yourself?"

"Yep, none of my friends could take the time off." Betsy giggled. "I've got my own cabin, even though I understand normally you have to pay extra for a single. Hello, there's Kent. I suppose he's in the same boat as I am. See, he isn't wearing a wedding ring. Not that I care; I don't think my parents would be happy if I hooked up with an exterminator."

"He must be interested in art to attend the preview."

Betsy poked her. "Maybe he came for the free champagne."

"It looks as though the rest of your colleagues had the same idea," Marla noted, observing the familiar faces of their tablemates among the guests. She felt a vibration underfoot as the vessel steadied itself from a large swell.

The doors burst open, and Kate and John strode inside. They spotted Marla at once and headed over. Dalton reached her at the same time as his parents.

"Mom, I thought you were going to the casino. And where's Brie?" He handed Marla a glass of champagne. She took a sip, enjoying the fizz as the cool liquid slid down her throat.

"Brie went to the teen mixer in the disco. I read

about this event in the newsletter and decided to stop by. We've been looking for a new picture for our family room. Hi, Marla. Do you have an interest in art?"

"I don't know much about it, so I'm here to learn. I'm sorry about the mix-up with our seats at dinner."

Kate patted her shoulder. "Don't worry, we'll work things out. I hope your cabin is comfortable."

"Yes, it's great, thanks."

Recognition dawned in Kate's eyes as she glanced beyond Marla. "Oh, look. Some of the people we met in the dining room are here. I'll introduce you."

She dragged over a young woman with a slender build and shoulder-length brown hair. "Marla and Dalton, I'd like you to meet one of my dinner companions. You won't believe this, but her name is Martha Shore."

CHAPTER 3

"Martha Shore? What a coincidence. We even look alike." Marla studied the woman, who could have stood in for a carbon copy of herself. Glossy mahogany hair, dark brown eyes, and a long neck above a well-endowed chest. Martha's hair was even the same length as hers, tumbling onto her shoulders instead of curving inward at chin length. Was it a coincidence that Martha was seated at the same dining-room table as her prospective in-laws?

"Your mother-in-law was telling me about you," Martha said in a low contralto voice. "I gather there was a mix-up at dinner, but there're too many of us to switch." Martha twisted one of her dangling earrings.

"What do you mean?"

"We have three people from the museum at my table, and you'd only have two seats available at yours."

"You work at the same art museum in Tampa as the people at my table?" Marla said, blinking.

"Sure do. I'm the gift shop manager."

No wonder the people at Marla's table had given a start of recognition at her name. Someone at the cruise line must have confused her with Martha Shore and exchanged their dining-room assignments.

"Hey, Martha," said Betsy while Marla digested this notion, "you guys all got your cruise tickets as free-bies too, right?"

"Yep. I don't know why everyone's come to the art preview, though. Like the bug man over there. How can he afford to buy any of this stuff?"

"Maybe he came to check out the chicks," Vail cracked before moving off with his parents and leaving Marla with her newfound friends. "I'll save you a seat," he called over his shoulder.

"Kent may have gotten the same invitation on his door as I did," Marla suggested. "After all, who can pass up the chance to win a free raffle?"

Betsy jabbed her. "You got a separate note? So did I. I wonder if the others in our group found one on their doors, too."

"What about the rest of these people? They're not with the museum," Marla replied.

"Hello, probably everyone got that flyer on their bed. Plus the preview is listed in the newsletter. The only difference is that we get two extra raffle tickets when we register. Let's ask Brooklyn if he got the same invitation." She led them over to a large man with mocha skin. "Marla, this is Brooklyn Jones. He's in charge of the museum café."

"Pleased to meet you." Brooklyn's ready grin ac-companied his deep, rumbling chuckle.

"Nice shirt," Marla said, admiring the tropical rum drinks depicted on his colorful top.

"Thanks. You that gal at the other table? Your boy-friend came around during dinner."

Marla's shoulders tensed. These continual refer-ences to the seating snafu were getting tedious. "We were wondering if you'd received a private invitation to the art preview?"

"Sure, didn't you?"

"I think I'm receiving messages meant for Martha here." Marla noticed how Martha stiffened. "Someone must have mixed up our names. That could be how Dalton and I ended up at the wrong dinner table."

"You may be right," Betsy said, nodding. Her glossy brown hair, straight down her back, swished as she spoke. "Are you saying only people from the museum got this free raffle ticket offer, and you received Martha's by mistake?"

"Yes, and that means someone on the cruise staff knows the members of your group. But then again, if all your tickets were booked together, that makes sense."

Brooklyn pointed a large finger at a nearby couple. "Ask them if they got the same deal. I'm gonna save us some seats."

He sauntered off with Martha Shore, while Marla glanced at the pair he'd indicated. The guy was a hunk with a shock of black hair, deep-set eyes, and sculpted arms like a bodybuilder. He looked as though he'd be at home camping in the woods, unlike his companion. The lady's refined gestures and redheaded elegance seemed more suited to hosting a soirée.

Betsy made the introductions. "Marla, this is Cliff Peters and Helen Bryce."

Cliff gave Marla's hand a hard squeeze, while Helen clutched her Gucci handbag and smiled. Betsy determined that the pair had received the same invitation to the art preview.

"What do you do at the museum?" Marla asked them, holding out her glass for a circulating waiter to refill.

"I'm head docent," Helen explained, "and Cliff is chief of security. We're so excited to be on the cruise."

"Me, too." Bustling activity at the other end of the room told her they needed to be seated soon. "I think we'd better go find our chairs," Marla said, excusing herself. Signaling for Betsy to follow, she veered down the center aisle.

"Thank goodness your fiancé saved me a seat," Betsy told her. "I wouldn't have wanted to be near Thurston Stark. Have you noticed how he brags continually about all the trips he and Heidi have taken?"

Marla grinned. "He likes to sound important. Do you have much contact with him at work?"

"Not really. I'm the public relations specialist, so I work with Bob, who's our business manager, and Olly, the director. Thurston is chairman of the foundation that supports the museum."

Balancing her glass and handbag, Marla shuffled through a row of seats toward Dalton, whose bored expression made her feel guilty. She hadn't even noted his parents leaving. In her eagerness to make new friends, she shouldn't have neglected the main reason she came aboard: to spend time alone with him and his daughter.

Dropping onto the cushioned chair beside him, she nodded in gratitude. "Thanks for saving us the seats. Hopefully, this won't take too long and we can join your parents."

His lips curved in an understanding smile. "Mom is having fun in the casino. Don't worry about her."

"Man, are you lucky to find such a nice guy," Betsy commented, tugging on her elbow. "I'm going to the singles mixer tonight, so maybe things won't be so dull hereafter. Hello, what's the matter with Olly? He looks as though he's seen a ghost. Holy mackerel!" Betsy's attention riveted on the man who'd just taken center stage. His boyish face and bow tie reminded Marla of Matthew Broderick in *The Music Man*.

"Welcome, ladies and gentlemen," the man said. "I'm Eric Rand, your auctioneer, and I'm here to explain what you can expect this week at our auctions." His eyes crinkled as he regarded the room packed with guests. "First thing you'll want to do is register with that lovely lady at the table in the rear. She'll assign you a numbered bid card. You'll keep this same number at all the auctions. Just for attending, we'll give you a free work of art at the end of each session, plus you'll be eligible for raffles where we give away art worth several thousand dollars!"

He swept his arm in a wide gesture. "You can get an extra raffle ticket by signing up for our special collector's card. The average credit is fifteen thousand dollars if you get approved, and you have thirteen months to clear your balance. That's thirteen months of no interest and no payments! Use our money to start your collections, folks. What could be a better deal? Whoo-hoo!" He circled his fist in the air.

Marla pursed her lips. "They sure come up with creative ways to take your cash," she muttered.

"No kidding." Vail glanced at her, a pained expression on his face. "Can we leave now?"

"This shouldn't take too much longer," she said, hoping it was true. A waiter came around pouring more champagne. She held up her glass for a refill.

"All sales are final once the gavel comes down," Eric continued, speaking into his headset microphone. "Since we're independent contractors, we have to add a fifteen percent buyer's premium. But don't forget, you're getting a hefty savings off retail prices. All our works come framed, matted, and shipped."

He paused to answer questions from the audience.

"We have sixteen hundred works of art to offer, folks, including originals from the classics: Picasso, Rembrandt, Dali, and Chagall, plus popular artists like Tomasz Rut, Kinkade, Tarkay, and Peter Max. We'll even include a registered certificate of authenticity to go with your piece. Whoo-hoo!"

"Do we hold the card up to bid?" a guest shouted.

"That's right. Occasionally we'll have what we call mystery items. The picture will be turned around on the easel so you can't see it, but if you're interested, raise your bidding card. After people bid, we'll show the piece. There's no obligation if you don't like it."

His eyes narrowed as he examined the front-row warriors, where the Smernoffs, Wolfsons, and Starks sat. They shifted uncomfortably, as though he were beaming telepathic thoughts in their direction. Marla glanced at Betsy. She seemed transfixed, her eyes glued to the auctioneer. Did the museum people know Eric Rand?

"Appraisals are available and recommended for insurance purposes," the auctioneer continued. "The first one is thirty-five dollars, with each subsequent appraisal fifteen dollars apiece."

"Another way for them to make money," Vail drawled.

"Each cruise, we offer a special collector's portfolio." Eric paused, his eyes sharp as lasers. "This week, we're especially fortunate to have a rare collection of Alden Tusk's signed suites for sale."

Betsy stiffened. "Holy mackerel, he can't be serious."

Others in the audience murmured among themselves while Marla's eyes widened.

"Bless my bones, I haven't heard his name in a long time," she muttered to Vail.

"Whose?"

"The artist." She lowered her voice and leaned toward him so no one else could hear. "Remember those unsavory photos I'd posed for in order to earn money to pay the lawyers after Tammy died?" She flushed at his curt nod. "Well, that wasn't my only modeling job, so to speak."

"What do you mean?"

"I did a legit modeling stint when I was still taking ballet lessons, right before Stan and I got married. An artist came into the studio and wanted a subject for a series of portraits. He hired me, and I posed for several sessions in my leotard and tights. His name was Alden Tusk. I never heard from him again, but he's popped up on the Internet now and then for winning awards. I'd love to find one of the paintings he did of me."

Vail's face brightened. Clearly, he'd expected a different sort of confession. "There's no telling what might show up at the auction," he said, patting her knee.

Eric's booming voice drew her attention back to the podium. "Many of you may not know that Alden Tusk painted a series of three pictures known as a triptych," he said, with a broad grin. "His series is complete, and it's on board the ship. Let me tell you, folks, this is the opportunity of a lifetime! Tusk's work has soared in value since his death. Whoo-hoo!"

Oliver Smernoff launched to his feet while Thurston twisted his head and raised his hand in a gesture to Cliff Peters. The rest of the museum crew looked astounded.

"How did you get Tusk's triptych?" Oliver demanded. "It was last shown at our museum. It belongs to us!"

"Our buyers scour the world for interesting pieces," Eric said, without acknowledging the question. Nor did he glance at the front-row occupants, focusing his gaze on those seated beyond. "We even commission some artists directly to produce work for our auctions. Last year, our company sold over three hundred thousand dollars' worth of art. Don't forget, these buys are tax and duty free. You're getting a bargain, folks, not to mention a sound investment. You don't want to leave without owning one of these fabulous pieces."

"Olly's wrong," Betsy mumbled, squeezing her handbag strap. "Alden's set doesn't belong to the museum. It was one of the works he'd donated for sale, before he, um, you know . . ."

"Before he what?" Marla asked, curious to learn what had happened to the artist.

"Sorry to cut this short," Vail interrupted, "but we have to meet my parents in fifteen minutes at the Meridian Showroom."

He rose, his meaningful glance making Marla remember her obligations. As soon as the last raffle number was called, she raced to join him in the rear of the room. First, she stopped to register for her bidding card and pick up her free picture, a signed seriograph by Picot. "I'll see you around," she mouthed, waving to Betsy from the exit.

Too bad she hadn't had time to follow up on Betsy's remark, Marla thought as Vail led her down three levels via the central atrium staircase. She'd enjoyed working for Alden, even for such a brief time. The young man had been an enigma to her back then, and now she wondered about the outcome of his career. She could always ask Betsy for more information tomorrow, or at the next art event.

Tempted to linger by the shops, she gazed wistfully

at displays of gold neck chains, Puerto Rican rum, perfumes, and logo shirts. Time for that later. Trailing Vail into the theater, she halted inside the entrance, awed by the tiered red velvet seats and glittery gold stage curtain. State-of-the-art lighting and sound equipment escalated her anticipation for the show. She spotted Brianna and ushered Vail in his daughter's direction. After stumbling her way through the row, she air kissed the teen. "Hi, honey, we've missed you. Did you meet any other kids?"

"Yeah, we're gonna hang out at the pool together tomorrow and maybe meet in the disco after dinner."

"Sounds like a plan." Marla squeezed between Brianna and Vail, with Kate and John on Brianna's other side. She felt the swaying motion of the ship and the engine vibration, more noticeable here than in the art gallery.

"We really appreciate you giving us this cruise," she said, leaning over to address Kate. "It was very generous of you."

The older woman smiled, lines crinkling beside her warm hazel eyes. "Consider it an engagement gift. We're so thrilled you and Dalton are getting married. We just can't wait to see your new house, too. From what he's told us about you, I know you two will be happy. All we ask in return is that you treat our son right."

Marla blinked. It was difficult for her to think of the stalwart detective as someone's child. "I'll do my best."

"Brie told us how you're teaching her to apply makeup and advising her on female issues."

She cleared her throat. "I've had enough teenage clients share their concerns. I'm glad Brie feels she can turn to me. I hope I won't disappoint her," she said, patting the girl's arm.

"She adores you." Chuckling, Kate added, "Maybe you can help me with my hair this week. It flies away in this humidity."

"I'd love to," Marla said, surveying Kate's wavy style. "If you wouldn't mind, I could trim your ends, too. It'll give more bounce to your hair and cut down on those flyaways."

"Super. How great is it to have a hairdresser in the family?" Kate said to the others, grinning broadly.

"She's a smart business lady, Grandma," Brianna remarked, pride in her tone. "You should see her salon. It's the coolest place, but her new one will be even more awesome."

"Oh yes, Dalton told me you're planning to expand. I hope you'll share your plans later."

"I'd be delighted." Marla smiled back. "And I hope you'll advise me on what's good to shop for in the ports." She couldn't believe how easy it was to talk to Kate. How unlike Dalton's former mother-in-law, who'd criticized her every move when she came to visit. Marla still didn't know how Kate and John felt about their religious differences but hoped it wouldn't be an issue between them.

"I want to buy you an item of jewelry," Kate told her, "something to show you how happy we are over your betrothal. Let me know if you have a preference for white or yellow gold. It'll give me an excuse to browse in the stores."

John rolled his eyes. "As if she needs a reason."

"Mom is a shopaholic at heart," Vail explained with a grin. "That's something you two have in common."

"What about me?" Brianna said. "I want a David Yurman bracelet. All my friends have one."

"Whoa, honey, that's awfully expensive," Marla said, touched by Kate's offer. She'd have to look for a gift to give her prospective in-laws in return. She still couldn't believe they'd accepted her so readily. How did they know she'd make a proper mother for Brianna when she wasn't even sure of it herself? As for Brianna, it actually gave Marla more pleasure to shop for the teen than for her own needs. She'd get Brianna something special, too, a remembrance from the cruise.

"We should check the shore excursion list," Vail suggested. "The tours might fill up early."

"You're right; we can look at the schedule after the show."

As if on cue, the lights dimmed. The curtain parted after a brief musical prelude, and a guy in a flashy royal blue jacket strutted on stage.

"Howdy, folks. I'm David Whetstone, your cruise director." His golden-boy looks would have gone over well in Hollywood. "Welcome to the *Tropical Sun*. I hope you're all prepared for a fantastic week," he said, with a wide grin. "Did you all enjoy your dinner?" A loud chorus responded with cheers. "We have award-winning chefs, and they'll make sure you can't resist their meals. You may come on board as passengers, but we'll roll you off as cargo."

When the laughter died down, he went on, "I need to caution you to pay attention to the signs around the ship. When you use the restroom, for example, you'd better heed the one that says to close the lid before you flush. Otherwise, you'll find out the meaning of the word *suction* in a very unpleasant manner."

More guffaws. "If you can't find enough to do, we have a special double-feature movie tonight: *Titanic* and *Poseidon*." Finishing his round of jokes, David introduced a Las Vegas–style musical review. Marla was surprised to see him among the singers. He had a pretty good voice, but then she supposed the requirements for entertainers were stringent. In particular, she enjoyed the glittering costumes with their elaborate headpieces, and the dance numbers. When the show finished, the cruise director returned to describe the next day's activities.

With a smile on her lips, Marla shuffled toward the exit alongside the rest of her group. "Now what?" she asked Vail. "We could go dancing, listen to piano music, or try the karaoke." With eight bars and lounges, they had almost too many choices. "Or we could check out the shops and the embarkation photos."

"I'm going to the casino," Kate stated. "John can mosey along with you, if you don't mind."

"Hell no, I'm turning in," the big man said, rolling his shoulders. "It's been a long day." He peered at them from behind his spectacles. "You kids have a good time. Brie, you should come along. It's past your bedtime."

Brianna turned a pleading face to Marla. "Can I go see the shops with you? I didn't get a chance earlier."

Marla put her hand on the teen's shoulder. "Sure, honey. I can walk you to your cabin afterward." Then she asked the girl's grandparents, "Would that be all right?"

"Hey, don't I have a say in this? She's my daughter." Vail hunched his posture like a protective male bear.

"You're coming along," Marla told him. "Brie will be happy to point out all the things you can buy her."

"Oh no, I'm letting her loose with the shopping demon." His face took on a resigned expression. "Mom and Dad, help me out!"

John chuckled. "Get used to it, son. See you in the morning."

"Be good to your fiancée, Dalton," Kate advised after her husband had sauntered off. "Watch what she looks at in the stores. Then you'll know what to get her for birthdays and anniversaries. Men have to learn how to be observant." She winked at Marla before heading away to conquer the slot machines.

"I like your parents," Marla told Dalton. Brianna walked beside her as they climbed two flights toward the indoor mall.

"They're smitten with you. I told you they would be."

Glowing with warmth, Marla led the way into the jewelry store on deck five, where she scanned the colored gems on display.

"It's tax free if you buy the stones without a setting," said a familiar voice from behind. Whirling around, Marla observed Sandy Wolfson at a counter showcasing watches.

"I'm not into fancy jewelry," Marla admitted.

"Me neither, except I've always wanted pink sapphires. I'm tempted to get myself something on this trip. If I wait for Bob to buy me a gift, I'll never get anything."

"Which port do you recommend for shopping?" Marla asked, wondering if the woman always kvetched about her husband.

Sandy shifted her handbag, an inexpensive canvas tote. "Cozumel is great. We cruise there every year. Bob prefers the western Caribbean."

"That's good to know." Glancing around to reassure herself that Brianna and Vail were occupied, Marla leaned inward. "I was surprised to see everyone from the museum at the art preview this evening. Did you receive a private invitation on your door?"

Sandy tilted her head. "Yeah, and I'm guessing our benefactor had the invitations sent to all of us."

Marla's pulse accelerated. "How so?"

"He booked us together, right? I'll bet it was Thurston. He donates a lot of money to the museum."

"Wouldn't he just admit it? Mr. Stark doesn't strike me as being the anonymous type."

"That's true, but then who else could it be?" Sandy's mouth turned down. "They should have given Bob a raise instead. He works so hard and never gets a word of appreciation."

"So why doesn't he leave? With his experience as an office manager, he could get a job anywhere."

"Nah, he won't budge. Bob complains a lot, but when push comes to shove, he's too timid to rattle the cage." Sandy lowered her voice. "I mean, even after that awful day, he wouldn't quit." She noted Marla's puzzled look. "You know, the day Alden Tusk fell off the museum balcony to his death."

CHAPTER 4

"**O**ur dinner companions are an interesting bunch, but I hope we get switched to your parents' table," Marla told Vail the next morning after breakfast. They were taking a brisk stroll around the outdoor sundeck after stuffing themselves with omelets from the buffet. Brianna had run off to join the teen program, while Vail's folks had headed to the shore excursion presentation.

"They're all kind of weird, if you ask me," Vail said, giving her a bemused glance. "What did you tell me about that artist dying at their museum?"

"Sandy said Alden Tusk fell off the balcony. I didn't hear how it happened, because her husband came by, and she shut up."

"So? We're on vacation. You don't need to know the details."

"I'd like to learn more about Alden's life. He impressed me as the starving artist type when I worked for him. All I remember are his piercing eyes, his scruffy beard, and his passion for painting. He lived in a small house with weeds overgrowing the lawn."

"And?"

"And maybe those portraits he did of me are worth something now."

"I'd think the odds are rare of finding one on the ship. Man, it's hot out here."

Marla raced to keep up with Vail's fast pace. The rising sun heated her back while a stiff breeze lashed her hair about her face. A couple streaked past, the guy wearing a white T-shirt and tan slacks, the woman in jeans and sandals. A jogger in bright red shorts sped past them all.

Marla glanced over the rail at the white-capped swells. She'd never seen water that deep royal blue before. It reflected the sky overhead, dotted with cotton-candy clouds. Salt air laced her lips. She licked them, thinking she'd better apply a lipstick with sunscreen.

Ding dong, ding dong. "Good morning, this is the captain, from the bridge," Captain Larsen said, while Marla wondered where else he might make his announcements from if not the bridge. "We have a light wind this morning with moderate seas. It should be perfect weather for you to enjoy yourselves. Our heading takes us on a southeasterly course, and I will keep you updated periodically on our progress. Have a nice day."

"Oh look," Marla said, "there's Cliff Peters. We met him last night at the art preview. He's the security guard at the museum and has a seat at your mother's table. Doesn't he look like a bigger version of Tom Cruise?" His thick black hair curled at his nape. "I wonder if he came on the trip alone. Betsy is looking to hook up with a guy, but I guess she isn't interested in him."

"All right, Miss Matchmaker," Vail teased. "What's that Yiddish word? A *yenta?*"

"That means busybody. And I'm glad to see you're learning the language," she added, grinning at him.

Ding dong, ding dong. "Good morning ladies and gentlemen. This is David, your cruise director. We have a fun-filled day planned for you with our shore excursion and port-shopping talks, diamond and gem seminar, jackpot bingo, and slots tournament. You'll find great deals in the spa and will want to sign up early for their signature treatments. Our shops are open, so check out the jewelry and perfume sales. Hope to see you soon!"

"Are we going to have to listen to that all day?" Vail groused, stopping to wipe the sweat from his brow.

"Probably." Drained by the heat, Marla felt her energy ebb. "I'm ready to get a spot by the pool. What about you?"

"I could eat again."

"Are you kidding? After you had an omelette with bacon, toast, potatoes, fruit, and a cinnamon roll?"

He spread his arms. "How can I pass up the opportunity to try the pancakes with strawberry sauce and whipped cream?"

"Fine, you go pig out. I'm changing into my swimsuit and reserving us some lounge chairs."

"Okay, but I might check out the gym before I return, if I can figure out how to get to the fitness center."

"It's forward past the solarium, on the same deck as the pool. I think the spa is there, too."

By the time she made her way to the pool, many of the seats already had towels thrown across them or bodies percolating under the tropical sun. She didn't know if Brianna or Vail's parents would join them but decided to save an extra place just in case. Searching for three vacant lounge chairs, she spied Heidi Stark's familiar face down one row. As she picked her way along, she felt the deck lift underfoot, tilting first to port, then to starboard, making her remember she was on a ship. By now, the rolling motion had become soothing and no longer bothered her. Same for the engine vibration that rumbled underfoot.

"Are these chairs free?" she asked Heidi. The scent of suntan lotion mingled with salt spray from water sloshing in the pool. Without waiting for a reply, she laid out her towel and reserved the next couple of chairs with her beach bag and a mystery novel that Nicole had loaned her. The other stylist was always trying to get Marla to read books, but all she had time for were *Modern Salon* and other professional magazines. Maybe now she'd actually be able to concentrate on a story.

"Hey, Marla," Heidi said in her childlike voice, glancing at her from behind dark sunglasses. "You're out early."

Marla sat and squirted sunscreen into her palm. The lotion had become very liquefied from the heat, so she rubbed it diligently on her arms and legs. "I gather it's going to get crowded later and all the chairs will be taken. I'm not interested in learning how to cross-stitch or in watching a fruit-carving demonstration. Besides, Dalton's parents went to the shore excursion talk this morning. They can tell us what we need to know, although we've already filled out our tour order form. Have you been to any of these ports before?"

"All of them." Heidi giggled. She looked like a Barbie doll with her blond hair tied into a ponytail, her taut bikini, and her leggy figure. "I'm not sure if we'll get off the ship at Roatan." Her nose wrinkled. "Like, it's so third world, you know?"

Marla glanced at the heated whirlpool, where two young women, a bald man, and a gawky youth soaked in the mist. "We're going on the Tabyana Beach tour. Dalton didn't want to do the jungle canopy adventure, and we'll go snorkeling on one of the other islands. So we'll do the beach and barbecue thing at Roatan. I hope it's worth fifty-five dollars each."

"The beaches are nice. Don't expect to go shopping, though. It's a total bore." Heidi waved her hand in a dismissive gesture. The large diamond on her left finger winked in the sunlight. Marla glanced at the woman's diamond-stud earrings and tennis bracelet with rocks sizable enough to have paid for her entire group's cruise.

Is that why Heidi had married a man twice her age, so he could shower her with jewels? She scanned the faces of passersby, wondering what was taking Dalton so long. People chatted and laughed, some of them sitting at square tables and eating food from the outdoor café, while glasses clinked at a bar nearby. Oh well. Maybe he'd decided to try the treadmill.

Stuffing her lotion bottle back in her bag, she kicked off her sandals and leaned back to relax. Her eyelids shut, and she let her limbs sag. Ah, now this was what she called a vacation!

"I can't believe the triptych is on board," Heidi blurted, after an interval in which Marla felt her cares slip away.

"Huh?" Her mind took a moment to reorient.

"Alden Tusk's work. Thurston was so upset about it."

Marla didn't move a muscle to open her eyes. "Where is your husband?"

"He's in the Internet Café. Dearest Thurston owns a number of car dealerships, and he's so conscientious. He just has to keep in touch with his key people even when he's away. He's totally a bull when it comes to business," Heidi said proudly.

"So why was he upset to see the artist's name come up at the auction?"

"Alden's triptych was one of the pieces that would have been auctioned at our museum's fund-raiser to establish a new children's art program."

"I see."

"No, you don't get it," Heidi said, clearly eager to gossip from the enthusiasm lacing her voice. "The afternoon before the gala event, when the museum was closed to the public, Alden fell to his death from the third-floor balcony. His triptych was a series of three paintings, and only the two outer pictures were found afterward. The middle picture had vanished."

"Really?" Snapping her eyelids open behind her sunglasses, Marla glanced at Heidi. "What happened to those two pieces?"

"They became part of his estate. I can't understand how Eric Rand fits in. It blew my mind to see him on board."

"Why?" she asked, unable to deny her curiosity. Betsy had seemed fixated on him, too.

Heidi turned her face to catch the sun's rays. "Eric was the museum curator at the time. He was fired over the scandal, and yet here he is, along with all three panels of the dead artist's set."

Marla swung her legs over the side of the lounge chair and stared at Heidi. "I don't understand."

"Eric was in charge when Alden tumbled to his death. As curator, he got blamed for the accident. Thurston said if it weren't for Eric's negligence, the tragedy never would have happened."

Tucking a limp strand of hair behind her ear,

Marla spied John Vail climbing down the stairs from the upper deck. Irene Smernoff, wearing a floral swimsuit, accompanied him. They were deeply engaged in conversation. Marla noticed Irene held a tall V-shaped glass containing a pinkish liquid. It looked like one of those tropical drink specials, but at ten o'clock in the morning?

Ding dong, ding dong. "Ladies and gents, this is Kevin, your assistant cruise director, inviting you to play jackpot bingo just beginning in the Sailaway Lounge on deck five. We have lots of money to give away and free rum punches, so we'll see you there. Don't miss this fantastic game!"

Distracted by the announcement, Marla forgot what Heidi was saying. Never mind that. What was John doing here without his wife? Hadn't he and Kate gone to the ports-of-call presentation?

"Save my seat," she muttered, leaping up. Stumbling over beach towels and bags, she forged a path toward John. Catching sight of her, he widened his mouth in a welcoming smile.

"Marla, I should have guessed I'd find you here." He patted her on the back. "You know Irene, of course."

Irene gave a nod, her frozen facial muscles allowing little more than a smirk. "I'm on my way to the salsa class. Do you dance, Marla?"

"Not ballroom dancing. I took ballet in my early years and even into my late teens."

Irene's eyes sparked. "Me, too. I've never given up my love for it, either. We have season tickets at home. Attending the theater is something Olly and I both enjoy."

"What about you?" Marla asked her future father-in-law. "Are there cultural events where you live in Maine?"

John tilted his head. "Sure, although you'll get me to a sports game faster than you will to a show. Kate likes that stuff. She goes with her bridge group all the time."

Irene nudged him. "You'll be going to plenty of shows soon, if I have anything to say about it."

"I hope you're right," he said, giving her a silly grin.

Am I missing something here? These two seem to have something going on between them.

"Where's Kate?" Marla demanded.

John's brow folded in a frown. "She's registering for the slots tournament. We stopped by the tour desk and bought an excursion to Tulum for us and Brie. I hope you don't mind if Brie goes along. We figured she'd like to see the Mayan ruins."

"It'll be fun for her. We had considered going, but Dalton doesn't have the patience to ride a bus for half a day. I'd rather go shopping in Cozumel."

"Good choice," Irene told her, then sipped her drink. "Oh, you're sitting next to Heidi? Is that an extra chair I see?"

"I was saving one for Kate and John, or Brie."

"I can't sit in the sun," John said. "Brie won't surface until lunch, and Kate is occupied. So you go ahead, Irene."

"If you're looking for Dalton, he may be in the sports complex," Marla suggested.

"What, are you trying to find things for me to do?" John scoffed. "Don't worry, I can entertain myself. I'm quite used to it by now."

You don't sound so happy about that, pal. Dalton had

told her very little about his parents. Certainly, they weren't as provincial as he'd let on. Could it be that he knew them less than he'd admit, or did he steer away from familial intimacy for a reason?

Marla's intuition made her skilled at sensing emotional nuances, and John's responses told her that something wasn't right at home base.

"Marla, can I get you a cocktail? I need a refill," Irene offered after he'd disappeared behind a glass partition designed as a windbreaker.

"Thanks, but I'm still digesting my breakfast. I'll go with you to get a cup of water, instead."

"I see you were talking to Heidi. She married for money, you know," Irene said after they were served by the handsome Jamaican bartender. Other boozers were getting their morning start, Marla noted as she jockeyed for a stool. She wondered if Irene made a habit of drinking every morning.

"Heidi seems fond of Thurston." The cool water refreshed her after sitting in the heat. She downed most of the contents in a few gulps.

"Heidi is more fond of Cliff Peters, darling. The security guard might have been more attentive to his job and prevented the accident if Heidi hadn't been around that day."

Marla straightened her spine. "You mean the day Alden Tusk died?" Maybe now she'd find out what really happened to him.

Irene nodded, fingering her gold hoop earring. She wore a heavy gold chain and a matching bracelet. "Heidi was supposed to be working with Brooklyn, our café manager, for the benefit that evening, but Olly ended up confirming the catering arrangements with him when Heidi disappeared."

"The fund-raiser was a dinner party?"

"Right. We had the patio set up with tables and chairs, and a florist was due to arrive later with centerpieces. Ordering the decorations was my job," Irene explained. "I was outdoors when I heard a man shriek in terror."

"And then what happened?"

"Everyone rushed inside. Alden lay on the tile floor. Oh, God, it was awful." Her hand shaking, she guzzled down a long drink.

"So the benefit was canceled?"

"Postponed. We had too many contributors to thank and art pieces that had been commissioned just for this event. The gala dinner took place on the following weekend."

"But without Alden Tusk's triptych, I understand?"

Irene's eyes narrowed. "Someone stole the middle painting. Helen Bryce, the head docent, thought it would reappear, because sometimes when she took tours around, a picture would be missing on the wall. She'd learn afterward that Eric had been repairing the frame, or that Thurston had taken the picture to an appraiser in town who couldn't make it into the museum."

"So the middle piece never turned up?"

"Not until now. I can't wait to see the completed set."

"You're very devoted to the art world, aren't you?"

"Olly and I have that much in common. He works in the field, while I'm a real estate agent for luxury homes. I just volunteer at the musuem." Irene hunched her shoulders, morosely regarding her cocktail. A soggy chunk of pineapple decorated the glass.

Marla spotted Dalton snaking his way through the throng. "Excuse me, there's my fiancé," she said, bouncing off her bar stool. "You're welcome to use our extra lounge chair until after lunch, if you want. Brie may join us then."

"Okay, thanks." Her gaze lifted. "And darling, do me a favor? Don't mention what we've been discussing to anyone at our dinner table."

"No problem," Marla replied, although gossip tripped on her tongue when she went to meet Vail. "Where have you been?" she demanded. "Did you see your dad? John was wandering around while your mom headed for the casino."

The detective looked dashingly handsome with a towel draped around his neck, his chest bare, and swim trunks taut in tantalizing places. His affectionate smile had her wishing for more intimate quarters.

"I was in the fitness center. They have some good equipment and a great view of the ocean. The spa and salon are next door, if you want to check them out."

"I'll get there eventually. Did you happen to get tickets for the wine seminar this afternoon?"

"Yep, on my way back to the room."

"Our chairs are next to Heidi. Oh look, Thurston finally got here." Meandering over, she greeted the heavyset man, who wore a polo shirt and shorts. Beads of sweat covered his ruddy complexion and flattened his light brown hair.

"Howdy, folks," he boomed. "Relax, lie back, and let the ship's staff take care of you. These days at sea are the best part of the cruise. For scenery, though, you'll want to try the Mediterranean. When we did the Greek islands—"

"Why, dearest," Heidi interrupted, "you gave those Greek gods some competition, didn't you? No one knows more about their mythology than you do. Tell them about the Acropolis."

Vail cleared his throat, and Marla caught his cue. Snatching her things, she flashed an apologetic grin.

"Sorry, but we have to meet Dalton's daughter. It's almost lunchtime. Besides, if I get too much sun now, I won't be able to lie out on the beach in Roatan. We'll see you later at dinner." *Unless we change tables. I don't know if I can stand another round of travelogues.*

By the time they collected Brianna for lunch, Marla had regained her appetite. They sat outside by the Outrigger Café, in a niche protected from the wind by glass windows. The square wood tables were bolted to the deck, which rolled gently from side to side with the ocean swells. Marla, accustomed to the motion, had even begun to block out the incessant loudspeaker announcements.

Kate and John had met up with them in the buffet line, foregoing a formal luncheon in the dining room. Brie started telling them about her afternoon schedule.

"What did you say comes after the water balloon toss and gladiator challenge at the pool?" Marla asked. Oh yum, those roasted sweet potatoes with a palm sugar glaze just melted in her mouth. The dish didn't necessarily go with the Thai chicken, coconut rice, and stir-fried vegetables she'd chosen, but who cared? Beside her, Vail stuffed his mouth full of carved turkey with cranberry sauce, pecan carrots, Lyonnaise potatoes, and red wine–braised beef, while Kate and John stuck to salads.

"After the pool, we're having ice cream and seeing a movie." Lowering her saucy eyes, Brianna bit into her slice of pepperoni pizza. She'd already tasted the Hawaiian and Margarita pizzas.

"Don't eat too many sweets between now and dinner," her grandmother advised from across the table.

"Tonight is formal night. You'll need enough time in the cabin to get dressed."

"Like, I know that already."

"Will you be going to the show with us tonight?"

"I'll see, Grandma. I may want to hang out with my new friends instead."

"Brianna," Marla said hastily to ward off trouble, "there's no reason for you to be snippy. Your grandmother means well."

"Sorry." Her sullen face said otherwise.

"Have you seen the Pirate's Grotto?" Marla asked brightly. "The entrance is on deck four, outside the casino. We popped in there last night. It has rocklike walls, so you feel like you're in a cave; strobe lighting; and disco music. The noise chased us away."

"I believe you have to be eighteen to get in," Kate cut in before Brianna could reply. According to the ship's rules, eighteen-year-olds could drink beer and wine with their parents' signed waiver but not hard liquor.

"Tomorrow night, we have a dance party in the Grotto," Brianna said, with a superior smirk. "Grown-ups won't be allowed inside." After shoving her chair away, she jumped up. "May I be excused? I'm done eating. See ya."

"Wait," Vail called. "It's not polite to leave before everyone's finished."

Brianna paused, her ponytail swinging. "Stop treating me like a baby, Dad. It's time you realized that I can be on my own. Gosh, you guys are so embarrassing! I can't stand being near you." With a flounce, she loped away.

"You'll have your hands full as her stepmother," Kate said to Marla, with a sympathetic smile. "Are you prepared to deal with teenage behavior? She's bound to get rowdier as she gets older." Lines of concern etched the older woman's forehead.

"I think she's just spreading her wings while we're on the ship. We have to give her some freedom so she can learn how to deal with different situations. It's good that she's made friends already."

"That's true." Kate put down her fork. "You know, it's not the best example for her that you two are sharing a cabin and aren't married. When are you going to set a date? I'm happy to help with the wedding plans."

Vail gave Marla a quizzical glance, clearly landing the ball in her field. "Uh, we're not quite sure yet," she hedged.

Kate tapped a finger on her chin. "Will you have a priest and a rabbi officiate together? I suppose you'll have the ceremony at a hotel where you can do the reception. A sit-down dinner works so much better than a buffet, don't you think? And it's okay to get chicken to keep costs down, although you'll still pay more than sixty dollars a head. We'll help out by paying for our guests, won't we, John?"

"Huh?" Staring into space, he refocused his attention. "Oh, yeah, whatever. Just make sure to let us know ahead of time so I don't make other plans." He gave his wife a challenging glare, making Marla wonder if those plans included Kate.

Another thought troubled her. Could Brianna's defiant behavior be a reflection of turmoil between her grandparents?

CHAPTER 5

Sunday afternoon, Marla joined the bridge tour, where she ran into Martha Shore, the lady who ran the gift shop at the art museum. Martha hovered in the rear ranks of visitors while a uniformed officer described the controls spanning the ship's command center.

"Hi there," Marla said to the other woman, with a friendly grin. "This is amazing, isn't it? We could be on the bridge of a spaceship with so many flashing dials. Look at this safety console. Do you think one officer mans all six stations at the same time?"

She noted buttons for fire and watertight doors, the public-address system, machinery controls, deck lighting, and a fire alarm. Oh, and another for ceiling panel surveillance cameras. Hmm. Where were those located? Probably in the casino.

"Quiet, I'm listening to the talk." Martha adjusted the turquoise top that matched her floral capri pants.

Well, excuse me for being nice. Switching her attention to the officer, she wondered if Martha was actually enthralled by his technobabble or admiring his wavy blond hair, ocean blue eyes, and lanky build. No wonder women fell for men in uniform.

"Our multipilot displays can be changed between radar, chart, and control functions," he said, beaming with pride.

"What's this?" a fellow in shorts bellowed, pointing to a unit off to the side.

"That's one of our wing consoles. It has joystick controls to maneuver the ship in harbor. We keep tabs on the underwater equipment over here," he said, drawing the passengers' attention to the cockpit. "This ship has two main propellers, stern and bow thrusters, fin stabilizers, and rudders."

At the navigational chart table, Marla leaned over, careful not to touch anything. "So are you having a good time?" she asked Martha, hoping to coax her into a conversation. "This must be like a busman's holiday to you with all your colleagues here."

Martha glowered at her, turning her neck at an angle so that Marla could see a couple of whiskers under her chin. The lady needed a wax treatment for facial hair. "I can't imagine who sent us the cruise tickets or why certain people were included," Martha said in her low contralto voice. "Kent Harwood isn't a regular employee, although he did his mold inspection that day. And Helen hung around even though the museum was closed to the public. What was she doing there, instructing the other docents? I don't recall anyone recruiting her to help with the party."

"What day was this?"

"Why, the day of Alden's accident." Martha's eyes grew round. "That's what the cops are calling it, but I'm not convinced."

"Follow me," the officer droned. "This is where our watch officers sit. You'll notice the captain's chair centered behind their two stations. Make your way forward between the steering stand and radio console, folks."

Seeing that Martha was about to join them, Marla stuck out a restraining hand. "You don't think Alden's fall was a tragic mistake? Everyone else seems to believe so."

"How convenient for them." Martha looked her squarely in the eyes. "Every one of the people from the museum on board this ship was present the day Alden died. Isn't it peculiar that we're gathered here at the same time as his completed triptych is for sale? Where was the missing middle piece all this time? If you ask me, I smell a rat."

Marla shifted her handbag. "What do you mean?"

The other woman's eyes lit, as though she were glad to confide in someone. "Well, I was in the gift shop doing inventory, and I heard music playing even though the sound system was turned off. I'm no musician, but it sounded like a flute. After a short refrain, I heard Alden cry out, and then the music stopped. It was horrible."

Martha scraped a trembling hand through her hair, hair that was too limp by Marla's standards. Besides a facial wax, she could add a decent cut and conditioning to her treatment list.

"Did anyone witness the artist's fall?" Marla asked.

"No one admitted seeing anything, plus I'm the only one who heard music playing. Most of the others were outside on the patio, setting up for the event."

"What did the cops determine?"

Martha twisted her chandelier earring. "They found a couple of screws loose on the balcony railing. Although it wasn't his responsibility, the curator got blamed for sloppy maintenance, plus he was at fault for letting someone snatch Alden's painting. That's really the reason why he got fired. Now he's on board with us as art auctioneer."

Truly weird. And what about the note left on her cabin door at their arrival? Suspecting it was meant for her companion, Marla sought a diplomatic way to introduce the topic. *I know what you did and I have what you want.* What could Martha have done that she'd kept hidden from the others?

And what did it mean that everyone on board the *Tropical Sun* from the museum was present the day Alden Tusk died? Could the benefactor who had supplied their cruise tickets have donated them, not out of generosity, but for some nefarious purpose? Just how far-reaching was this wealthy person's influence that he could manipulate Eric Rand as well? It crossed her mind that one of her dinner companions might even be that donor, watching all of them, waiting for . . . what?

Swept to the wing console with a crowd of fellow passengers, she lost her chance to continue their discussion. Nor did she get the opportunity at dinner. Interrupted by the wine steward, ship's photographer, and singing waiters, she barely concluded her meal before the next seating arrived. Martha Shore had already left her table by the time Marla sought her. Maybe they'd run into each other in San Juan the next day.

Early the following morning, Marla lounged by the pool and then browsed in the ship's gift shops along with Kate and Brianna to check out jewelry prices. As a concession to her betrothed, she'd agreed to go along on the El Yunque Rain Forest tour, but they'd still have a short time left in town afterward for shopping. Kate had picked up extra copies of maps with stores recommended by the cruise line.

After lunch, Marla lined the railing with the others in her party to observe the approach into port. A strong wind tossed her hair into her face as she watched the mountainous island emerge from the blue ocean canvas. Strips of sandy beach outlining the land grew larger as they neared at a slower pace, the ship gently rolling side to side.

At the tip of the island stood a massive stone fort, its flags rippling in the breeze. City buildings loomed tall as they sailed farther into the harbor, where the seawall gave way to parking lots and palms. Snapping photos, she jostled with other passengers for the best view.

Thirty minutes later, Marla handed her ID card to a security officer, who swiped it through a machine and handed it back. Upon exiting the ship, she halted with her group to pose for the ever-present photographers in front of a San Juan sign. Having viewed the outrageous prices for photographs in the gallery earlier, she doubted she'd be adding this one to her collection. Between the drinks, photos, shore excursions, and duty-free shops on the ship, their all-inclusive vacation could end up costing hundreds of dollars more. And she didn't even waste money on bingo or the slots!

Passing through the terminal outside to a covered walkway, she searched for their tour group leader. Taxis and buses waited just past the security gate. Beyond was a government building, Departamento de Hacienda, while another crumbling fort jutted on a distant hill. Flagstone sidewalks invited exploration, as did quaint structures with wrought-iron balconies and flowering plants. A maze of streets generally led upward from the pier. Marla's mouth watered at the sight of a Starbucks and a place called Mojito's Restaurant.

"Over there," Dalton said, pointing toward a tour host holding up a sign.

Marla trailed her fiancé toward the bus that would transport them to the rain forest. Unaccustomed to traffic noise after the tranquility of the sea, she winced at the brutal sounds of horns honking, engines idling, and motorcyles roaring along the busy street in front of the terminal.

A man stuck a coupon for Señor Frog's in her hand, while another guy yelled, "I give you a private tour, lady. Only ten dollar per person to take you around island."

"Let's go," Marla said to Brianna, urging her inside the bus. She didn't like the way the man looked at the girl.

Sitting next to Brianna, while Vail kept his mother company and John sat behind them, she relaxed in her seat as the bus entered traffic. "Look at the mountains in the distance," she said to Brianna.

"Awesome, they have McDonald's here," Brianna pointed out as the bus rumbled down the street, starting and stopping in the congestion.

"Look, there's Martha Shore," called Kate, gesturing. Sure enough, Martha ambled along the sidewalk with Brooklyn Jones. Engaged in a heated discussion, they nearly got run down by a charging taxi.

Craning her neck, Marla realized she and Vail were the only ones from their dinner table on this particular shore excursion. She'd seen the Smernoffs and Wolfsons get on the bus for the Bacardi Rum Distillery tour and almost regretted her choice until she reminded herself of her purpose: to spend quality time with family. Reaching out her hand, she squeezed Brianna's palm. It felt gratifying to share responsibility for the girl and to enjoy new experiences together.

"Don't tell me what to do," she heard John's curt tone.

"You know your skin is sensitive," Kate chided, twisting in her seat to regard him. "You should have let me put sunscreen on the back of your neck."

"We're going into the rain forest. The canopy will provide enough shade."

"I hope you're right. And why did you insist on bringing that heavy bag? We're going to be hiking on some rocky trails."

"It's *my* stuff. I'll deal with it." He compressed his lips. "See what I have to put up with?" he said to his son.

Marla felt a surge of sympathy for Kate. "Your wife is just concerned about you."

"I'd worry more about getting wet," Vail commented in a wry tone. "It's called the rain forest for a reason." The bus had started to climb from a residential district with pastel houses and overhead power lines into the green-covered hills, and a light mist curtained the outside air. None of them had thought to toss an umbrella into their totes.

Marla marveled at the lush foliage as the bus engine strained. She had to admit that the route through the city had given her a glimpse of Puerto Rico she wouldn't have seen otherwise. Florida being so flat, she rarely had the opportunity to go uphill and view scenic vistas like those revealed on the mountain road. By the time they reached the ranger station, the sun had broken through the clouds and turned the moisture into sprays of diamond-like dew.

Vail bounded ahead on the dirt path beside a running stream toward a waterfall cascading over a rock face. The guide stopped to point out pink wildflowers, ferns, and other plant life indigenous to the region. Vail and Brianna quizzed each other on the trees while Kate slung her arm through Marla's.

"Dalton always liked taking walks in the park," the redhead said, presenting Marla with a dazzling smile. "When he was growing up, we took him every Sunday to a conservation area near home with wooded trails. John carried a big stick, in case we came across any snakes, but I think it was more for show."

"So Dalton got his enjoyment of nature from you?"

"More likely from John. He's the adventurous one. Even now, when he should be enjoying what we have at home, he wants to go off on some half-assed jaunts to nowhere."

"How long has he been retired?"

"Six months. He's been working on his stained-glass projects. At least that keeps him busy."

Marla glanced at her future mother-in-law. "Do you work outside the home?"

"Honey, I put twenty-five years into teaching. Now I'm happy to volunteer at our church, keep up with my bridge games, and refurbish our house."

Marla paused to admire a cluster of wild orchids. Water gushed in the background from the waterfall, while the earthy scent of vegetation weighed the air. She couldn't hear what the guide up ahead was saying, but Dalton could fill her in. She was more interested in getting to know her future family.

"Do you get to Florida often?" she asked, already knowing the answer. Brianna had gone to visit her grandparents in Maine over Thanksgiving because she hadn't seen them for months.

"I don't like to travel that much," Kate admitted, her forehead folding into a frown. "That's why I was so upset when John suggested we get a Winnebago to tour the country. All of a sudden he has time on his hands, and he wants to be a nomad. He can go on his own as far as I'm concerned."

Marla heard Kate's resentful tone and again wondered about any underlying issues between the pair. "You came on this cruise with us," she pointed out.

"That's different. We wanted to be with you. We're even thinking of buying a place in Florida so we can come down during the winters. John's been talking to a real estate agent."

Kate halted beneath an overhang of a tree with broad green leaves. "You know, if you get married in December, I could come down early to help out. Unless you want to use the chapel on this cruise ship." She grinned broadly.

Marla took a step backward. "That wouldn't be fair to my mother. She'd want to be at our wedding. It doesn't have to be any big deal. Dalton and I have been through this before."

Kate's face softened. "Anyone can see how taken you are with each other. You keep looking at him and vice versa. I'm so thrilled for you both. You're a delightful young woman, and I know you'll make him and Brie so happy."

"Thanks." Her cheeks warmed. "I find I'm liking this mothering thing. I can never replace Pam, but I'll do my best to love her child and look after her husband."

The older woman chuckled. "As if Dalton would let anyone look after him. He can be stubborn, but he says the same thing about you. You're a perfect match, even if you do butt heads on occasion. I suspect he finds that stimulating."

So did Marla. She smiled inwardly as she urged Kate to move ahead. They rejoined the group for the trek along the mountain path that ended just as the heavens opened up and it poured. They made it inside the bus just in time.

Once they reached the downtown area, the sun had dissipated the clouds. Heat reflected off the pavement, intensifying the odor of exhaust fumes and garbage overflowing from a nearby can. A gentle sea breeze stirred the hairs on Marla's arm and freshened the air.

Checking her watch, she realized they'd better hurry to do their shopping. John excused himself to return to the ship, while the rest of them scooted toward the recommended shops.

"Daddy, can we go in here? They have Reef sandals," Brianna said, darting into a store along Calle de la Tanca.

Marla strolled in after her, browsing the souvenirs, opal inlay jewelry, beachwear, and T-shirts. Vail studied the Bacardi rum selections, while Kate checked the blackboard with lucky cabin numbers to see if any of them had won a tanzanite pendant.

"Today isn't our lucky day, at least not in this place," Brianna's grandmother said, eyes twinkling. "Where to? You and Dalton could shop for wedding rings at A Touch of Gold," she told Marla in a bright tone.

"That's okay," Marla said, backing toward the exit. Time to go, before Kate showered her with any more nuptial tips.

"I'll take these," Brianna said, dumping a decorated shirt, sun visor, souvenir shot glass, and sandals on the counter.

Vail gave Marla a bemused glance as he pulled out his wallet. "It's a good thing we didn't spend all day shopping," he remarked.

"Oh yeah? Wait until tomorrow, when we're in St. Thomas," Marla said, with a grin.

Outside, they headed uphill, past a shop selling Tommy Bahama clothing, a Payless ShoeSource, and the San Juan Fitness Club. Veering around a red motorcyle parked at the curb, they reached Calle Fortaleza. Families with strollers, tourists, and pigeons competed for the right-of-way against noisy buses, motorcycles, and older-model cars.

Pausing at a shady square on Calle de Cristo, Marla consulted her map. A woman slept on a nearby bench, close to where a street worker collected trash. Plants in large ceramic pots lined the cobblestone street. A horse and carriage trotted past, carting a young couple on a romantic ride.

"Let's go in here," Marla said, indicating a jewelry store a few doors away from the Coach outlet. "They offer free piña coladas. I'm dying for a drink."

"Oh, good, I can look for ankle bracelets," Brianna cried, rushing inside.

"Look who's there," Vail said after he'd entered. "The guy from our dinner table."

Marla spotted Thurston Stark examining a selection of watches. "I'm going to talk to him. Kate, will you see if you can find what Brie wants?" While Vail meandered off with a bored expression, she approached the museum foundation chairman.

"Hi, Thurston. Getting any good buys? Where's Heidi?"

He gave her a friendly smile. "Hello, Marla. I see

you brought the whole family shopping with you. Heidi is in the back looking at the sale items. If you're heading there, please tell her to come up front, will you? I'd like her to see this necklace. It's not as though we can't afford the good stuff. Har har."

Marla gave him a sharp glance. His chuckle had an insincere ring. Had there been an inkling of truth in his statement?

A gleam of gold caught her eye, and she wandered to a display case. Maybe she could find a new pair of earrings for work. Nothing exciting jumped out at her, so she made her way toward the rear, stopping to admire a collection of Caribbean hook bracelets. Too expensive in gold. Would Brianna like one of them in silver as a gift?

As she rounded the corner, she halted. *Good Lord.* Heidi Stark had her arms around Cliff Peters. The museum's security guard appeared to be giving Thurston's wife more than a sociable greeting. Marla cleared her throat before they heard her and sprang apart.

"Oh, hi, Marla," Heidi said, with a nervous giggle. "We were just, um, saying hello."

Cliff gave Marla a two-fingered salute. "Heidi was telling me how bad she felt about, uh, leaving her terriers at the kennel. Poor baby."

Marla didn't buy their act. "Your husband needs you," she told Heidi in a cool tone. The woman wore a black tank top with turquoise shorts. Around her neck, she sported enough gold chains to open a store branch.

"I'll just, like, mosey on along then," Heidi replied in her girlish tone.

"Here you are," Thurston's voice boomed after she'd joined him. Marla had followed her, uncomfortable at being left alone in Cliff's hulking presence. She noticed Heidi stroke a teasing finger down Thurston's jaw. Expanding his chest, he gazed at her adoringly. "I've found the perfect necklace to go with that red dress you bought recently. The rubies aren't too small, are they, baby?"

"Oh no, dearest. They're totally amazing." When he turned to the display case, Heidi aimed a scorching glance at Cliff and jerked her thumb at him. The security guard took the hint and slunk toward the exit.

Vail approached, handing Marla a cup with a frosty cream concoction. "Be careful, it's really cold," he said, but she'd already taken a sip. The liquid froze her throat so she couldn't speak.

"Marla, come here," Brianna called. "I like these two ankle bracelets, but I can't decide. They would look great together," she said hopefully, while Vail snorted.

"Let me see." Swallowing, Marla examined the selections. "This one's too thin. It might break easily. I'd say this other choice is your better bet."

"Okay." The teen shrugged, her ponytail swinging. "See, Grandma, I told you she'd like that one the best. Can we look at rings next?"

"Not here," Vail barked, pulling out his credit card. "Go see what stores are down the street. I'll meet you."

"Did you find any earrings you liked?" Kate asked, tapping Marla's arm as they emerged onto the street.

"Not yet. I think the shopping will be better tomorrow."

Marla picked her way along the uneven pavement, passing stores selling amber jewelry, discount perfumes, native handicrafts, and liquor. Halting to wait for Vail, she nearly ran smack into Oliver Smernoff. The man took a moment to recognize her.

"Marla, how ya doing? Find any bargains?" The museum director gave Brianna an oblique glance. "I don't see you ladies holding too many shopping bags."

"Dalton has them; he's just behind us," Marla explained as Kate slipped into a linen shop. "This is his daughter, Brianna. She is staying with her grandparents on the ship. They're the people Dalton and I were supposed to sit with at dinner. Where's your wife?"

Oliver grimaced. "Irene went back to the *Tropical Sun* after our tour. She always has trouble walking. It's those damn heels she wears. Totally impractical."

"Oh, how was the rum distillery?"

"Interesting, but I don't care for lectures. I should have brought my iPod." He hummed a little tune for emphasis.

"We went to the rain forest. It was beautiful but a long ride. At least we got to see some of the terrain along the way."

"I wonder what Thurston did," Oliver mused, shading his face with his hand. "He and Heidi have been to San Juan before."

"We ran into the Starks at a jewelry store."

"No kidding? I'll bet the old man couldn't resist buying Heidi another bauble." He waggled his eyebrows. "Like she doesn't have enough already, you know? I shouldn't criticize him, though. He dotes on that gal, and he's mighty generous when it comes to the museum. Thurston is one of our biggest contributors. His name makes the platinum circle every year." He squinted. "Oh look, there's Martha."

Marla spied the gift shop lady across the street.

Waving, Martha Shore hurried over to join them. "Hi, guys. Olly, I'm glad I caught you. We need to talk."

His gaze darkened. "What about, Martha? I don't want to drag past events into my vacation."

"It's not about that. You need to keep an eye on Bob Wolfson when we're in Grand Cayman. Here's why." She drew him away, out of Marla's earshot.

"Darn, I'd like to hear what they're saying," she told Brianna, at her side.

"Who cares? I'm hungry. Can we go back to the ship?"

"As soon as your father joins us. What could be taking him so long?" Scanning the street, she noted Kent Harwood veering toward Martha and Oliver, who remained huddled together in low conversation.

"Let's go look in the window of that hammock store," Marla suggested to Brianna. "Maybe we should get one for the backyard at our new house. We could string it between the orange trees."

"Cool." Buying her excuse, Brianna accompanied her until they paused a few feet away from Kent's broad backside.

"Find any good buys for the museum gift shop?" Kent was saying to Martha. Oliver didn't look very happy. His shoulders hunched, and he had a glowering expression on his face.

"Nothing I can't get at the gift shows back home," Martha replied. "Have you been shopping?"

"Well now, I'm looking for lots of things, but you won't find many of them in the stores here. Take those Brighton belts you have in the museum store, for example. I might want to buy one as a gift, but how would I know if you have the item in stock?"

Pulling a toothpick from his pocket, he stuck it in his mouth.

Martha's brow wrinkled. "You can ask. If we don't have it, I could order the item from a catalog, or you could take the sample from the shelf."

"How often do you do inventory?"

"Once a week."

"Which day?"

"I don't see why it concerns you, Kent. Have you been following me?" Martha fingered her earring.

"Nah, what gives you that idea? Hi ya, Mr. Smernoff. Hope you're having a good time. Never cared much for San Juan myself."

He sauntered off, leaving them staring after him.

Marla glanced at Brianna. Why would the mold inspector be interested in the museum's gift shop inventory? It made no sense for him to care about Martha Shore's routine.

Unless . . . he was inspecting for more than mold.

CHAPTER 6

"What do you mean, Martha is missing?" Marla asked Helen Bryce at the on board art auction Monday night.

"We're sharing a cabin together, and we went shopping this afternoon," Helen replied. "We got separated when I wanted to go back to the ship, and Martha said she had something else to do. When she didn't show up for dinner, I thought she must have grabbed a quick bite at the Outrigger Café." Brushing aside a strand of auburn hair, she slumped into the seat beside Marla.

"We were late in sailing," Marla offered. "Your roommate had plenty of time to get back on board. Did you check all the public lounges?"

The museum's head docent, wearing an attractive moss green silk blouse with black slacks, clutched her handbag. "Security paged me. They said she didn't make it back from Puerto Rico, and the captain had to sail without her. I spoke to someone in Guest Relations who filled out a report about her last-known whereabouts. I can't imagine what happened to her."

"What will she do if she's stuck in San Juan?"

Helen shrugged. "Get a flight to our next port perhaps. She left her stuff on board. I searched all over the ship, but there's no sign of her, and then I was in a rush to get here."

"Tell me about it. I got this invitation for free raffle tickets on my door again, and I didn't even look at it until the waiters were marching around singing "Finicule Finicula" in the dining room. The note is addressed to Martha, like the last time. I expected to see her here anyway."

Deserted by Brianna and Vail, who'd strolled off to browse the photo gallery, and Kate and John, who were listening to music in Deadeye Dick's Pub, Marla had attended the auction alone.

"More champagne, madam?" said the bar attendant, poising a bottle over her glass.

Marla rubbed her stomach. "No, thanks, I'm too stuffed from dinner." This had been Italian night, and she'd overindulged with a salad of sliced mozzarella and tomatoes, veal scallopini, angel hair pasta, and tiramisu for dessert.

"What should I do about Martha?" Helen asked. "I've spoken to the others in our group, and no one has any news."

"If you wait until the auction is finished, I'll go with you to Guest Relations. Their security team must have notified the authorities in San Juan."

Eric Rand donned his microphone headset while his assistant plunked a canvas onto an easel facing the audience. As before, the Smernoffs, Starks, and Wolfsons sat in the front. Betsy hustled into a far corner, giving Marla a little wave. She took a seat next to Brooklyn Jones. The others from the museum, Kent Harwood and Cliff Peters, sat separately.

"Hello, folks. For those of you who haven't been here before, my name is Eric Rand, and I'm your auctioneer. If you see an item that interests you, please raise your bidding card. My lovely assistant up here will write down the winning numbers. You can make an appointment to return for delivery arrangements when you hand in your cards at the end."

He pointed to the first piece. "Here we have a Muhammad Ali signed photograph. Photos of this size on the sports memorabilia market are exceedingly rare. Gallery price is five thousand four hundred dollars. Do I have an opening bid for twenty-two-fifty? There you go, sir. Twenty-three hundred? Right on. Who wants it for twenty-three-fifty?" He scanned the audience. "No one? Are we done? Going once, going twice, third and final warning, sold for twenty-three-hundred dollars! Whoo-hoo!"

One assistant took that item away as another young man in a logo shirt positioned a brightly colored painting on the easel.

"Look at this Peter Max, folks. Max is the living Picasso, with the hottest collectible art on the planet today."

Marla squinted at the picture. It looked like a sailboat on the ocean with a red sunset, but the lines seemed blurry to her vision. She gripped her bidding card but didn't raise it.

". . . It's gonna go once, it's going twice. Third and final warning. Sold for fifty-seven-hundred dollars! Whoo-hoo!"

She tuned out while more modern works, additional keepsakes from sports stars, and Betty Boop pictures revolved in quick succession.

"And now we have one of our mystery suites," Eric said, while his assistants added a couple of more easels to display three pieces of art facing away from the audience.

Marla jerked upright as Helen gasped beside her.

"Those could be Alden Tusk's triptych," the head docent rasped, her sea green eyes wide as she stared forward.

Eric tugged on his yellow and gray bow tie. "Listen up, folks. First come, first served for our set of mystery pictures tonight. Gallery price puts these at five thousand dollars apiece. Who wants to give an opening bid for twenty-seven-seventy-five each? Use your collector's card, folks, and don't pay anything for thirteen months. Put our money to work for you."

Thurston Stark's hand shot up, and so did Oliver Smernoff's. Through the forest of raised bidding cards, Marla also saw Kent Harwood's number. Out of curiosity, she raised her own. Judging by the numbers being vigorously copied down by the assistant, the mystery items were more popular than the regular auction items.

At each incremental price, many hands went down, but the people from the museum kept in the race. Thurston, red faced, bounced in his seat, while Oliver clenched his teeth and looked like he'd swallowed his tongue. Kent, a wolfish expression in his eyes, grinned every time the bid increased.

Marla saw Irene lean sideways and mumble something into Oliver's ear. Scowling, he snapped something back at his wife and then returned his attention to the auctioneer. His jaw slackened when the gavel came down.

". . . Sold for a total of ninety-nine-hundred dollars. Whoo-hoo!" Rand cheered, pumping his fist.

Oliver aimed a poisonous glance at his rival bidder. Thurston shrugged, raising his hands, but he appeared pleased. Heidi elbowed him, adjusting her legs for maximum exposure. The museum's foundation chair responded by kissing her cheek.

Yuck, Marla thought. *He's old enough to be her father, and he treats her like a newlywed. Maybe he holds stock in Viagra.*

While the audience collectively held their breath, the auctioneer's assistant turned the pictures around. "Look at this fantastic collection by Tarkay, a true mover and shaker of modern art, folks," Eric said, gesturing at the watercolor portraits of ladies in conversational groupings.

Thurston slouched forward, hanging his head, while a look of triumphant relief settled over Oliver's complexion. Marla twisted forward to view Kent Harwood, who was smirking at them both.

"Tarkay is one of the top-ranking artists in today's world," continued Eric, pacing back and forth. "We're a direct source for his fabulous works of art, and we'll have more than forty original pieces for sale during our cruise."

Feeling a wave of fatigue, Marla sagged in her seat while numerous other works were moved forward. Another mystery item brought forth an enthusiastic response, but since it was only one piece, her dinner table mates made a lukewarm effort to win the bid. When the gavel came down on the last item, Marla stretched to her feet.

"I'll go to Guest Relations with you to ask about Martha," she said to Helen. "Then I'm supposed to meet Dalton. You're welcome to join us in the Starlight Lounge for a drink."

Twisting an emerald ring on her right hand, Helen cast her a grateful glance. "Thanks, but I'd better check our cabin again to see if I have any phone messages, and then I thought I'd go on-line. Martha could always contact me by e-mail."

Marla smiled reassuringly. "She'll turn up, even if she has to take a plane home."

"And leave her luggage here? Doubtful."

Marla didn't care to think about the implications of the museum's gift shop manager being missing for more nefarious reasons than just getting caught up in shopping. Remembering the creepy look one of the men on shore had given Brianna, she shuddered. That wasn't a place where she'd want to be left behind. "Let me know what you find out, will you?"

"Okey dokey." Helen rose reluctantly, as though unsure what to do first.

"Let's get in line," Marla said, gesturing toward the registration desk where people waited to hand in their bidding cards. She exchanged her card for a free seriolithograph.

"Isn't this lovely?" Helen said, pulling her eight-by-ten picture from the envelope. The colorful tropical scene, red beach chairs in front of a cabana overlooking a harbor with sailboats, was a work by Fanch Ledan called *Volets Caraibes*.

"It'll look nice on one of the walls in our new house," Marla said, pleased with her acquisition. They'd all received the same signed picture, albeit with different numbers in the limited series.

Helen pointed to Marla's diamond engagement ring. "Are you getting married soon?"

"We haven't set a date. I'm a little nervous about taking the plunge for a second time."

A sad expression crossed Helen's face. "I can relate. For a long time, I wasn't ready to date anyone else."

"Are you divorced?"

"Widowed. Bill had heart disease."

"I'm sorry." They moved toward the exit, proceeding down the foyer steps and into the corridor. "Did your husband support the art museum when he was alive?"

"Sure, that's how I got involved with the docent program. I love learning about art and wish I had the money for my own collection, but I have to be grateful Bill left me enough so I don't have to work. My volunteer activities keep me quite busy." She brushed a speck of lint off her slacks.

"Where were you—" Marla began, intending to ask about the night Alden Tusk died, but just then Helen spotted the Wolfsons.

"Excuse me," Helen interrupted, "but there's Bob. Maybe he'll come along to my cabin to see if I have any messages."

Hey, what about me? I offered to go to the purser's desk with you. Watching her scurry away, Marla wondered why Helen would even approach the museum manager to accompany her. But when she saw the woman's body language, another message came through loud and clear. Bob's wife figured it out, because Sandy snatched his elbow and propelled him away.

And to think I felt sorry for you, Marla said silently to Helen's retreating back. *You're nothing more than a man-eater disguised as a lonely widow. Keep away from my guy, lady.*

"Hey, Marla," Betsy said, poking her. "I guess none of us won the raffle again, huh?"

"Nope. Some lucky devil walked off with three thousand dollars' worth of art. Oh well, there's always tomorrow night. I could've plotzed when they brought out those three mystery pictures. Didn't you think they might be Alden's?"

"Too bad they weren't. Eric is keeping us in suspense." Betsy fell into step beside her.

They descended the central stairs to deck five. Maybe Dalton and Brianna would be on the promenade. Glancing around, Marla sniffed beer fumes coming from the pub but didn't spot Kate or John inside. Nor were any members from her party in the Cargo Café, shops, champagne bar, or Sailaway Lounge.

"I think Oliver was mad that he lost the bid," Betsy said. "Irene spoke to him at the last minute, and so he wasn't paying attention when Eric called the final number."

Marla gave her companion a curious glance. "Speaking of Oliver, I saw him in town today talking to Martha Shore. Kent was there, too. Now Helen is concerned because no one has seen Martha since the ship cast off. Apparently, she was left behind, and we sailed without her."

Betsy's eyes widened. "No shit? Poor gal. I wonder what she'll do. Man, I wouldn't want to be stranded in that port."

"Me neither. I'm hoping she'll catch up with us in St. Thomas tomorrow if she can get a flight."

"You said it. I can see why Helen is worried."

Marla hoped to get voice mail from Helen later on saying the gift shop manager had turned up safe and sound on the island, but by the time she located Vail, enjoyed a drink with him in the fourteenth-floor lounge, and returned to their cabin, no one had left a message.

"Do you think I should give Helen a call?" Marla asked Vail, as she removed her necklace. "She might have heard from Martha via e-mail."

"It's late. I wouldn't bother her until morning." His gaze darkening, Vail watched her slip out of her dress. "In the meantime, I can think of a way to put your mind at ease."

"Oh, really?" Stepping closer, she stroked his chest with her finger while the air-conditioning cooled her underwear-clad body. "Show me."

Ding dong, ding dong. "Good morning, ladies and gentlemen, and welcome to St. Thomas. This is the captain from the bridge. . . ."

Marla threw her mascara wand on the bathroom vanity when a knock sounded on their door. Feeling rushed because they'd woken late, she'd been hurrying to pack her bag for the day and put some finishing touches on her makeup. She heard Vail, who'd opened the door, greet someone in the hallway.

"Marla," he called, "there's an officer here asking us about Martha Shore."

She reacted to his businesslike tone by scurrying out. A white uniformed man with a crew cut and clipboard stood there. He had a lean build, blond hair, and cold blue eyes.

"So sorry to disturb you when you're getting ready to debark, but I have to ask a few questions. Mrs. Helen Bryce has filed a missing person report on her roommate, who failed to return to the ship yesterday before we sailed."

"Are you with Security?" Marla asked, her heart sinking. This meant Martha must still be out of touch with everyone.

"I'm Carl Jenkins from Guest Relations. Our manager has put me in charge of this investigation." Wearing an earnest expression, he consulted his paper. "I have here that Ms. Shore was last seen shopping in

San Juan by yourself, Kent Harwood, and Oliver Smernoff. Is this correct?"

Marla gestured for him to enter, and then she sank down on the sofa. She noticed how Dalton shook his head in resignation. *Hey, don't blame me. At least this isn't another murder . . . yet.*

"Dalton's daughter was with me," she told the officer before addressing Vail. "Did you see us talking to Martha and Oliver?"

Pacing, Vail crossed his arms in front of his chest. "I was stuck in the jewelry store. By the time I came outside, you and Brie were down the street at the Guess outlet."

"Do you know where Ms. Shore was heading next?" Carl asked, scribbling notes.

"Speak to the others. They talked to her after me."

"Did the lady say anything at all to indicate she might not be returning to the ship?"

"No, she didn't." Clasping her hands, Marla examined a spot on the carpet. "Does this happen often that people don't make it back on time?"

"We get the occasional stragglers. We'll give them about twenty minutes before we raise the gangplank. People get busy shopping or sightseeing, and they forget to watch the time. It's costly for us to remain in port, so we can't wait too long."

"Doesn't your security team know right away if someone hasn't come back? They swiped our cards when we left the ship. You should be able to confirm who's missing."

"Yes, ma'am. We paged the lady on board just to make sure she didn't slip through unnoticed."

"I was unaware she hadn't shown up until I saw her roommate at the art auction last evening," Marla said.

She glanced at Vail who hovered near the door, clearly anxious to be on his way. Doubtless he wanted to avoid any investigative work while on vacation. So what if this didn't concern them personally? She felt bad for the woman. Hopefully, Martha had kept her passport, but she'd still have to get a hotel room, contact the airlines, and such. What a hassle.

"Can you verify the passenger's physical description, ma'am?" Carl asked. Gripping his pen, he regarded her with a level gaze.

"She, um, sort of looked like me."

"Did you get in touch with the authorities in Puerto Rico?" Vail interrupted. Marla gave him a startled glance. He might not appear to be involved, but his mind must be running in detective mode. Force of habit, she thought with a smirk.

"Yes, sir. They are conducting a search, but no one answering her description has come forward." Carl returned his attention to Marla. "Can you tell me which areas on the ship Ms. Shore liked to frequent?"

"I didn't really know her that well. I ran into her on the bridge tour, and she seemed interested in the talk. Elsewhere? We didn't come across her in any of the lounges. Maybe she liked to hang out in the casino. I don't gamble, so I don't spend time in there. Nor do I make use of the spa."

"Did the lady have any medical complaints?"

"How would I know? I just said we were barely acquainted." Her brain registered his words. "Oh, do you think she might have gotten sick on shore and sought medical help?"

"It's possible."

"Will anybody check the hospitals? I mean, how awful to be stuck in a foreign place alone and to become ill."

"It's being covered. Now, can you tell me who else Martha Shore associated with on the ship, besides her roommate and the other two people mentioned earlier?"

Holding up her hand, Marla counted on her fingers. "Cliff Peters and Brooklyn Jones. They're assigned to her table in the dining room. Along with Helen, plus the folks at our dinner table—they all work for an art museum in Tampa," she told the officer. "Did Helen inform you that they received their tickets courtesy of an unknown benefactor? And how we've been getting private invitations to the art auctions on board?"

"That's not so unusual," Carl said, "especially if these people work in the art field together."

"Someone on the ship's crew must know about them," Marla persisted. "Someone like the ship's auctioneer, who previously had been employed as curator at the museum."

"He left the Tampa facility months ago," Vail pointed out. "How would he have kept up with the employees and volunteers?"

"Beats me, but someone brought them here for a reason."

Carl interjected, "Is there anyone else whom Ms. Shore associated with, to your knowledge?"

Ignoring him, Marla addressed her fiancé. "Should I tell him about the note?"

Vail shrugged. "Why not? But make it quick. We have to meet the tour group outside." He tapped his watch for emphasis.

At the last minute, they'd signed up for the excursion to Coral World after arguing whether they should do Blackbeard's Castle, Magen's Bay, or spend the entire time shopping. Dalton had balked at the latter, while Brianna had wanted to explore snorkeling. They'd finally compromised when Kate and John said they would like to visit the underwater observatory.

Marla had saved the original note from their cabin door. She pulled it from her purse and unfolded the worn sheet of paper. "This was addressed to Martha, same as the private invitations to the auctions that I received. At first, I assumed my name had been spelled incorrectly, but when I met the other people from the museum, I realized I must've been getting messages meant for Martha."

"I see," Carl said, taking the paper from her hand and scrutinizing it. "Any idea what this means?"

"No clue. I haven't really discussed this particular message with any of our tablemates, and I hesitated to bring it up to Martha. Those words could mean anything, but they sound sinister to me."

Especially since Martha has gone missing.

CHAPTER 7

Marla passed through the security gate toward Havensight Mall, where people congregated with their tour groups. St. Thomas had so many choices of things to do that in her opinion, it was easiest to do nothing and go shopping. But she had never been to the island and confessed to a curiosity about the mountainous wonder that awaited them. The harbor facing Charlotte Amalie was entrancing enough with sailboats bobbing in the water.

She watched people depart for the snorkel excursion, helmet dive, jet boats, and Atlantis submarine. The crowd going on the Kon-Tiki raft were already into party mode, laughing and dancing their way behind the guide, a woman holding up a big sign. Marla could imagine their boisterous return after they sampled a few rum punches on the ride.

Shading her face, she halted beside the group going to the Kayak Marine Sanctuary. "Do you see Brie or your folks anywhere?" She reached into her purse, rummaging for her sunglasses among the guidebooks she'd shoved in there before they left. She kept her key card pass in the zippered compartment along with her passport and traveler's checks.

"What a mob," Vail complained, scanning the passengers milling about. "We should have just taken our own taxi."

"You're probably right." Vowing to buy a hat, she wiped the sweat already beading her brow.

"It took me fifteen years of marriage," said a guy to another man standing next to her, "but now I understand that when a woman says she's going shopping, that doesn't necessarily mean she's buying."

"No kidding," the other fellow said. "When my wife shops, she can't make up her mind, so we go from store to store."

"Personally, I think it's genetic."

Marla smiled to herself. She noticed both husbands carried large canvas shopping bags, no doubt prepared to escort their wives and pick up their own souvenirs.

"Oh, there's Brie," Marla said, spotting the teen's lavender Bebe shirt as she squeezed through the security gate in front of her grandparents. Shoveling her way through the crowd, Marla hugged the girl. "Hi, honey. We've missed you."

Kate beamed at her. "You look fresh and bright this morning."

"I'm excited about seeing the island. It's such a beautiful place, with the town at the base of the mountains and the picturesque harbor."

"We need more than one day here," Brianna stated, bouncing from foot to foot. "I'd love to go to the beach. Magen's Bay is supposed to be one of the best. I don't want to spend the whole afternoon shopping."

"But there's so much to buy here!" Marla exclaimed. "Jewelry, liquor, linens, perfume, island coffees and rum balls. And next to AH Riise is a place that just sells David Yurman."

"Oh yeah? Maybe they have the bracelet I want."

"You've been eager to see Coral World," Vail reminded his daughter, patting her shoulder. "Don't let Marla turn you into a shopping fiend."

"Too late for that," John remarked in a dry tone. He stood beside his wife, tall and stalwart, with a bored expression. Straightening his glasses, he jerked his thumb at one of the buses. "Are we heading over or just standing here?"

Once inside the bus, he took a seat next to a handsome older man while Marla and Kate sat next to each other, and Vail kept his daughter company. Marla heard the stranger introduce himself as an exseaman to John and soon they were chatting like old buddies. Peculiar, she thought. He opens up to someone he doesn't know more than he does to us.

"I'll tell you a funny story," the Navy guy said in a manner that reminded her of Wilda Cleaver, the psychic who'd inherited a salon from Marla's dead rival. Wilda began her long-winded tales in a similar fashion, and Marla had heard enough of them to cringe when anybody said they had a story to tell. She got an earful of the man saying how he'd given a young midshipman a requisition for fallopian tubes in the days before there were women on ships, and how the crew had sent the poor sap around in circles until he'd ended up asking the captain for help.

John responded with loud guffaws and started telling his own war stories, which she would've liked to hear, but Kate touched her arm and struck up a conversation. "Look out the window, Marla. Isn't this island beautiful? I'm so glad Dalton has you to share these adventures with him and Brie."

She met her future mother-in-law's warm gaze. "I hope we'll be able to do more traveling. I've hardly been anywhere."

"Dalton says you're expanding your salon. Won't that make you even busier?"

Here comes the reprimand, she thought. *Kate will inform me how being a good stepmother means staying home more.* "Actually, once we get up and running, I'd like to cut back my hours. But I've put too much hard work and effort into establishing a name in the community to step away entirely. Besides, I really like working behind the chair. It's just so gratifying when a client looks great and feels better about herself."

"Well, I really admire your skill and ambition. I couldn't combine working and raising children myself, but things are different today. You'll manage; you have lots of energy."

Marla's mouth dropped open. "Thank you, Kate. I appreciate having your support. It isn't always easy," she said, thinking of the dressing-down she'd gotten from Vail's former mother-in-law, Justine.

"When you and Dalton are married, you'll have to call me Mom. Unless that's what you call your own mother?"

She laughed. "Ma is going to like you. I'll bet you have a lot in common."

"Yes. When am I going to meet her? We'll have to coordinate our dresses for the wedding. Have you chosen a color scheme?"

Her bright tone notwithstanding, Marla caught a hint of underlying anxiety in her tone. *Surely she isn't afraid I'll change my mind?*

"Uh, not yet. Maybe something will strike me on this trip when we don't have so many distractions." Pointing out her window, she added, "Another McDonald's? They're everywhere." Their bus chugged past a chain drugstore and gas station before turning onto the route to take them across the island.

Her attention diverted to the winding ride through verdant hills colored by flaming-red royal poinciana trees, pink azaleas, green banana plants, and white oleanders, along with hibiscus, bougainvillea, and frangipani. As the bus rounded a hairpin curve, they were met by an ocean vista. She glimpsed dark and mysterious islands rising from the distant sea.

Speaking of mysterious, Marla remembered she'd wanted to question the museum people about Martha Shore. Vail had advised her to forget about the woman for now, but she couldn't dismiss her so readily. At the very least, she should talk to the woman's colleagues to see if Martha had mentioned plans to remain in Puerto Rico. She hadn't seen Helen among the tour groups. Had the widow stayed on board to track down her roommate?

Marla pushed aside her questions when they arrived at Coral World. Filing off the bus, she wondered if this excursion would be anything like Crystal Cay in Nassau. She'd enjoyed the underwater observatory there until someone shot at her in the Marine Gardens. Helping cousin Cynthia with a fund-raiser, Marla hadn't expected her search for a saboteur to turn so deadly.

Brianna led the way to the structure poised over the water and they descended to a lower level where viewers peered at the coral reef through huge windows. Schools of tiny fish swarmed in unison like a wave, undulating in the current. Colorful parrot fish, funny-looking trumpet fish, and other varieties of brilliant sea life kept Marla entranced.

"Awesome, look at that brain coral," Brianna exclaimed.

Marla nodded. "I like how that branch type of coral waves back and forth. There's just so much to see down here." The coral came in all shapes and sizes, waving or billowing as if blown by a wind. Watching it brought her a strange sense of serenity. Just beyond the window's viewing range, the reef dropped away, and the water became a murky, impenetrable aqua.

Vail stepped up to her side. "It's easy to forget about the outside world in a place like this."

"Is that why you like going to parks?" she said, turning to gaze into his craggily handsome face. "Studying the trees makes you feel more tranquil?"

"That's right. Nature lacks the ugliness that mankind exhibits."

"Mankind also has beautiful accomplishments, like ballet, music, and art—things most people don't have time for these days, myself included," she retorted. "I'm enjoying the art auctions on the ship, because I'm learning something new, and they're fun."

"So much fun that Oliver Smernoff nearly belted his wife because she made him miss the final bid on that mystery piece," he drawled.

"Those people have something going on beneath the surface. Like this undersea life, the ripples affect everyone. I'm interested in learning the truth about Alden Tusk, besides caring about what happened to Martha Shore."

"We're supposed to be on vacation, remember?"

"That doesn't mean I'm going to sit back while bad things happen to people I know."

"Marla, darling, let's go upstairs to see the stingrays," Kate inserted, taking her elbow.

Marla acquiesced, grateful for the intervention before she got into an argument with Vail. "This is similar to a place I visited in Nassau," she told her future mother-in-law as they climbed a spiral staircase to the upper level. "I'll stop here briefly, but then I'd like to check out the shops. We don't have much time before we have to be back on the bus."

"Maybe you should do your wedding in tropical colors," Kate said while they stood in front of a picture window viewing the sharks, stingrays, lobsters, spider crabs, and big fishes that swam past. "Peach or coral would be lovely. Your mother and I could wear turquoise for contrast."

Marla tilted her head. "I don't know. Do we really need a color scheme? If anything, it'll be a small affair, likely at a country club."

"Or a hotel. Sometimes you can get a better deal depending on the season."

She glanced at Kate's eager hazel eyes. "Did Dalton have a big church wedding with Pam?"

"Oh, yes." Kate smiled sadly. "She looked like an angel in her ivory gown. The flowers were magnificent, and the organist did a stupendous job. My friends talked about their wedding for weeks afterward."

"I hope it doesn't bother you that I'm Jewish. Despite our cultural differences, we respect each other's traditions." She hated the waver in her voice, but this was a sensitive issue after being harangued by Pam's parents and her own mother on the subject.

Kate placed her hands on Marla's shoulders and regarded her squarely. "I don't care if you're from Mongolia as long as you love my son and granddaughter."

Touched by her words, Marla leaned forward and hugged her. "I do, and I love you, too, for saying that."

"So will you look for a priest and rabbi who can do a mixed-faith marriage, or will you get a justice of the peace?" Kate persisted, with a grin that lit her face.

"Who knows?" Marla flung up her hands. "I'm hitting the shops. Do you want to come?"

"I'd better see where John went. He wandered off again, as usual."

"He does that a lot, doesn't he?"

"It annoys the hell out of me. The man just can't stay put. And now he wants to take all these trips? I don't understand why he isn't happy when we have so much to do at home."

They exited together, wincing in the bright sunlight. As a light breeze lifted her hair, Marla whipped a pair of sunglasses from her handbag.

"So he wants to explore the country. That's a nice goal for retirement. He's earned the right for leisure travel."

Frowning, Kate faced her. "You don't get it. He doesn't just want to tour the states and see the sights. He wants to follow the different art shows."

Marla mulled over her words while she browsed the Caribbean crafts store alone. Dalton had taken Brianna to get a hot dog at the snack bar. He preferred to wait for a more substantial lunch in town. Meanwhile, Kate had discovered John haggling over some paintings done by a native artist who crouched on the ground spray painting pictures of alien landscapes. Colorful, but too far out for Marla's taste. Certainly not after she'd been introduced to artists like Fanch and Peter Max.

Wait a minute. Did Kate say John wanted to attend *art shows?* How peculiar, unless this had always been an interest of his. From Kate's tone, Marla didn't believe that applied. So where did this sudden interest in art come from? And why had she seen him shmoozing so intimately with Irene Smernoff on board the ship? Their conversation had been animated, as though they were discussing more than idle shipboard news.

Could it be possible . . . had they known each other *before* the cruise?

Eric Rand came to mind. The ship's art auctioneer had a history with these people. Why not her future father-in-law? But John hadn't been attending the art auctions, except for appearing briefly during the preview. So his interest couldn't be in collecting modern works of art. What then?

A horrible suspicion crossed her mind. What if they hadn't been seated with the museum people by mistake? What if they'd been set up, and John was somehow involved?

She wondered, for the first time, who had actually bought their cruise tickets. Had it been John, or Kate? He could have put in a request to sit with the museum crowd. Then he might have been seated at Irene's table. Their seat mixup could still have been an error on the cruise line's part. Either way, she'd try to keep better tabs on him, if not for Kate's sake, then for Brianna's. The child was staying in their cabin, and Marla didn't want her embroiled in any intrigue.

Despite Marla's good intentions, she lost track of John in town after a bus ride through the verdant mountains, a few stops at scenic vistas overlooking the sea, and a lurching halt in front of a street market. They drove on the left side of the road in St. Thomas, which gave her a kick, but the bumpy ride lessened her appetite. Not so for Vail, however. His nose for food led them straight to Café Amici, down an alley by AH Riise, which was where Marla had promised to take Brianna for David Yurman jewelry.

"That man refuses to carry a cell phone," Kate complained about her husband as she took a seat in a wicker chair. They'd found an empty marble-topped table on the outdoor terrace.

Greenery cascaded over a stone building to Marla's left, while ceiling fans rotated overhead. Listening to the New Age music playing in the background, she felt her tension ease. A warm breeze caressed her skin like a kiss from the ocean.

"John said he wasn't hungry and would meet us in the liquor store," Marla said, hoping to wipe away the worry lines on Kate's brow. She didn't like to see dissension between them.

"Dad needs some space," Vail told Kate. "He says you nag him all the time to do chores at home, and he has his own things to keep himself busy."

"Yeah, and they don't include me."

Sensing Dalton's mother was about to deliver a diatribe against her husband, Marla cut in.

"Hey look, there's Helen! Looks like she's tagging along with the Wolfsons. I'm glad she didn't stay on board the ship."

"That's nice," Vail said in a resigned tone. "So, Brie, what are you getting to eat?"

"I just had a hot dog, Dad," Brianna said, as though he were the dumbest person on earth. "This is, like, totally a waste of time. We could be shopping already."

"We've got all afternoon," Marla reassured her. Feeling relaxed, she ordered a rum punch and a vegetarian pizza from the waitress, who was wearing an apron over black pants and a T-shirt. Dalton ordered shrimp and asparagus pasta, while Kate got a salad and Brianna just had a Coke. Bristling with impatience, the teen kept glancing toward Main Street, where bustling shoppers crowded the sidewalk.

"Can I see your map?" the teen asked Marla, sweeping her hair back and retying her ponytail.

"Sure, honey." She dug into her tote bag. "I brought

these coupons from the ship, too. Here's one from Diamonds International. You can get a free charm bracelet there. Someone mentioned Cardows for jewelry and said they have a discount section in the back. If you want to fill this card out, we might win a reversible ring."

"Can you put that stuff away?" Vail announced. "Here come our drinks. Besides, I don't want Brie to turn into a shopaholic, like you." His tone held no censure, just amusement.

Nonetheless, Marla pursed her lips. "Be grateful I like shopping at outlet malls and sales racks." She sipped her rum punch, tasting the liquor with approval. She hated ordering a mixed drink that cost a lot and held nothing more than sugar water. She'd better drink it slowly, or she'd be too sloshed to recognize a bargain when she saw one.

After lunch, Vail and his mother hustled off toward Main Street to hunt for John, while Marla and Brianna tackled AH Riise. She'd meet her fiancé later inside the immense store that held jewelry, crystal, cosmetics, designer eyewear, liquor, perfume, and Caribbean gifts, among other things. Stepping inside, Marla felt she could spend all day in this consumer palace. Located in a series of restored nineteenth-century Danish warehouses, the family-owned business that began as an apothecary had turned into a maze of duty-free wares to tempt the traveler.

Dazzled by the display cases, Marla had to ask for directions to the David Yurman boutique. She helped Brianna make her selection and then wandered into other departments to compare prices with those at home. Over by the watches, she spied Bob Wolfson trying on a Rolex. She knew the brand because his wife was haranguing him that they couldn't afford it.

"It's perfect for you," said Helen, simpering beside him.

Sandy Wolfson gave the redhead a venomous glare. "Don't you want to look at the skin care products? You could use a more effective foundation to hide your wrinkles, if you're trying to look younger."

Helen lifted her chin. "*You* might want to visit the fashion department, darling. Your wardrobe could use updating."

Seeing the thunderous look in Sandy's eyes, Marla hastened over. "Oh, hi, Helen," Marla said brightly. "Can I get your opinion on something?" Taking the woman's arm, she steered her away before she could protest. Sandy Wolfson cast her a grateful glance before turning back to her husband.

Checking to see that Brianna had rejoined her grandparents and Vail, Marla directed her attention to Helen Bryce.

"I'm glad you decided to come into town. Any further news on Martha's situation?"

The museum's head docent shook her head. "Not a thing. I didn't see the point of staying on board. The ship's security staff is doing everything they can to track her."

"That's good to hear. Listen, Dalton and I want to shop for wedding rings. Do you have any recommendations on where we should look?"

Helen shrugged, her slim shoulders boosted by shoulder pads inside her turquoise top. "Your guess is as good as mine. It's more a matter of finding what you like."

"So you've been to St. Thomas before?" Marla asked.

"Oh, sure. Bill and I came here on several cruises.

In fact, this is where I got my emerald ring." She held up her hand, wriggling her fingers.

"How long has it been since . . . ?"

"Bill passed away two years ago." Helen smiled, the corners of her eyes creasing into tiny lines. "I've made a life for myself. It's lonely at times, but I have my sons. If only I hadn't messed with their futures."

"What do you mean?"

"I sold something I should have kept for them. I didn't think I could get it back until I got that note on my cabin door."

Marla's interest piqued. "What note?"

"It was addressed to me personally. I don't understand how someone could have learned my secret." Helen leaned forward, lowering her voice. "If I tell you, you'll keep quiet, won't you? I have to talk to someone about it."

"My lips are sealed."

"I sold my life insurance policy to an investor. I made a mistake, but I needed the money. I'm in a better position now, and I'd like to buy it back, but I can't locate the buyer. That note means he may be on the cruise."

Marla almost burst with curiosity. "And the note said . . . ?"

"I know what you did and I have what you want."

CHAPTER 8

"I got the same note on my door, only mine was addressed to Martha Shore. At first, I thought the sender had spelled my name wrong." Marla regarded Helen's stunned expression. "I wonder if everyone from the museum got one."

"Holy macaroni. That's weird."

Marla leaned against a jewelry counter. "I've been thinking what it must mean. And now . . ."

"What?" Helen prompted.

She tilted her head. "All of us, if you consider I've been getting messages intended for the gift shop manager, have received personal invitations to the art auctions. It's highly likely they're from the same person who put the cryptic note on our door the first day of the cruise."

"Okey dokey, I see where you're going with that train of thought. It would have to be someone who knows all of us."

"More than that," Marla pointed out. "This person knows everyone's cabin number. I don't see how that's possible unless it's a crew member."

"Eric Rand!" Helen gasped.

"I've thought of him, since Eric is the ship's auctioneer plus your former curator." She scratched an itch on her arm. "Obviously, he's aware of your interest in art, but how could he have learned you'd all be on the cruise together unless he sent the tickets? Is he that financially well-off?"

Helen's eyes widened. "Not that I recall. He made a decent salary as curator, but I have no idea what these art galleries pay their people. Anyway, how would he have learned about my life insurance transaction?"

"He wasn't the buyer, was he?"

"Well, it actually went through a broker." Helen gripped Marla's arm. "If there's any chance I can buy back my policy, I have to do it. I had no right to take away my sons' security. They'll need that money if anything happens to me. Kate says you're good at solving mysteries. Help me regain ownership."

"I'm not sure what I can do."

"If Eric isn't involved, it has to be one of us, someone who knows our secrets. But why tease us with that note?"

"The message might be meant as a threat. Your secret may not involve anybody else, but who knows what other people are hiding? Someone brought all of you on board for a purpose."

"You're right."

Helen waved at Sandy and Bob, who'd reappeared schlepping several bundles. They halted by the Lalique counter, while outdoors beyond the open doorway, a jitney rattled past on the crowded street. "Take Bob, for instance. I know what he's up to, but his stupid wife will never figure it out."

"Oh really, and what's that?"

Helen's eyes glittered. "Martha was the one who clued me in. She said Oliver questioned her about some gift shop items that were on the expense record but weren't in her inventory." She smoothed her slate gray pants. "Bob needs someone more adventurous like me who can appreciate a risk taker."

What? How did Oliver's remarks relate to Bob? Marla stared at Helen as the woman stalked off after her prey. Bob, adjusting his eyeglasses, squared his shoulders at her approach.

Deciding to look for her own group, Marla sauntered into the liquor department, which also housed Caribbean gifts. She caught sight of Brianna studying a selection of silver hook bracelets and hurried over. "Hi, hon. I'd love to buy you one of these. Do you see a design you like?"

Vail and his dad were in a debate over different brands of rum, while Kate had wandered toward an alleyway where works of native art were displayed. Glad to have a moment alone with the girl, Marla draped an arm across her shoulder.

"That one with the dolphin is neat," Brianna said. "Do you think it'll go with my David Yurman bracelet?"

"Why not? You can wear more than one on your wrist."

"Grandma bought me these earrings," Brianna said, reaching into her purse. Vail had finally consented to allowing his daughter to get her ears pierced.

"Those are lovely," Marla said, admiring the teardrop design in white gold.

"Hey, Marla," Vail said, approaching, "Mom says we should go into Ballerina Jewelers for wedding bands."

She swallowed, feeling the nuptial noose tighten around her neck. "I just want to get this for Brie; then I'll be ready to move on. See if the bracelet fits, honey."

After making her purchase, she parted ways with

the teenager and her grandparents, who'd promised to stop by the beach before heading back to the ship.

"I'd like to get something for your mom," she told Vail as they headed across the busy street. Squealing brakes competed for decibels with car radios and motorcycles. Fresh sea air dispelled the exhaust fumes but not the heat vapors that rose from the asphalt. Respite from the sun came only in the shade from awnings or palm trees.

He guided her with a hand on her midback. "How much more time do you plan to spend here? I don't want to be late for dinner. They have lobster on the menu tonight."

"Are you thinking of food again? We just ate." Marla shook her head. Men had large appetites, both for sex and for meals.

"I'm always hungry. Let's look in here." Inside the jewelry store, he asked for the recommended salesperson. "We're interested in wedding bands," he said, his voice firm.

Marla remained silent. Was she ready for this step? Getting wedding bands meant a commitment, and even though she wore a diamond engagement ring on her finger and they'd put a down payment on a house together, she'd hesitated to set a date. Now there would be no avoiding it, and she already had enough on her plate between moving into a new salon and furnishing a new home. Then again, for Brianna's sake, she and Dalton should be married before they merged their households.

"Shall we get yellow or white gold?" Vail asked, jarring her thoughts.

"Uh, I'd like white gold this time." *Bite your tongue, Marla. You shouldn't have put it that way.* Vail wasn't too fond of her ex-spouse, Stanley Kaufman.

"How about these brushed-gold designs? I kinda like that look," he said, pointing. "Or do you want one with diamonds?"

She smiled at him. "Nothing too fancy that I can't wear to work, thanks." Hooking her arm into his, she thought how lucky she was to have him. He'd been learning to consult her before making decisions that affected them both, and she appreciated his effort. They were each pigheaded, butting their heads often, but the challenge acted as a stimulant to their relationship. She almost wished they were already married.

Making their decision, they took their wrapped package and bustled out the door for more shopping. Marla found a pink pearl necklace for Kate, trinkets for her colleagues back home, and a few other items later on at Havensite Mall by the pier, including a Mont Blanc pen for Vail, after he boarded the ship ahead of her.

Burdened by her bundles, her feet hurting, and dying for a drink, she stumbled up the gangplank. She handed her identity card to the security officer, stuck her packages on the moving belt through the X-ray machine, and passed through the metal detector gates before being allowed to proceed.

"You had me worried," Vail said, jumping to his feet from the bed when she entered their cabin.

"Last-minute shopping," she said, tossing her packages along with her handbag onto the couch. Grabbing the water bottle on her nightstand, she swallowed several gulps in quick succession. Satisfied, she peeled off her sweat-soaked top.

"I hope you left some money on the credit card for the rest of the trip," Vail drawled, sauntering toward her with a gleam in his eyes.

Her blood heated. "No problem. Look, if you

don't let me take a shower first, you're gonna regret it. I won't be long."

No joke there. The shower stall, shaped in a circle the size of a New York sewer cover, didn't allow for much movement. At least the ship wasn't rocking since they were docked, but she had to stick her legs in the sink to shave them afterward.

Vail, who'd been pacing impatiently, drew her into an embrace when she emerged from the bathroom wearing her underwear. She'd just lifted her chin to kiss him when the phone rang. Cursing, Vail broke off to answer, his tone curt.

"Yes, we're back okay. . . . No, we hadn't heard about it. When did this happen? . . . Christ, we just saw her in port."

"What is it?" Marla asked, reaching for her clothes.

Vail raised a hand. "I see. What condition is she in? Is she conscious? . . . All right, you can tell us more at dinner. Thanks for checking in."

He replaced the receiver, his mouth a grim line. "That was Kent Harwood. He wanted to make certain we got back from shore okay. Apparently after she returned to the ship, Helen took a tumble down a flight of steps, one of those narrow curving stairs on an outer deck. She hit her head and was admitted to the infirmary."

Marla's jaw dropped open. "Oh gosh, will she be all right?"

"Harwood doesn't know the details, but he said he'd try to find out. We'll talk more about it at dinner. Finish getting dressed, will you? You always take too long with your make-up."

His uncharacteristic short temper alerted her to his distress. He hadn't been so upset when Martha was missing. Maybe now he actually believed someone meant them harm. Not *them* exactly, but the museum people.

On their way into the dining room promptly at six o'clock, they passed a miniature boat filled with fruit by the entrance. The waiters, wearing colorful tropical shirts, scurried around while a steel band played Caribbean music in the background. Pausing by Kate and John's table to greet the elder couple and Brianna, Marla noted Helen's empty seat.

"Helen didn't make it," said Cliff Peters, looking scruffy despite his open-collared shirt and Dockers slacks. His brusque manner didn't seem suited to the elegant surroundings.

Marla's heart skipped a beat. "What do you mean?" she asked the museum's security guard.

"She's in sick bay. Had some sort of accident." He stuck a bread stick in his mouth.

Marla let out a sigh of relief. Oh, he hadn't meant that Helen had, well, gone to Davy Jones's locker, or whatever the seagoing expression was called.

"We know," Vail said. "Kent phoned us."

"Yeah, what's with him, dude? He's, like, just a bug man, but he's been nosing around like some damn cockroach."

Isn't it your job to nose around at the museum? Marla thought, wondering how he'd ever gotten a job in security.

"Don't sweat it, man," Brooklyn Jones cut in. He looked like one of the band members with his dark skin, tropical shirt, and easy grin. "I'm more worried about Helen. I told that gal not to wear those tipsy shoes on the ship."

"Kent promised to see what he could learn about her condition," Marla said. "Brie, what are your plans for tonight? We have tickets to the ice show at nine, remember?"

"We're making costumes for the pirate party later tonight," the teen said, buttering a roll. "I'll just stick with you guys until then."

"Okay. I'd like to attend the art auction at ten-thirty. Kate, will you join me?"

The older woman smiled. "No thanks, dear. John and I are going to the Love and Marriage Game Show."

John grimaced, his lack of enthusiasm evident. "I agreed to check it out, but I didn't promise I'll stay."

Marla took that as her cue to leave. "See you later," she said, steering Vail toward their own table.

After ordering a crabmeat and avocado appetizer, salad greens with papaya and pineapple, and broiled lobster tails accompanied by garlic butter sauce, she addressed their companions.

"Tell us about Helen," she said to Kent Harwood after greeting the others and inquiring about their shore excursions. Vail, munching away on a crispy conch fritter, kept his ear tuned in her direction.

Kent shrugged, an easy proposition in his loose-fitting jacket. It needed a good press, like the rest of him. His jowls sagged, and his hair hung in stringy strands about his weary face. He may have gone snorkeling, but he could have made himself more presentable. Betsy had been on one of those tours, and she looked as bouncy and fresh as a new perm.

"I stopped by the infirmary," Kent replied. "They said Helen couldn't have any visitors. They're monitoring her condition but think she'll be okay if nothing further develops." He chewed on a toothpick, waiting for delivery of his Bimini grouper. He was the only one at their table who hadn't ordered lobster.

Marla noticed he always skipped the soup and dessert courses, as though watching his weight. At least he had more discipline than Dalton, who'd loosened his belt at least once that evening.

"Did she trip and fall?" Betsy asked, licking her fingers. She'd gotten the seafood cocktail with brandy sauce for her appetizer. "Poor thing. This will ruin her vacation."

"No one saw her tumble down the stairs," Kent told Betsy before scanning the others. "Right?"

"You know, mister, I don't care for your tone of voice," Thurston Stark snapped. "Are you implying one of us had a hand in Helen's accident?" His eyes twitched. *Blink, blink.*

"Am I? You tell me. It's mighty strange that Martha doesn't make it back to port, and then her roommate is put out of action. In my mind, I'm wondering who's next?" Chomping on his toothpick, he glared at the museum foundation chair.

Marla glanced at Vail. She hadn't shared with him the conversation she'd had with Helen, in which Helen had confessed selling her life insurance policy. Helen had also mentioned knowing what Bob was up to before she ran over to snag his attention. Hadn't Martha Shore said something similar to Oliver Smernoff in San Juan? She'd mentioned to the museum director that he should keep an eye on Bob when they docked at Grand Cayman.

Her gaze swung to where Wolfson sat beside his dowdy wife. Sandy had a smug grin on her face for some reason, while Bob wore his usual sour expression. What did Martha and Helen, and quite possibly Oliver, know about him that could be dangerous?

"I wonder when Alden Tusk's triptych will be up for sale," Irene commented. "Are you all attending the art auction tonight?" Sipping from her martini glass, she eyed them like a beauty contestant might survey the competition.

"Of course we're going, aren't we, dearest?" Heidi said.

"Wouldn't miss a chance to pick up some new works for our collection, baby." With a fond glance, Thurston draped his arm around her.

Across the table, Oliver hummed along to the tune of "Yellowbird," playing in the background. Irene, casting him an annoyed glance, drew her elbows inward, as though she couldn't stand his proximity. "Aren't you sorry you couldn't get your seats changed?" she called to Marla with a sniff.

"I feel bad that Dalton's parents paid for our trip and we're not even sitting with them," she acknowledged.

"Who the hell paid for ours?" Bob grumbled. "I'd like to find out who knows so much about us."

"I'll bet you would," Marla muttered under her breath. Next to her, Vail raised his eyebrows.

Bob gave the foundation chair a shrewd glance. "You're not pulling the wool over our eyes, are you?" he asked Thurston.

Thurston slapped a hand to his chest. "I may be generous in my contributions to the museum, but regrettably, it wasn't I who thought to treat everyone to this voyage."

"You think he's the only one with money?" Irene demanded, appearing affronted. With a jerky motion, she tucked a strand of teased hair behind her ear, showing off the diamond stud on her lobe. "Some of us just aren't as showy with our wealth."

Oliver wagged his finger. "Thurston is very kind to make such large donations to the cause, and remember, I'm beholden to him for our children's art program. I would never have gotten it off the ground if it weren't for his support of our fund-raiser," he told his wife in a chastising tone.

"Speaking of the fund-raiser," Betsy spoke in a quiet voice, "can someone tell me how Alden's missing panel came to be here?"

"Talk to Eric Rand," Irene suggested. "He's got what it takes . . . to get answers," she concluded, although Marla figured that wasn't what she meant. Her husband's face purpled but he kept silent, while Marla got the impression Irene had just won a battle of wills between them.

"I just love that cute bow tie that Eric wears," Heidi purred in her little-girl voice.

"Listen," Thurston said, hunching his shoulders, "if y'all let me make the high bid on Tusk's series, I'll show my appreciation by making a significant contribution toward the museum's next traveling exhibit."

"Oh, we're not going to let you have all the fun," Irene said, her voice dripping sarcasm. "Are we, darling?" She nudged her husband, who'd been gnawing on a piece of lettuce.

Swallowing, Oliver jabbed his finger in the air. "Certainly not. I already have some of Tusk's work in my collection. I'm not passing up a chance to get what could be the highlight of his career."

"Alden considered that piece to be his redemption," Betsy mumbled. "Said it would give him back a part of his soul that he'd lost." The others stared at her. "What? I'd . . . admired his talent. We . . . we communicated with each other." Her face flushing, she lowered her head.

After a moment's silence, Oliver laughed. It was a harsh, grating sound. "No kidding? You're our public relations specialist. You had to be in contact with him to arrange for publicity."

"Sure, that's it." Betsy lifted her chin, beaming brightly. "So who's going to the ice show later on?"

She effectively switched the conversation to a more neutral topic and chatter flowed easily from then on. But Marla sensed she hadn't been entirely truthful and indeed knew more about Alden Tusk than she let on. Resolving to delve into their history at the art auction, Marla dug into her lobster tail when it arrived. Enjoying their meal became paramount, but she bit back a remark when Dalton ordered seconds and then thirds on the seafood. *Lord save me, we'd better add that treadmill to our new house.* She knew Ma's boyfriend had a predilection for buffets, but now Dalton was turning into a *fresser* as well. Did all men expand their waistline after they found a woman?

"Aren't you too full for dessert?" she finally said after the waiter cleared their plates. "I'm going to order the coconut cake. You can have a taste."

"Nope, I can't pass up a slice of Key lime pie." He waved off the wine steward who circulated with after-dinner drinks in fancy-colored cups.

She patted his thigh. "Just keep eating, and you'll need to get your wardrobe adjusted before we leave the cruise."

He gave her a wolfish grin. "Keep your hand there, and I'll need something else adjusted instead."

One appetite led to another, and they paused for an interval in their cabin before venturing forth to join Brianna and her grandparents. The ice show was spectacular, better than the theater productions. After it concluded to a standing ovation, Marla strolled toward the photo gallery alongside the teenager.

"Did you find out what happened to that lady who

fell down the stairs?" Brianna asked, giving her a concerned glance.

"You're an angel to care, you know that?" Marla said, squeezing her in a brief hug. "Mr. Harwood said Helen should be all right. I hope she doesn't have to spend the rest of the week in the infirmary, though. That would be an awful vacation."

"She doesn't have her roommate anymore, does she?"

They halted before a rack showing formal portraits from the previous evening. Passengers could pose for free in front of various backdrops, but the eight-by-ten photos cost nearly twenty dollars each. Kate had expressed a wish for a family picture.

"We haven't had any word on Martha, if that's what you mean," Marla answered.

Brianna shook her head as though Marla were daft. "I mean, if Helen is lying there in an infirmary bed, she has nobody to bring her things from her cabin."

"Oh. That would be a thoughtful gesture, wouldn't it?" She glanced at her watch. "I only have fifteen minutes until the art auction, and aren't you supposed to meet your friends?"

"We're meeting at ten-thirty. I can be late."

"I'll tell you what. In the morning, before we arrive at St. Maarten, I'll stop by sick bay. Even if Helen is conscious, she's probably sleeping by now. The nurse may let me in to see her tomorrow, and then I'll ask Helen if she wants me to bring her anything. I'll tell her it was your idea."

Marla smiled, pleased with her plan and the potential chance to question Helen.

CHAPTER 9

At the art auction, Marla sat on the sidelines, away from the museum people who had claimed front-row seats. She'd arrived early to find Oliver Smernoff talking privately to the auctioneer, who repeatedly shook his head as though replying negatively to whatever Oliver was saying. With a snarl, Oliver took his seat, while the auctioneer's assistants flanked him for escort to center stage.

Irene, already on a refill of her bubbly, shifted away from her husband's bulk with a distasteful glance. She caught Eric Rand's eye and lifted her shoulders in a questioning gesture. He gave a barely perceptible nod, then straightened to search the crowd. His glance seemed to fall upon Kent Harwood, sitting several rows back. The exterminator slumped in his chair, passing on the free champagne while he idly thumbed through the catalog provided by the gallery showing samples of works for sale. A toothpick hung from his mouth like an attached tentacle.

Up front, Eric spoke into his headset microphone. Tonight he wore a pale-yellow shirt, black trousers, and a lemon and steel bow tie. He'd fixed his graying hair in a brushed style like a television newscaster and flashed a smile worthy of a toothpaste commercial.

"Ladies and gentlemen," he said after explaining the rules for any newcomers, "tonight we'll start off with a fifteen-hundred-dollar piece by Fanch. He's considered one of the top ten artists today. Look at the vibrant colors in this beautiful serigraph. Don't you get the impression that someone has just left the room, from the blazing fire in the fireplace and the bowl of fruit on the table?"

Marla admired the picture that looked like someone's living room overlooking a view of city skyscrapers. But at the opening bid of six hundred thirty dollars, she let it go. She passed on the Kinkade piece, the art deco work of Erté, an attractive female form by Bellet, and an abstract work by Alfred Gockel. At least it looked abstract to her uneducated eye.

"I can't believe they sell all these pieces," she confided to Betsy, sitting beside her. The brunette lounged in her seat and cracked her knuckles. Her face held a pinched but alert mode. "I mean, I don't have several thousand dollars just to throw out on this stuff."

". . . A bid for twenty-five-hundred dollars," Eric's baritone voice boomed. "Do I have an advance to two thousand five hundred fifty? No one? Are we done at twenty-five hundred? Going once, twice, third, and final warning," he yelled, banging his gavel. "Sold for twenty-five-hundred dollars. Whoo-hoo!"

Marla sipped her champagne, feeling her seat vibrate, although the ship barely seemed to be moving. Her eyes bulged when she noted the assistants setting up a couple of more easels and propping three pictures on them, backs to the audience. Three mystery pieces! Could this be Alden Tusk's set?

After putting her glass flute on the floor, she

straightened. Her hand shot up with a bidding card along with most of the other people in the room. But when the price escalated to over $3,000, she quit the race. To her surprise, Betsy kept her arm up. Marla hadn't gotten the impression that the public relations guru had much money, but she could have been wrong. Or maybe Betsy figured Alden Tusk's work was worth it. After the majority of people dropped out, Betsy competed against Thurston Stark, Oliver, Bob Wolfson, and Kent. Marla did a double-take at the bug man. Why would *he* want Tusk's paintings?

Thurston Stark, she could understand. The foundation chairman collected art and made no bones about his wealth.

Oliver seemed to prefer music, but it could be he was putting his bid in for his wife's sake. She seemed more cultured and at ease in the art world, but then again, hadn't Irene mentioned he shared her interests?

Bob remained an enigma. He complained about how he wasn't adequately compensated as business manager for the museum, and yet he was practically bouncing in his seat each time Eric Rand raised the price.

At the end, Thurston won out again. No one could have been more disappointed when the auctioneer turned the pictures and revealed a suite of watercolors by Tarkay. The ornate gold frames were probably worth as much as the pictures, Marla figured, admiring the colorful scenes.

She'd seen a Tarkay she'd liked earlier, a signed serigraph on wove paper depicting two ladies having tea in a café. Maybe she should consider getting some art for her new salon, in which case she could deduct the cost! The risqué picture by Rut that came up next for bidding, a seminude couple entwined in an embrace, certainly couldn't be shown on her walls. Fanch's style appealed to her, but his work was priced beyond her means. Maybe she could find a lesser artist for a more reasonable cost.

"Remember the triptych by the late Alden Tusk that I mentioned we'll be offering for sale on this cruise?" Eric Rand was saying when her mind refocused. "You don't want to miss that fantastic opportunity. We're going to give you a sneak preview beforehand, so be sure to attend every night if you want a glimpse of this amazing set."

"Holy mackerel, he's got to be kidding," Betsy said, cracking her knuckles again. She must fall back on that habit when she got excited, Marla realized, because Betsy rarely did it at dinner.

After the auctioneer called the raffle, Marla stood and stretched her arms above her head. By the time she looked around, the auctioneer had vanished, letting his assistants straighten up. She noticed several closed doors toward the sides of the gallery, workrooms or offices perhaps.

Obviously, Eric didn't care to mingle with the guests, or else he had more pressing business elsewhere. She'd like to talk to him to find out where he had obtained Tusk's completed work, especially the panel that had been missing from the museum. Perhaps that's what Oliver had been questioning him about earlier. Hoping he'd share any response, she glided over to where the museum director milled about with his colleagues.

"We're going out on deck for the pool party," Irene said to Heidi, who clung to Thurston's arm. "What about you, darling? Want to join us?"

"No, thanks, dearest Thurston and I are headed

to the promenade for a cup of coffee," Heidi replied in her girlish tone. From the way she was rubbing against him in her skimpy black dress, she had other plans in mind.

"Sandy, how about you and Bob?" Betsy cut in. "I'm craving some ice cream. Wanna get a sundae with me?"

"Sorry," Sandy replied in a tired voice. "I'm turning in early so I'll have enough energy for tomorrow. We have a full day in St. Maarten. And Bob doesn't need the extra calories."

Taking his wife's elbow, Bob steered her away. "There you go, putting words in my mouth again."

Betsy smiled at Marla. "So, are you free, or do you have to rejoin your family?"

Marla glanced at her watch. "I have to meet Dalton, so we can make our plans for tomorrow."

"Oh, are you going on any tours?"

"Yeah, over to Marigot on the French side, then to a beach. I need to get up early so I can visit the infirmary. I want to see if Helen is okay and if she needs anything."

Several pairs of curious eyes swung in her direction. "What?" Betsy said to the others in their party. "Marla may not work for the museum, but she's our friend. She's talked to Helen a couple of times and is concerned. What's wrong with that? The rest of you should be so caring. Like, has anyone heard any news about Martha?"

Shaking their heads, the members of the group broke up. Marla left, intending to make good on her promise in the morning.

On Wednesday, she hit the buffet before heading down to the infirmary, on the bottom deck. After gobbling a mushroom omelette and croissant along with bacon, hash browns, and sautéed onions, she passed on the smoked salmon and bagels, fresh fruit, sliced luncheon meats, cheeses, pastries, cereal, and yogurt. Who could eat all that for breakfast and still make it off the ship?

Feeling stuffed, she waddled into the elevator next to Dalton, who'd insisted on accompanying her.

While the lift descended, he patted his belly. "That meal should keep us until lunch."

"I should hope so. We'd better do a lot of walking today."

"We can always climb the stairs." He peered beyond the open doors when they arrived at deck one. "Are you sure this is the right place?"

Striding into the corridor, she noticed the GANG-WAY sign and a utilitarian crew section but no sign of sick bay. "Maybe we should have taken the elevators on the other side of the ship."

"Let's go around that corner. It could be behind the elevator bank."

"There's a crewman. We could ask him." She'd spotted a fellow in a nondescript uniform lugging a bucket of paint.

"No need." Vail stalked ahead, his chin jutting forward. "We'll find it."

Typical male, unwilling to ask for directions. Much more aware of the ship's vibration at this level, she backtracked to their point of entry and discovered a door emblazoned with a big red cross.

"Here it is," she called, noting the small sign indicating the medical center. "Looks like they don't want to advertise so much, but they could put up a banner telling people where to go."

More importantly, the hours were posted for seeing the nurse: eight in the morning to twelve noon, or two to six in the afternoon. The doctor had shorter hours: from nine to eleven in the morning or from four to six. Marla would try to remember that if she felt ill.

After pushing open the door, Vail held it for her to enter first. What met her eyes wasn't what she'd expected. Her only view of infirmaries on ships came from watching old movies. But this wasn't a big ward with hospital beds lined up. Instead, she had stepped into a typical waiting room such as she'd find at home in the local doctor's office.

The door to the inner sanctum remained open, and beyond she could see a nurse's station staffed by medical personnel in white uniforms and clerks busy with paperwork. One of the women looked up at her approach.

"Hi, one of your patients is a friend of mine," Marla said, her heartbeat accelerating. She couldn't help it. Hospitals did that to her. "I wanted to inquire about her condition and ask if I could visit her."

"The patient's name, ma'am?"

"Helen Bryce. And I'm Marla Shore. This is my fiancé, Dalton Vail." Resisting the urge to wring her hands, she gave a hopeful smile. As though sensing her anxiety, Vail gave her a reassuring pat. He left his hand on the small of her back.

"If you don't mind waiting a few minutes, I'll come out to talk to you," said one of the nurses, wearing a stethoscope around her neck. She was a thirtyish woman with curly natural blond hair.

Obediently, Marla retreated to a blue upholstered chair in the waiting room. Her gaze scanned the amber and cobalt carpet before rising to a vending machine that dispensed throat lozenges, Band-Aids, and Benadryl tablets.

"If we have to wait long, I'm going to need those," Marla said, pointing to a sign that read: SEASICK TABLETS ARE ON YOUR RIGHT. Acutely aware of the ship's rocking motion, she swallowed. A Toshiba television stood silently on a shelf, while framed pictures of flower gardens and Mediterranean villas took up wall space.

A teenager banged his way inside. Tugging at his baggy shorts, he limped along in a pair of sandals. "I hurt my foot," he whined to the receptionist, who leaned over the counter to survey his open wound.

"Come on inside," she told him, while Marla gnashed her teeth. Now they'd have to waste more time here.

Leaning forward, Dalton rested his elbows on his knees. "We're gonna have to meet our tour group. This was a bad idea."

"I didn't expect a delay this early in the morning." She pursed her lips, prepared to postpone their visit, when the nurse strolled out to greet her.

"Miss Shore? I'm Wilhelmia from South Africa," she said with a pleasant accent. "How may I assist you?"

"I'm worried about my friend Helen. I heard she fell down some stairs and cracked her head. Is she awake?"

"Indeed, and she'll be fine. It's only a mild concussion, but she's very dizzy when she sits up. We'll have to keep her a few more days for observation and to make sure there's no internal bleeding. We have X-ray machines plus a fully equipped laboratory, but unfortunately, we don't have the capability to do MRIs or CT scans."

"I didn't know you even had that much equipment." She'd thought of shipboard amenities as basically being first-aid stations, but she supposed they had their share of heart attack victims. For surgical emergencies, they could probably airlift people. Hadn't she seen a helipad somewhere?

"We are prepared like any emergency room at home," Wilhelmia replied in a serious tone. "We have fully equipped private and semiprivate hospital rooms, crash carts, and also a morgue."

Thanks, pal, I really wanted to know that. "Would I be allowed to see Helen? I'll be quick. I just want to ask if she needs anything from her cabin."

The nurse shook her head. "Normally we permit visitors, but Helen expressly requested that we admit no one."

"Please, she might want to see me. I'm not one of her colleagues and we've . . . become friends. Can you just ask her if I can come in?" She saw the nurse glance at Dalton, who stood studying the contents of the vending machine. "Not him. I'll be alone."

"Wait here." A few minutes later, the nurse ushered her inside. Marla passed by the nurse's station and entered the room indicated behind a partially drawn curtain.

Helen lay flat in bed, her pale face framed by her auburn hair. An IV line snaked from her arm to a hanging bag on a pole.

"Hi, Helen. Thanks for seeing me. How do you feel?" She noticed the head docent's left arm was in a cast up to her elbow.

"I'm sore all over, and I feel as though someone used my head for a punching bag, but I guess I got off lucky with just a concussion and a broken wrist."

Marla winced. *Ouch.* "I couldn't believe it when I heard about your accident. I'd just spoken to you in St. Thomas. What happened?" She pulled over a chair and took a seat. From Helen's bright expression, Marla surmised she welcomed the company. If Helen showed signs of fatigue, though, Marla would leave. Crossing her legs, she gave an encouraging smile.

Helen plucked at her covers with her free hand. "I had a note on my door when I returned. It said I could get what I want if I took the forward elevator to deck twelve and went outside to the stairs that lead down to the bridge view. I'd just stepped onto the landing when someone hurtled by and bumped me."

"And you lost your balance?"

"Presumably. At least that's what I told the doctor. But in reality, that person didn't brush past me accidentally."

Marla's breath hitched. "What do you mean?"

Helen narrowed her eyes.

"I got pushed, honey."

"No way."

"I'm just mad that I missed who did it." She turned on her side to regard Marla more closely but squeezed her eyes shut. "Oh gosh, I get so dizzy. The doctor said it should go away in a few days, but it's hard to believe I'll ever be able to sit up straight again."

"You will. I've had a concussion myself. As long as there aren't any complications, you'll be on your feet soon."

Helen's lids flew open. "I hope you're right, because I'd really hate to miss the rest of the cruise. I won't be able to get off at the ports, but I'd at least like to enjoy the meals without feeling as if I'm going to throw up."

"Haven't they given you something for nausea?" She remembered the sickening feeling from the room spinning after she'd conked her head in a car accident.

"Suppositories. I couldn't keep down any pills."

Rising, Marla pushed her chair back. "I don't want to tire you if you're feeling ill."

"Don't go yet. I'm worried, Marla. Something happened to Martha, and we still don't know that she's safe. And now something bad happened to me."

Tell me about it. "Assuming someone is behind this, why do you think you were targeted? Or Martha, for that matter?" She had to stop by Guest Relations to see if they had any news on the gift shop lady.

"I'm not sure, but I'd sure as hell like to know who's pulling our strings."

"Back in St. Thomas, you'd mentioned Bob Wolfson's name. What exactly were you referring to?"

Helen averted her gaze. "Forget I said anything, Marla. Has he asked about me at all?" Tension strained her tone.

"Everyone has been concerned, especially Kent Harwood. He even came down to the infirmary to check on you." She didn't want to say that Bob had remained silent while they discussed her condition, and that Sandy had looked almost gleeful. "We were trying to figure out who might know so much about all of us, or rather, all of you. Kent seemed to imply that your accident and Martha's disappearance might be related."

"Really?" As she regarded Marla, Helen's expression crumbled. "Now I won't get my insurance policy back, will I? That last note was just a trick. I'll never recover what I lost."

Marla hesitated. "How well did Betsy know Alden Tusk? I mean, she did the publicity for your fundraiser, so she had to advertise the artist's collection, but do you think she saw any of his paintings before they were displayed to the public? Your words made me remember what she said at dinner. Alden viewed his triptych as a type of redemption."

"I wonder what she meant by that. Now that I think about it, I can't recall who brought Alden to the attention of the museum in the first place." Helen put a hand to her head. "If only this headache would go away, I could think more clearly."

"Who usually schedules exhibits for visiting artists?"

"That would be Olly's job, but I don't think it applies in this case."

"Why not?" Resisting the urge to check her watch, Marla folded her hands in her lap. She should have enough leeway to get off the ship in time.

Helen's face scrunched in thought. "Olly came up with the idea for a children's art program, but Bob said we'd need extra funding to get things rolling. He's the one who proposed a gala dinner to raise money. I found out about it only because Olly asked if I could get my docents to help that evening."

"So how did that work? Were different artists scheduled to have their work sold?"

"Well, Alden's name sort of popped up as a rising star. Betsy said it would create a buzz if his work was featured because he was already getting great press."

"So you're saying that Betsy was influential in snagging him for the fund-raiser?"

Helen shrugged. "I suppose. She knew how to contact him, and it was a done deal before anyone could blink."

"Interesting." Marla sniffed the pungent smell of antiseptic amid a bustle of activity outside the room. "I went to the art auction last night. It was quite lively when they showed a mystery set with three panels.

Everyone tried to outbid each other, especially the members of your group. They were disappointed when it wasn't Alden's work."

"I'll bet."

"Eric is keeping people in suspense, so he must know what's so important about those paintings. He said he'd give viewers a sneak preview, but it hasn't happened yet."

"Betsy might have seen them already," Helen remarked.

"How could she?"

"At the museum, I mean."

"Oh." Marla tried to figure how that would be possible. "Weren't the paintings crated when they arrived?"

"They would've been unpacked in preparation for viewing after dinner. Actually, that would have been Eric's job as curator."

"Did he accept delivery, or could someone else have gotten a peek upon arrival?"

"You could have a point. As for right before the show, anyone wanting an advance look would have had to get past security. The exhibit was roped off."

"How many guards were on duty that night?"

"You'd have to ask Cliff Peters. I can tell you this— Thurston went apoplectic after the disaster when he discovered the middle panel was missing. I think he intended to bid on the set for himself."

"But how did he learn the triptych was incomplete, unless he saw the two end panels with a gap in between? Would he just go by Eric's claim that the center one was gone?"

"A number of people pushed their way into the exhibit hall during the commotion following Alden's accident. Eric appeared just as surprised as anyone by the missing piece. He'd set up the display beforehand."

"Someone must have been awfully quick to swoop in there and steal the center panel."

"True." Helen pressed a hand to her forehead. "I've got a headache, so I'm afraid we'll have to finish our discussion."

"One more question." Marla leaned forward. "How could the triptych have ended up here?"

Helen's troubled gaze met hers. "After Alden died, his works of art went back into his estate. His executor donated some of them back to the museum, but the rest would have been sold. Anyone could have bought the two end pieces, perhaps the same person who'd swiped the middle panel."

"Through an intermediary, I imagine." Collecting her purse, Marla stood. Dalton must be bored stiff waiting for her outside. "Thanks for talking to me," she told Helen. "Can I bring you anything from your cabin?"

"No, but you can do one more thing that'll help give me some peace of mind. Speak to the countess. She may know what happened to Martha."

CHAPTER 10

"Who's the countess?" Marla demanded, anxious to leave the infirmary and explore St. Maarten.

"Surely you've seen her at the blackjack tables. She makes it a point to sit next to Sandy."

"I didn't know Bob's wife likes to gamble."

"Holy macaroni, haven't you seen her at the bingo games?" Helen said. "That's a favorite pastime of hers at home, along with gardening and volunteering at the horticultural station."

"So who's the countess," Marla repeated, "and why is she so friendly to Sandy?" And where does Sandy get the money to throw out at games of chance when Bob keeps whining about how he's the underdog at work?

"She's an older woman, quite possibly in her seventies, with fluffy blond hair. With her makeup and fancy chiffon outfits, she reminds me of a film star from the nineteen forties. You must have spotted her around the ship."

Marla gave her a thoughtful glance. "I've only passed through the casino on my way to somewhere else, so I haven't noticed her. I'll keep a closer watch. Why do you think she would know about Martha?"

Helen narrowed her eyes. "She's been keeping an

eye on us, and I swear she and Sandy must be hatching something together. I've tried to insinuate myself into her graces, but I don't seem to count where she's concerned. I'm thinking maybe it's really something of Bob's that she wants."

"How did you hear about her title? Where is she from?"

"I overheard a crew member addressing her. She speaks with an accent but I couldn't find out anything else."

Marla patted her arm, careful not to touch the IV tubing. "I'll see what I can learn. You get some rest now."

She scurried into the waiting room, where Vail sat frowning over a paper in his lap, a pen poised in his hand. Her heart warmed at the sight of him. A lock of hair, ebony streaked with silver, tumbled across his forehead. His chest, broad and solid, stretched his knit shirt taut, while hip-hugging jeans enfolded his muscular legs. A coil of heat wrapped in love assaulted her. What other man would wait so patiently while she visited a sick friend?

"I'm ready," she announced, retrieving the beach bag she'd left in his care.

"I've got one more question," he said, pointing to the daily trivia sheet available each day from the ship's library. "What did ancient Egyptians do when their family cat died?" Rising, he rolled his shoulders before showing her the answer choices.

"I don't know. Fasted for seven days or burned their clothes?"

"Nope, they shaved their eyebrows," Vail said, reading the correct response on the back.

"Good for them. Let's go."

He held the door open for her. "How's Helen feeling?"

"She's dizzy, but that'll pass. The worst thing is she broke her wrist." She paused, facing him. "Helen thinks someone pushed her down the stairs."

"No kidding. Who?"

"She didn't notice."

He gave her a skeptical glance. "Then it could have been anyone, even another passenger in a hurry. As long as she'll be all right, I wouldn't worry about it. Worry instead about catching our tour group."

They emerged onto the pier and stood staring at the green-covered mountain peaks while the wind whipped their hair. Marla grappled in her purse for a couple of bobby pins and stuck them on either side of her part. She'd been growing out her bangs, and hair kept falling into her eyes. It would be easier to manage when her layers were longer.

Another cruise ship had already pulled into port ahead of them, one of the Carnival line. Ashore, she observed houses nestled amid the slopes beyond a sandy beach. The water, a dark teal, lightened to aqua with the rising morning sun. Their tour group was supposed to meet in front of the Philipsburg courthouse, and passengers had been advised to take the water taxi into town. Walking to the booth, they met up with Kate, John, and Brianna.

"Where have you guys been? We were getting ready to leave without you." The teen's tone held more worry than anger.

Marla gave her ponytail an affectionate yank. "Sorry, I stopped by the infirmary to visit Helen."

"How is the poor woman?" Kate said, while John distributed their transportation tickets. His face held a resigned look as though this excursion hadn't been his idea. At least he was being a good sport to come along.

Marla climbed onto the open-air boat rocking on the water. "Helen will be fine." She raised her voice to be heard over the engine and the island music blaring from a loudspeaker. The vessel vibrated as they got under way. A stiff breeze cooled her neck as they sped along the water toward the center of town.

"Do you have a swimsuit?" she asked Brianna, sitting beside her on the long bench.

"Under my clothes," the girl replied, gesturing to her shorts and tank top. "Man, look at all those shops. I hope we'll have enough time to browse after the tour."

"You're the one who wanted to go to the beach, muffin," Vail reminded her.

"Yeah, but Grandpa said we should go to the French side first. That's why we picked this tour."

Marla gave the older man a sharp glance. This excursion had been his idea? Why visit Marigot on the French half of the island? St. Maarten and St. Martin, the Dutch and French sides, had been coexisting for nearly 350 years. But they would have had enough to do if they'd just stuck to Philipsburg. Did John have an ulterior purpose, other than simple curiosity, for wanting to visit the French side?

The town sucked her in with its warren of narrow streets crowded with shops, tourists, and noisy vehicles. The buildings seemed to absorb heat from the pavement, causing her body to film with sweat. Running into a Burger King to use the bathroom, she took short, shallow breaths in the furnace-like air.

Outside, she crossed Front Street to meet her group by the courthouse. Scanning the heads, she saw no

one from the museum crowd. Betsy had gone to swing
among the treetops on the rain forest adventure tour,
while the Wolfsons had signed up for the butterfly farm
and nature parks. Heidi had mentioned something
about the shipwreck snorkeling tour, but she doubted
Thurston would go along. Maybe Cliff had accompanied her, although Marla thought he'd mentioned
mountain biking.

Hoping her party had made the right choice for
fifty-four dollars per person, she filed after the others
onto the air-conditioned bus that would take them
through the hills. It looked cloudy over the mountain range, but she hadn't bothered to bring an umbrella. She also wore a swimsuit under her clothing,
so it wouldn't matter if she got wet. Sitting in the window seat beside Vail, she twisted forward to regard
Kate across the aisle.

"You've been in the casino, right? Have you met a
blond woman known as the countess?"

Kate's expression brightened. "Oh yes, dear. Charm-
ing lady. She doesn't speak English that well, but she
takes such an interest in the people around her."

"Is that so?"

"She sat next to me at the slots one night, and we
struck up a conversation. She asked me all sorts of
questions. I gather she cruises a lot and likes to meet
people. Veronique told me how her husband died,
and she manages their properties now. They didn't
have any children." Kate beamed at Brianna, who
stared out the window in the adjacent seat. "Poor
lady. She has no idea what she's missing." Her glance
swung to Marla and her son. "Are you two, uh, planning to add to your family?"

Marla coughed. "We, um . . . listen, the tour guide
is talking. Did she just say the island has thirty-five

beaches? And that's a salt pond over there. The salt turns light pink when it matures and is ready for reaping."

Vail squeezed her hand, his eyes crinkling. "Give it a rest, Mom. We're not at that stage yet."

Gulp. I hope we're never at that stage, thank you. Taking care of one teenager is enough for me.

Turning her head, Marla gazed out the window while pondering the identity of the mysterious countess. Why would she have befriended Sandy and then Kate? Could she be pumping them for information, or had Helen guessed correctly that she was in cahoots with Sandy? And if so, for what reason?

The bus sped past structures painted turquoise, lemon, coral, and suntan. Dogs ran loose in streets dotted with palms and banana plants. Many of the tin-roofed houses had wall air-conditioner units protruding from them, while others just had open windows for natural ventilation. Goats and ducks roamed the weed-filled yards, and overhead, utility lines flanked the roadside.

As the lovely nutmeg-skinned tour guide—whose name was Michelle—rambled on, their vehicle climbed a winding hillside, exposing a panoramic view of the ships in harbor and the glistening sea beyond. A more affluent neighborhood came into sight, where red flowering trees, Spanish barrel-tile roofs, and modern architecture prevailed. Then they drove farther up, the engine straining, as a cliff dropped off on the right side with only a guardrail for protection. Cactus grew wild along the road, competing for space with ferns, vines, and yellow wildflowers visited by delicate white butterflies.

"All of our produce on the island is imported," Michelle spoke into her microphone. "The Dutch side still uses guilders, while on the French side, euros are standard."

"This tour should have started an hour earlier," someone in the backseat grumbled. "Look at this traffic! We didn't need to come here to get stuck on the road."

"Why do we have to go to a beach?" another lady groused to her husband. "We live in Florida."

Marla almost agreed with her as the bus crawled along the two-lane road. Eventually, they reached the summit of Cole Bay Hill and began their descent toward Simpson Bay Lagoon. As they approached Marigot, she noted street signs in French, two-story homes decorated with religious ornaments and carved balcony railings, and a distinct absence of traffic lights.

Once they reached their destination, passengers spilled from the bus like ants from an anthill. Forgoing the native craft market for lunch, Marla and company found an outdoor café and plopped down at a round table. An orange umbrella shaded them from the strong midday sun, occasionally mitigated by a passing cloud. A waiter, whose pale face and long curved nose reminded her of an ibis, tossed over menus. No, make that a rooster. His hair was so moussed, it stood straight up.

She slapped a hand onto her paper place mat before it blew away. Flags flapped outside storefronts and palm fronds rustled in the tropical breeze stirred by the sea.

Glad she'd fastened her hair back with a couple of bobby pins, Marla perused the menu choices and decided on an avocado and shrimp salad.

"It looks as if we're going to have a long wait," John complained, glancing at his watch and then down the street. He tapped his fingers impatiently.

"Those other people haven't even been served their drinks yet, and they got here first. I think there's only one waiter, and he seems overwhelmed by the crowd."

"Relax," Kate told him. "We'll still have enough time to look around."

"Oh, here you're willing to explore, but at home you don't want to go anywhere." His gaze dropped to his wrist, making Marla wonder why he'd insisted they take this particular tour.

"At home, I have plenty to do. I can't just take off without a lot of advance planning," Kate retorted.

Marla blinked. This sounded like an old argument. She cast a sly glance at Vail. He sat stoically, his lips compressed.

"Grandma, what should I get to eat?" Brianna cut in. "They don't have anything normal."

"Normal being a hamburger, I suppose?" Vail said, the corners of his mouth curling up.

Kate turned her attention to the teenager. "How about the lobster lasagna with bisque sauce? Or the grilled red snapper?"

"Yuck. Maybe I'll stick with the garden salad."

"Excuse me," John said, scraping his chair back as he hopped to his feet. "I'm going to look in that store with the hot sauces. Order me the salmon with coconut milk and ginger."

"Hey, if you're going shopping, can't I come with you?" Brianna inserted. "We could check out the West Indies mall over there."

Marla followed her gaze past the Restaurant Largo Café to the large building housing an indoor shopping center. "Wait until we finish our meal, hon. Then I'll go with you." Her attention switched to John's retreating form. He had a long, lean torso like Vail.

The waiter arrived to take their orders, after which Marla excused herself to use the bathroom.

"You shouldn't drink so much coffee when you know we're going ashore," Vail chided her.

"Tell me about it. I'll just be a minute."

Grasping her purse, she stepped inside the café, crowded with tables, and made her way to the rear, where a door was labeled W.C. *Isn't that a British term for water closet?* The restroom turned out to be a one-person affair, and she had to wait. Thankfully, she'd brought her bottle of hand sanitizer, because she needed it when she was through.

Stepping outdoors, she noticed her iced tea had arrived but not her meal. Nor had John returned. Glancing up the street, she squinted at the sight of him scurrying into another shop. She'd better tell him their drinks had come.

Passing by storefronts with tempting displays, Marla wished she had time to browse the jewelry in Oro de Sol, cameras in Maneks, and Swarovski crystal in Little Switzerland. John had gone into a gift shop featuring fine arts and crafts.

Peering in the window, she noted he wasn't alone. Irene Smernoff looped her arm through his and smiled brightly at a clerk in a dress shirt and tie. John was talking earnestly, gesturing at something on the countertop.

Marla hesitated, curious to hear what they were discussing but not wanting to be accused of following her future father-in-law. Leaning in a nook by the open doorway, she nodded at a passing couple.

"It's well worth the price, and we can promise you more where that comes from," Irene trilled. Leaning forward, she gave the shopkeeper a view down her cleavage in a designer sundress that could have graced a garden party. "You won't find anything else like this, I guarantee it."

Bless my bones, are they selling something to this guy?

A street-washing machine rumbled past, spraying water onto the sidewalk. Marla leaped back, tripping on an uneven piece of pavement and tumbling onto her backside right at the store's entrance. Several pairs of eyes darted in her direction.

"Oh, hi . . . um, I was just coming to get you, Dad." Gritting her teeth to a jarring pain in her hip, she struggled to right herself. The contents of her handbag had spilled out, and she found herself in the humiliating position of crawling on her hands and knees to retrieve her wallet, comb, styling brush, breath mints, Tampons, and other personal items while Irene snorted with laughter. *Her stiff facial muscles must prohibit a real belly laugh*, Marla thought. *How unfortunate for her.*

John belatedly came to her assistance. "Here, let me help you." Rescuing her emergency penlight, he handed it over before hauling her to her feet. Behind his eyeglasses, his gaze darted toward the museum director's wife.

Irene stood in front of the counter, blocking Marla's view of the items on top. "You can go," she told him. "I'll finish up here."

"Sure, fine. Thanks a bunch," John stammered. He charged out of the store with Marla at his heels.

"What was that all about?" she demanded, brushing dirt off her shorts as she rushed in his wake.

"Nothing important. Something in the store caught my eye, and Irene figured she could get me a good price for it."

What, you think I'm some kind of schmuck? Tell me another story. "And just how did Irene happen to be here? She didn't come on our tour."

"She took a taxi from the Dutch side. Cost her a whole lot less than we paid."

"Where's her husband?"

"Oliver is across the street, checking out the native market behind the Coconut Juice House. They're taking the catamaran yacht tour from the marina."

"They could have joined us for lunch." She waved to Vail, who'd been anxiously scanning the street. He stood as he saw them coming.

"They get lunch on board along with complimentary rum punches." John gave her a grin reminiscent of a snake that had just swallowed a rat. "In case you haven't noticed, Irene can't pass up the opportunity to get a free drink."

Nor did she pass up the opportunity to meet you in Marigot. You can't fool me with your prattle.

"It's not free if you consider the cost of the excursion, plus the taxi ride to get over here." She plastered a cheerful expression on her face as they approached their restaurant table. "John got carried away with his shopping," she told the others. "I retrieved him before he could buy Kate an expensive piece of jewelry."

"I should be so lucky." Kate twisted her paper napkin. "Where's our food? We're spending a wicked amount of time at this place."

"You're the one who told Grandpa to relax," Brianna reminded her grandmother. "Look, the waiter just brought those people their meals. We should be next."

After Marla took her seat, Vail nudged her and

waggled his eyebrows. She knew he was questioning her, but this wasn't the time or place to discuss what was on her mind.

They found time later at the beach, where rough waves and clumps of seaweed discouraged swimming. While Brianna and Kate soaked up the sun, and John lounged in a hammock slung between two palms, she and Dalton took a walk.

Clouds clustered over the range of mountains, but at the shoreline, the sun shone brightly overhead, and the turquoise water sparkled. Wearing a sun visor and dark lenses, Marla squished her bare toes in the damp sand. She glanced at Vail in appreciation. Clad only in a pair of swim trunks, his torso gleamed with suntan oil. Her body responded with a coil of warmth. *I'll have to take the guy to the beach more often.*

"What took you and Dad so long to return at lunch?" Vail asked, noticing her eyes on him.

"He'd gone window shopping, and I went to tell him our drinks were ready. What's going on between him and your mother?"

Vail placed one long, muscled leg in front of the other. "What do you mean?"

"Surely you're not oblivious to the fact that they have problems. He rarely touches her, and you've heard his snide remarks. Or maybe you turn the other cheek on purpose?"

He swept his gaze to the horizon. "Dad isn't happy. You know he recently retired. He wants to go out more and try new things, but Mom is stuck in her routine. She refuses to alter her lifestyle to the point of ignoring him."

"I can't believe she ignores him. Maybe she resents the intrusion after having the house to herself all these years. It'll take a period of adjustment on both their parts."

"Could be, but it isn't going so well to start."

"What kind of things does he want to do?"

"Travel, tap into his creative side, take classes. Mom doesn't want to do anything different." He kicked at a piece of driftwood in their path. Ahead was another section of beach, marked off by a rickety fence that ended at the sand. That area didn't appear as populated as the stretch beyond, in front of a hotel. Beachgoers there splashed in a cordoned-off lagoon. She could hear their laughter as they strolled onward.

"Kate probably has her friends and her own activities," she offered. "John has to make a new life for himself without relying on his wife."

"His version of a new life is pretty radical."

Before Marla could ask what he meant, she glimpsed a sight up ahead that made her do a double-take. *Lord save me, that looks like a person's bare butt. It can't be, can it?*

"Dalton, look at that lady over by the lime-colored umbrella. Is she wearing anything?" The woman turned, and Marla's jaw dropped. A pair of hanging breasts swung into view. She almost stopped in her tracks, staring in disbelief.

"Good God," Vail muttered.

Quickly averting her gaze, Marla resumed her pace. She focused instead on the ocean, but her attempt to preserve decorum proved futile. She elbowed Vail. "Look at that guy wading in the water. You can see his, uh, you know, sticking out." Stark naked, the man did nothing to hide his scrawny body.

"None of these people have equipment I'd write

home about," Vail drawled, nodding at an older couple lounging naked on a couple of beach chairs.

Reversing direction, they hurried back to their tour group. "You'll never believe what we saw," Marla told Kate, who'd waved her over to an empty chaise. "There's a nude beach next to ours. The people are out in the open just as fresh as when they were born."

"No way," Brianna said, sitting upright. "I wanna go see."

"You stay right here," Kate ordered, giving the teen a stern glare. "Such a sight is not for young eyes."

"It's not as though I haven't seen a boy's thingie before."

"What?" Kate and Marla sang in unison.

"Billy Underwood showed me his in third grade."

"I hope you weren't playing doctor," Kate huffed.

"With Billy? Ugh, what a jerk."

Kate threw Marla an exasperated look. "We'd better get back to the bus. The shops are waiting for us in Philipsburg."

They gathered their towels; collected John, who'd been snoozing in his hammock; and boarded their ride back to the capital city of Dutch St. Maarten.

After a frenzied hour of shopping, Vail's shoulders slumped and his eyes glazed. "Look," he said, clutching several packages, "if you gals want to stay longer, I can return to the ship with Dad."

"I'm ready to head back," Kate announced, her face flushed from the heat. "We may have to wait in line for the water taxi. I don't want to cut it too close."

Am I the only one who isn't done? Marla thought with dismay. Brianna's slouched posture and glassy expression indicated the teen needed a nap. They should all get back on board, but she'd seen a pair of earrings in one of the stores that matched the David Yurman bracelet Kate had bought Brianna. She'd love to buy them as a surprise for the girl. And maybe she could find some good men's gifts if she had time alone.

Besides, she hadn't checked out the Belgian chocolate shop, Guavaberry Hut, or Trader Bob's Emporium.

Spotting a familiar brunette along Front Street, she waved. "There's Betsy in front of Diamonds International. I'll hook up with her and meet you later, if you all want to go back now. Dalton, would you mind taking these packages? I can't schlep these plus my purse anymore. My arm feels as though it's going to fall off."

He acquiesced with a weary nod. "Are you sure? I don't want to leave you alone."

She gave him a reassuring smile. "Betsy's signaling to me. I'll be fine. We'll head back to the ship together."

Relishing her freedom, she hastened toward her new friend. They exchanged greetings before hustling into the shops.

"My tour was awesome!" Betsy gushed, tapping Marla's arm. "I've always wanted to traverse the tree canopies in a rain forest, but my muscles will be sore for the rest of the week." Out on the street, she halted abruptly in front of a fine-arts gallery, her face blanching when she spotted a painting in the window. "Holy mackerel! That's impossible."

Impatient to move on, Marla squinted. "What is it?"

Betsy pointed a wavering finger. "T-that painting . . . it's a work by Alden Tusk. We have the exact same piece back home in the museum."

CHAPTER 11

"How can the same painting be here if it's back home in your museum?" Marla asked Betsy.

"I have no idea. Alden never painted a similar picture twice. Someone must have made a copy." Striding inside the shop, Betsy demanded to see the owner.

Marla followed, hoping to inquire about Alden's ballet portraits. She'd love to find one of the paintings with herself as subject. Who knew what it would be worth today?

"Where did you get that painting in the window?" Betsy demanded of a man with a walrus mustache who'd hurried over.

"Hello, ladies. Our buyer obtains the pieces for our shop," the proprietor explained. "If you're interested in that particular item, I'll give you a good price."

Betsy pursed her lips. "The artist was my friend. We have a similar canvas hanging in the museum where I work. Alden would never have painted two of the same scenes. This tableau is quite memorable, with a young boy gazing at a tree stripped of leaves. His mournful expression leaves an emotional impact."

Marla, glancing out the front window, spotted Thurston and Heidi Stark strolling by. Suddenly, Thurston stopped, his eyes bulging as he caught sight of the painting on display. He bent toward his wife, murmuring a few words into her ear. Then he dashed off across the street, signaling to someone Marla couldn't see from her vantage point.

Curious, she excused herself from Betsy's company. Outside on the sidewalk, she spied Thurston arguing with Cliff Peters in front of an alleyway. Heidi remained frozen in place, staring at them with an unreadable expression.

"What's wrong?" Marla asked her. "I noticed Thurston freaked out when he saw this painting. Betsy says it's by Alden Tusk, but the original is in your museum."

Heidi slowly turned her head and regarded Marla with an icy expression. "Drop it, Marla. This isn't anything you need to concern yourself about." Her girlish voice seemed incongruous with her harsh words.

Marla gave her an appraising glance. Despite her strappy heels, butt-high shorts, and revealing top, she didn't sound as clueless as she appeared. Her eyes flashed before she turned and stalked away.

Undoubtedly Thurston hammered at Cliff about the reproduction. Marla would love to hear what they were saying, but as she jostled through the thinning crowd, she saw Brooklyn Jones waving from a produce market.

Hustling over, she regarded the large fellow. Glowering, he leaned toward her and spoke in a gravelly tone, "Don't pay them no mind, sister. Thurston and Cliff got somethin' to fight over. You don't want to stick your nose into their business."

"Thurston is upset, and rightfully so," she explained. "First Alden Tusk falls to his death in the museum, and now one of his paintings turns up here, or at least a close copy. Cliff isn't doing a very good job as security manager."

"That ain't got nothin' to do with it." He picked a weighty papaya off a stand and examined the fruit as though fortunes were etched in its skin. "Mr. Stark understands how things are between young Mr. Peters and his wife. You'd be blind if you've missed it. Those two are tight as a strangler fig."

Marla's gaze searched for Heidi, but the blonde had vanished. Smart shikseh to stay out of her husband's warpath.

"So why doesn't Thurston fire Cliff?"

"He lacks the authority. Olly calls the shots, and it suits him to keep Cliff around." Rapping her shoulder, Brooklyn moved his face so close she smelled his garlic-scented breath. "Maybe Olly likes having a security guard who's so easy to distract."

"Meaning?"

"Uh-uh. I've said enough." Putting the papaya back, he strode a few paces to a display of guavas. "You taste the liquor they make here on the island? Pretty strong stuff."

Someone bumped her elbow, and she felt a tug on her handbag. Clutching the purse against her side, she whirled around and saw a kaleidoscope of people. Any one of them could have jostled her, but the tug had been hard, too hard to be accidental. Rummaging in her bag, she breathed a sigh of relief when her fingers found her wallet and passport.

As Brooklyn meandered off, Marla scanned the street for Betsy, but her friend had gone. Sniffing a blend of ripe fruit warmed by the sun and exhaust fumes from cars choking the street, she hitched her breath. Here she'd done the very thing Vail had cautioned her against—ending up alone. She needed to catch the water taxi and get back to the ship.

Waiting for the traffic to ease so she could veer

around a patch of cracked pavement, she shrugged off an eerie feeling of being watched. Did they have pickpockets on the island? Or was she imagining things based on Martha's disappearing act?

She'd just crossed the road when a flash of movement caught her eye. Entering the Guavaberry Mercantile farther down Front Street was an older woman with teased blond hair, a heavy application of makeup, and a silk blouse and skirt. She looked too elegant for an ordinary tourist and too well dressed for a native. Wondering if this could be the elusive countess, Marla hurried after her. Charmed by the cherry-red cottage with gingerbread trim, Marla entered the emporium. Inside to the left stretched a mahogany bar topped with liquor bottles and disposable plastic cups.

"Hello, missy," said the bartender, a large-girthed dark woman with a singsong voice. Her wide smile revealed yellowed teeth. She wore a turban, the fabric matching her flowing caftan. "Would you like to sample our famous island guavaberry drink?"

Marla glanced to her right, where shelves stocked with hot sauces, cookbooks, boxed rum cakes, and souvenir glassware took up space. Beyond the front section, which may have been the living- and dining-room space of a converted house, sat a cloth-draped round table with two chairs. A beaded curtain separated the rest of the place from the public. The strips of beads wavered, as though someone had just passed through.

"Where's the woman who just came in here?" Marla demanded. Behind her, she heard a bell tinkle over the door as another patron entered.

The bartender's gaze flickered momentarily with recognition. "She went back to get ready for a reading. You got business with the countess? I'll give you a drink while you wait. You taste this, you wanna buy."

Marla shifted her purse, watching the man who'd come in from the corner of her eye. He wore a black T-shirt and baggy pants and had the swarthy complexion of a native. Her skin prickled. He appeared to be browsing the gift items, but she'd swear his intent wasn't on shopping. Never mind him. The bartender had mentioned the countess, so she was on the right track.

"You say the countess is here for a reading? Do you tell fortunes?"

"Madame Nadine reads your signs, lady," the proprietress said in a haughty tone. "I have the gift, same as my mama before me. You want an appointment? Rules say you gotta sample my brew first. I know you'll wanna buy a bottle for your friends back home."

"Okay, fine, I'll buy a couple of bottles. Just tell the countess I need to talk to her, okay?"

"Countess Delacroix don't talk to just nobody. Why you wanna see her?"

"A friend of mine gave me her name. I have some questions to ask about a mutual acquaintance." Then, suddenly afraid she wouldn't be able to communicate with the Frenchwoman, Marla queried, "She does speak English clearly enough, doesn't she?"

The bartender laughed, a wheezy sound coming from deep within her chest. "She done speak seven languages, lady. It's all that vanilla. Makes her smart."

"Vanilla?"

"You don't know why she's so rich? True vanilla is expensive, and Countess Delacroix's family owns many plantations. See those shelves over there?" She pointed toward a row of labeled brown bottles. "I carry her product, pure Mexican vanilla extract. You go to

Cozumel, and you'll find lots of bottles for sale, but it ain't always real."

Marla glanced at the man, who was busy perusing a selection of Caribbean coffees. He'd paid no heed to their discussion, but he wasn't in any hurry to make a purchase either.

Madame Nadine poured a few ounces from two different bottles into the plastic cups. "You there, mister. Come taste a free sample. You'll like this better than that other shop down the street. My prices beat theirs, too."

"Thanks, I could use a shot," he said, sauntering over.

Marla took a step back, observing his stubbled jaw and hard glacier eyes. "Look, I have to get back to my ship. Is the countess coming out or not? She shouldn't have to prepare for a reading. I've had one by a psychic, and Reverend Hazel held my eyeglass case for vibes." Her predictions had been right on the mark, too, but then Cassadaga, Florida, was known for its certified mediums.

Feeling parched as well as frustrated, Marla snatched one of the little cups and gulped the contents. Her throat constricted as the strong liquor scorched her esophagus. Its fruity taste left a pleasant aftermath, making her consider its possibilities as a gift for her brother back home.

"Wait here," Madame Nadine told her. "I'll go get Countess Delacroix for you."

Watching her disappear behind the curtain, Marla was startled to feel a tap on her shoulder. She spun to face the man hovering by the bar. A grin split his face like an ax cleaving a tree trunk, giving her the impression he didn't smile often.

"Try this," he said, holding up one of the little

cups. "It's sweeter than the other. People from the States like it a lot better."

Marla grasped the cup, wondering what was taking Madame Nadine so long to retrieve the countess. Maybe she should have followed her through the curtain. Without thought, she downed the liquor, then set the empty vessel on the polished countertop. That should quench her thirst until she got back to their cabin.

Glancing at her watch, she winced. "I can't wait any longer. Will you tell Nadine that I had to leave? I've wasted too much time here already." She was beginning to think she'd been bamboozled about Countess Delacroix even being there. Likely the woman had left through a rear exit.

And likely Dalton will be white with worry over my absence.

Berating herself for lingering, she hastened toward the door. Midway there, a twinge of queasiness hit her stomach. Oh great. She shouldn't have drunk alcohol on top of that meal from the French café. Or maybe the liquor didn't agree with her system. Who knew what extra ingredients it contained.

Planting a hand on her abdomen, she wavered. Her face flushed, a wave of heat moving from the top of her head to her toes. Were those walls moving inward, or was it the enclosed, stuffy atmosphere making her see things?

Lurching toward the exit, she stumbled again as dizziness overwhelmed her. *Get outside!* a warning in her head shouted. Her vision narrowing, she forced herself to put one foot in front of the other. Voices murmured from behind, but she couldn't make out what they said. She gasped as her stomach clenched with a sudden, sharp pain, and then all went black.

* * *

Marla awoke as suddenly as she'd conked out. Her eyelids fluttered open, and she found herself lying flat on her back staring up at a flaky ceiling. Blinking, she tried to clear her muddled mind to determine what had happened. Her forehead throbbed, making clarity of thought difficult. Tempted to close her eyes, she forced herself to remain awake.

Get out of here, flashed a familiar refrain. Oh yeah, she'd been in a hurry, for some reason.

Groaning, she flexed her arms and legs. Her elbow and knee joints moved and nothing hurt. *That's good. Now figure out where you are, pal.* Physically, she appeared to be intact except for the sluggishness that felt similar to caffeine withdrawal.

Groping with her fingers, she explored the hard surface she lay on. Not a bed, so she wasn't in a hospital. Had she been in an accident and taken in by a bystander?

She swung her gaze around the four blank walls surrounding her, noting the little vented window high up and the solid white door. Puzzlement wrinkled her brow, intensifying her headache. Not a very welcoming room. Maybe she'd notice more if she sat up.

Struggling upright, she folded her legs Indian style for support and rubbed her hands over her face. Oh gosh, what happened? She couldn't remember . . . Wait, she'd been in the shop. Vanilla . . . guavaberry liqueur. She'd tasted some and then passed out.

Lord save me, did I miss the sailing?

She couldn't be on board the *Tropical Sun*. From the window, she glimpsed an electric wire strung outside. That meant she was still on St. Maarten. Could this room be at the rear of Madame Nadine's emporium? Possibly the bartender had returned to the storefront and seen that Marla had taken ill. Madame Nadine could have brought her back here until she recovered enough to fend for herself.

Focusing her bleary vision on her watch, she widened her eyes. It wasn't too late! All passengers were supposed to be aboard in fifteen minutes, but the ship wouldn't leave port for another half hour. She couldn't reach the pier by water taxi in time, but by a land route, yes. If she could rouse herself to leave and find a driver.

Moistening her lips, she craved a drink of water to erase the cottony dryness in her mouth. Her stomach felt queasy, and an edge of lethargy still sapped her energy.

Maybe it was the heat. Without air-conditioning, the room acted like an oven, making her suck in short, shallow breaths. How long could she last before succumbing to heatstroke? And if this was Madame Nadine's place, why didn't the woman come and check on her?

Sweat dripping down her chest, she pulled herself to her feet. Standing motionless, she waited until her body stopped shaking before staggering toward the exit. She tried to turn the doorknob. Hope dispelled when it wouldn't turn.

Rattling it with more force, she gave up after the door refused to budge. Futility resulted when she banged her shoulder against the wood. Was it stuck from being warped or locked on the other side?

Maybe Madame Nadine had dumped her in here, and the door had jammed on the way out. Or she had left her in here on purpose. The countess could have put her up to it to avoid contact. If that was the case, surely the countess was long gone by now. Pounding on the wood, Marla shouted for help.

"Madame Nadine, are you there? Let me out!"

Voices came into earshot. Male voices chattering in a language she couldn't understand.

Suddenly afraid, she slumped to a sitting position, her pulse racing. What if she wasn't at the back of Madame Nadine's emporium?

The men stopped outside her room. Someone tested the doorknob, which held fast. Snickering, one man uttered a remark in a foreign language that caused the other guy to laugh. Fear pelted her like needles of ice. She recognized his gruff tone. He was the same man she'd met in the shop.

Holding her breath, she waited until the pair moved away, their voices rising in argument. Finally, they retreated far enough for silence to reign.

She exhaled in relief. Tuning her ears, she listened for street sounds but didn't hear any car engines, vendors hawking their wares, or motorcycles. For all she knew, she could be somewhere inland, far from the ocean.

A chill crawled up her spine like skeletal fingers playing upon her vertebrae. Is this what had happened to Martha Shore? Someone slipped her a Mickey and locked her up in San Juan? And was the intent to kill or merely to keep her from getting back to the ship?

Not that it mattered. If she stayed in this place much longer, she'd die from the heat. Perspiration poured off her face, and she hyperventilated. Her mouth hung open, and her limbs felt weighted down with flaccid immobility.

Think, Marla. Dalton needs you. So does Brianna. You have to get out of here.

Shaking her head, she felt some of the mental cobwebs dissolve. Whatever she had drunk must have been quick acting. Did Madame Nadine slip it into her cup in cahoots with the man, or did he do it when she was distracted? Remembering how she'd had the sensation of being watched on the street, she realized he could have been following her. Madame Nadine may have had nothing to do with her predicament.

But then who was he, and why had he accosted her?

Not wanting to be around when he returned, she rose and shuffled to the door. This was her only way out, and if it wasn't bolted on the other side, she had a chance.

Wondering if the door itself could be removed, she examined the hinges. Although rusted, she didn't think they'd give easily. Picking the lock was her only resort, but what to use?

Her gaze fell upon her handbag. Thank goodness she still possessed it. The person who'd dumped her in here probably wanted to erase any evidence of her presence. Or else he hadn't noticed how she'd had it cross strapped over her shoulder.

Unfortunately, she'd removed her nail file and Swiss Army knife to pass through the ship's security clearance. What else did she have that could be useful? Snatching her handbag, she dumped its contents on the floor.

Pouncing on a cellophane-wrapped mint, she tore at it like an animal. She'd never thought of a restaurant mint as a trophy, but this was a prize like none other. Popping the candy into her mouth, she relished it as a child would a stick of sugarcane. The sugar taste brought saliva into her mouth and gave her a boost of energy.

Now to get out of here. She scraped through the contents of her handbag—wallet, sunglasses, lipstick, comb, powder compact, mini hairspray, hand sanitizer, Tampons, pens, and business card case—but found nothing she could use as a lock pick. Stuffing everything back inside the handbag, she flipped a strand of hair behind her ear.

Her fingers touched metal.

Bobby pins.

Schmuck, you should have thought of this trick before. Grabbing a pin, she straightened it and bounded to the keyhole. A little maneuvering might work on this old door. Grateful to Vail for his lesson in lock picking, she stuck the pin inside and jiggered it. Nothing happened.

Come on, you stupid lock. Sweat dripped down her face as she continued her efforts, the pin becoming slippery between her fingers.

She tilted the angle, feeling for a latch. A clicking sound told her she'd hit her mark. Another twist of the doorknob, and the lock released. Thank God.

Cracking the door open a notch, she peered around its edge. Another room faced hers across a short hallway. It appeared much like this one, unfurnished and deserted. At the end of the corridor was an opening to a weed-filled yard.

Hoping the men weren't outside, she crept to the passage. *Oh, shit.* Her heart sank when she saw them chatting by a cluster of banana plants, dragging on their cigarettes. Forget that idea.

One route eliminated, she turned back and padded down the hallway, careful not to make a sound. Thankfully, the rest of the small house appeared deserted. She cracked open the front door, then ventured outside, her wobbly legs carrying her as far as a rickety white fence before she heard a shout from behind.

Adrenaline boosted her energy. Flapping open

the fence gate, she dashed across the street and wove through several backyards in a residential neighborhood.

Assuming she could elude her pursuers and catch a ride, it should be a shorter hop to the port from here than downtown Philipsburg, with its congested traffic.

Spying an old Chrysler rumbling down a side street, she clutched her handbag and charged after it, waving her hands. "Help, please. I need a ride."

The driver stopped and peered at her through an open window. "What you doin' here, sister? You get lost?"

Grateful he spoke English, she observed his missing front tooth, age lines, and steel-wool hair. "Yes, that's right," she said in a breathless rush. "Please, I need your help. I'll pay anything if you'll take me to the port. I'm on one of the cruise ships, and it's going to leave without me unless I'm there within the next ten minutes."

Realizing she must look a mess with her limp hair, sweat-stained shirt, and cracked lips, Marla gazed at him imploringly until she heard a triumphant cry from off to her right. A quick glance told her the two men were on her tail. Without waiting for a reply, she threw open the passenger door and hopped inside the vehicle.

The islander grinned. "All right, missy, you got a deal. An old guy like me can always use some American dollars."

"Thanks so much." She leaned back against the cushion as he pressed the accelerator. The car lurched ahead with a belch.

"Oh, don't thank me yet. My gas tank is down low. If we don't stop for fuel, this trip will be over before it starts."

CHAPTER 12

"**D**on't ever leave my sight again," Dalton snapped, pacing their cabin. "You're lucky the captain waited to leave port."

Marla opened her eyes. She lay flat on her back in bed with a cool washcloth on her forehead. They hadn't made it to dinner and had ordered room service instead. Already she felt better after a hot shower, light salad, and coffee.

"I have you to thank for the delay," she said.

After searching for her throughout the ship, Dalton had urged the security officers at the gangplank to hold their departure. His pleas had been answered when her savior's car had screeched to a halt by the gate. She'd rocketed down the pier, up the ramp, and into his waiting arms.

"I've never been more worried in my life. You'll be the death of me yet. Didn't I warn you not to go anywhere alone?"

She winced at his hoarse tone. "I'm sorry. One minute I was with Betsy, and the next minute, she'd gone. I saw the countess and hurried after her."

His smoldering look could have started a fire. "Is that woman responsible for what happened to you?"

"Which one, Madame Nadine or Countess Delacroix?" Marla swallowed, her throat dry from the memory. "I don't know if either one of them had a hand in my situation. The man who entered the shop was definitely involved. I recognized him in the house where I ended up. When I was distracted, he could have put something in my drink."

Vail plowed stiff fingers through his peppery hair, which seemed to have sprouted more silvery roots since their embarkation. "I thought you said the bartender pushed those liquor samples on you."

Folding her hands under her head, Marla gazed at the ceiling. "Madame Nadine admitted she did business with the countess. It appears Countess Delacroix's family owns vanilla plantations, and Nadine sells vanilla extract in her shop. They could be conspiring together, but for what purpose?"

"You tell me. And why knock you out of the picture?"

She gave him a steady glance. "Remember, I spoke to Helen at the infirmary. I'd assume that whoever injured her doesn't want her to talk about what she knows. Such as, the countess has been kibbitzing with Sandy Wolfson in the casino."

"So? If they've been seen together, their association is hardly a secret. There's something else at stake." His mouth tightened. "I'll locate that so-called aristocrat and interrogate her. No one will hurt you again." After snatching his wallet from the desktop, he stuffed it in his pocket.

"Shouldn't we ask the security team to report my attack to island police?" Marla asked.

"Go ahead, for all the good it will do."

"I'll come with you then, and we can stop off at Guest Relations." Tossing the washcloth onto the nightstand, she swung her legs over the side of the bed.

When no ensuing dizziness resulted, she stood up. "What did you tell Brie and your parents?"

"That you were too tired from shopping. They'll save seats for us at the second show, unless you don't feel up to it?"

"I'm fine, and we should ask your dad about his relationship with Irene." Collecting the fliers for that evening's gift shop specials, she stuffed them into her Coach handbag. Dress code for tonight was casual, so she'd donned a pair of black slacks and an embroidered coral top. She reached for her lip gloss, then smeared it across her mouth.

"What are you talking about?"

"I saw them together in Marigot. They were in a fine-arts store negotiating with the proprietor. Your father gave us an excuse at the lunch table so he could run off to meet her."

"That's preposterous."

She spun to face him. "What's even more interesting is that Betsy spotted a painting in another shop window. She claimed it was an exact replica of one by Alden Tusk in their museum. Thurston was passing by. He took one look and his face paled."

"And this is your concern, why?"

"Your dad is acting weird, Martha Shore is missing, Helen got pushed down the stairs, and now someone's trying to put me out of action. Isn't that enough? As for why I'm a target, we've already discussed that. Don't you want to find out what's going on, especially if your dad is involved?"

Vail's expression hardened. "I'll admit things aren't as rosy between him and Mom as I'd expected, but I can't believe he's mixed in with this museum crowd."

"If you want to interview somebody, then find out how he knows Irene and why they're conniving together." Unfolding the *Tropical Tattler*, she checked the list of evening activities. "Other than a digital camera demo and a cigar club meeting, there isn't much going on until after the show. Let's look in the casino for the countess, and if she isn't there, we'll hunt for Brie. We should spend more time with your daughter."

"Sounds like a plan."

On the way to the casino, Marla stopped at Guest Relations to talk to a security officer. He wrote down her description of the house where she'd been locked up but said not to expect much in the way of a response from island authorities. The young man seemed more concerned about the cruise line's reputation if she let the media know she'd been mugged.

Satisfied that she had filed a report, she entered the casino. Vail wandered off to check the blackjack tables for the countess, while Marla patrolled the slot machine aisles looking for Kate. She found her future mother-in-law propped on a stool diligently dropping coins into a machine with flashing lights.

"Hi, Mom," Marla said, tapping her on the shoulder. "Sorry we missed seeing you in the dining room. I got back too late from shore."

Kate half rose to give her an affectionate hug. "Dalton was worried about you."

"I know. I got carried away and forgot to look at my watch. It won't happen again. Where's Brie?"

"She's waiting with John to get into the theater. They'll save our seats for the late show." Kate dipped her hand into a huge plastic cup filled with quarters and resumed her play.

"I hope Brie had a good time on the tour. We didn't expect to be stuck in so much traffic, and the beach could have been nicer. We'll have to let her choose the next excursion."

"That's thoughtful of you." Kate smiled, her eyes crinkling like worn dollar bills. "You'll make a fine mother."

Marla's cheeks warmed. "I hope so. It's a new experience for me."

"I don't have any doubts," Kate said. "Remember how I told you John and I are considering buying a condo in Florida? We could rent a place in the meantime to help you arrange wedding details."

At least Kate didn't suggest they stay at Marla's house, unlike Vail's former in-laws. Her considerate attitude made Marla feel even more kindly toward her.

"I'll have enough to do moving my salon," she confessed, "so I might take you up on your offer." *Although I'm not sure how my mother would react. I haven't exactly talked to Ma about wedding plans yet.* "We don't know when our house will be ready, but it shouldn't be long afterward. For Brie's sake, we want to be married before combining households."

"I'll talk to John. He's been consulting a real estate agent, but not about rentals. Prices are sky-high on property in South Florida. It's hard to find anything affordable."

"Tell me about it." If it weren't for the substantial portfolio she'd inherited from Aunt Polly, Marla wouldn't have been able to contribute toward the new home's down payment. As Marla thought over Kate's words, a lightbulb popped in her brain. "Irene told me she's a real estate agent. Maybe John has been asking her for advice. I've seen them together a few times."

"Really?" Kate's eyes rounded in surprise. "I'll ask him, but my bet is they're discussing his stained glass hobby. John thinks he's good enough to enter juried art shows. I imagine he's trying to convince Irene to sponsor him."

Could that be the real reason why John kept crowding Irene? He was serious enough to want to exhibit his work? That would explain his desire to travel, if he hoped to participate in art festivals around the country. It could also explain the tension between her prospective in-laws. Perhaps John felt Kate didn't appreciate his talent and his compulsion to succeed. And maybe Kate feared his new ambition would drive him away from her, not to mention wreak havoc on her established routine.

Opening her mouth to pose a question, Marla noticed Vail's frantic arm signal from around the corner. "I've got to go," she told Kate. "We'll talk more about this later."

She'd just rounded the end of the aisle when she spotted Countess Delacroix rising from a seat beside Sandy Wolfson at the next row over. Behind the Frenchwoman hovered a mustached gentleman dressed in a white dinner suit. He had slicked-back hair and a deep tan. Waiting until the couple strode a sufficient distance from Mrs. Wolfson, she hastened to their side. From her closer vantage point, the countess seemed shorter than she'd first appeared, a full head below Marla's five feet, six inches.

"Excuse me, I've been wanting to meet you. My name is Marla Shore, and I just love your outfits," she gushed, hoping the woman bought her introductory remark. "Where do you shop?"

The countess's smile erased years from her expression. "I am Veronique Delacroix," she said with a pronounced accent. "This is my companion, Claude Rabaud."

"*Enchanté*," the gentleman said, bowing. He appeared as the perfect image of a gigolo keeping company with a wealthy older woman. From his amiable countenance, he didn't mind the role.

"I shop in Paris," Countess Delacroix replied. "It is still the best place, in my opinion, for high fashion."

Wishing she had the money to spend on Parisian clothes, Marla cast an admiring glance at the older woman's red and black tulle ensemble. The loose top and skirt flowed together with an outward flair.

"Those shoes are fabulous," she said, staring at the heels of the woman's shoes, crafted in a clear Lucite-type material. Their painted floral design matched a flower barrette in the countess's coiffed blond hair.

"*Merci.* Now if you will pardon me—"

"Can we talk in private?" Marla said quickly. "I'd be honored if you'd join me for a drink in one of the lounges. I saw you in town today entering the guava-berry liquor store, and I have some questions about the proprietress."

"*Vraiment?*" The countess turned to her companion. "Claude, I can catch up to you later, *non?*"

He caught the drift, nodded, and meandered off, jangling some coins in his pants pocket.

"All right," the elder lady said, with a puzzled frown. "Madame Nadine is a friend of mine as well as a business acquaintance. I am curious as to why you are interested in her."

"We'll discuss it, but first I have to tell my fiancé where we're going. Come along and I'll introduce you."

After agreeing to meet Vail at the show, Marla led the countess to the Nautilus Lounge on deck four. Selecting a quiet corner away from the piano player, they settled at a small round table with a flickering oil lamp. The countess picked up the bar menu and studied the wine selections.

After they'd ordered their drinks, Marla leaned forward. "I saw you enter the emporium in port, but by the time I got there, you'd disappeared."

The countess raised a penciled eyebrow. "You followed me?"

"Well, yes. I'd hoped to catch up to you. We have a mutual friend, Sandy Wolfson. She'd mentioned your name," Marla lied.

"Ah," Countess Delacroix said, with a noncommittal shrug. "Then why do you ask about Nadine?"

"You weren't in the shop when I entered. Madame Nadine gave me a sample of her liquor while I waited for you to return."

"It warms your throat, *non?*"

"Actually, it tasted very strong, too strong for me. I had a bad reaction."

"How unfortunate. You must be careful what you drink in the ports, although I have never known Madame Nadine's customers to be displeased."

"I'm sorry I missed you. Where did you go?"

"I used the restroom and left through a back door, after I heard customers come inside."

"I wish you had still been there, because I could have used your help. After drinking the liquor, I passed out. When I woke up, I was locked in a strange house some distance away."

"Indeed? That must have been truly frightening. Who brought you there, and for what purpose? And why are you telling me about this, mademoiselle?"

"Someone wants me out of the way," Marla explained. "It relates to events that have transpired among my dinner companions. Sandy is one of the people involved. Did you just become friends on this cruise?"

"What concern is that of yours?" the countess snapped.

She related the whole *megillah* about Alden Tusk and the museum gang. "Now Martha is missing, Helen got pushed down the stairs, and someone detained me in St. Maarten. Naturally, I'm concerned. Who's going to be next?"

The countess sighed. "I suppose I should explain. My business with Sandy Wolfson concerns vanilla beans. How much do you know about the industry?"

"Nothing, really." Allowing her muscles to relax, Marla sank back against the cushioned seat. Fatigue ebbed into her limbs. She hadn't rested enough after her ordeal.

"Then listen. Vanilla is the only edible fruit of the orchid family," the countess began, tapping her long fingernail on the tabletop. "It is an extremely valuable crop. The plant stock is native to Mexico, but the beans are also grown in places like Indonesia, Madagascar, and Tahiti. Variations in soil and climate account for the differences in flavor."

"I see. So what is your interest in this commodity?"

The countess tilted her head. "My family has been engaged in the industry for many years. Although we've expanded into Central America and the South Pacific, Mexico remains the primary location for our plantations. That is why it is so critical for us to obtain Bob Wolfson's property."

"Huh?" The waiter chose that moment to appear with their wineglasses, and his interruption was followed by a loudspeaker announcement. "You were saying something about Bob Wolfson's property?" Marla prompted after peace descended.

Sipping her French vintage wine, the noblewoman

regarded Marla from across the table. "I have been talking to Sandy because her husband is too stubborn to sell his land. It is adjacent to one of our plantations."

"He owns land in Mexico?" Glancing at her watch, Marla cursed under her breath. Twenty minutes until the show started. While she yearned to hear what the countess had to say, being with her family took priority.

"Can you believe the man had told his wife nothing about the real estate purchases he's made during each of their yearly cruises?" her companion countered. "Mrs. Wolfson was totally in the dark. *Mon dieu*, I had no idea she was so ignorant when I approached her. It came as quite a shock to the poor woman."

Marla struggled to focus. "So you want to buy a piece of property that Bob owns in Mexico? And his wife didn't know anything about it? Why is he investing his money there?"

"Ah, you do not understand much, do you?"

You're supposed to be enlightening me.

The countess paused, swirling the wine in her goblet. "The legend of the Totonacas began in blood, and so the goddess returns to extract her toll again. You see, Wolfson does not appreciate this valued heritage. He plans to build a resort when his holdings are large enough. Such sacrilege will despoil the land meant for growth. Tonoacayohua is offended. The goddess has infected the mortal's colleagues with tendrils of evil in retribution for his selfish acts."

"What legend are you talking about? What goddess?"

"It began in the Land of the Resplendent Moon. The ruler was blessed with a beautiful daughter, who dedicated her life to serve Tonoacayohua, the goddess of crops.

"One day while gathering flowers in the forest, the girl came upon a young prince. He fell in love with her and persuaded her to run away with him. The priests stopped them and beheaded the doomed couple. Their hearts, cut from their bodies, were given as an offering to Tonoacayohua."

"That's awful."

"I am not finished. In the spot where their blood spilled, a bush grew. From the earth sprang a vine that twisted around the bush like a pair of lovers embracing. Orchids sprouted on the vine, and when the flowers died, slender green beans developed, releasing a powerful perfume. Thus, vanilla was born from the blood of a princess and thereafter offered as a tribute to the goddess."

Marla took a moment to absorb her words. "Great story, but getting back to reality, let's think about what happened to me in St. Maarten. I've concluded that someone drugged my drink. A man entered the shop after me, so it could have been him. The only other person would be your friend, Madame Nadine."

"That is absurd. Nadine would have no reason to harm you. More likely it was that man who followed you inside. He could have been an islander hired by . . . whoever wanted you to be delayed."

Marla grabbed the check from the table and scribbled her signature. "Who do you think is responsible? Please tell me what you know," Marla urged when the countess rose to leave.

"Ah. If we had the answer to your question, mademoiselle, the game would be over. That is the whole point of this voyage."

More bewildered than ever, Marla hustled toward the theater. She had just enough time to sink into her saved seat and mutter a greeting to her relatives before the lights dimmed. Drat, she'd wanted to discuss the countess's information with Vail. She hoped his detective brain could figure things out, but it would have to wait.

Turning her attention to the dance troupe on stage, she dropped her jaw. Holy hot rollers, their costumes didn't leave much to the imagination. If this were a movie, their thongs and feathers would earn an R rating.

Mesmerized by the pounding music, flashing strobe lights, and glitzy numbers that followed, she forgot her concerns until they filed from the theater at the end.

"Did you learn anything from the countess?" Vail asked her in an undertone.

"I found out why she's so interested in Sandy Wolfson, but she hinted at other things I don't understand. We'll talk about it later."

"No fair," Brianna chimed in. "I wanna get the scoop."

Turning to the teen, Marla hugged the girl. "You're on this cruise to have fun, honey. Have you been down to the photo gallery to see if the photos are up from St. Maarten? We could stop by there, and I want to see the silent-auction items at the lounge across from the atrium steps."

"Do you really think Eric would show the triptych this openly? My guess is he's saving it for a mystery item on the last night," Vail said on their way past the lower entrance to the Pirate's Grotto.

"You're probably right. In the meantime, maybe I'll find one of the pictures Alden painted of me," she replied.

Splitting from her family at the martini bar, Marla

wandered along, gazing at the paintings on display. Unfortunately, she didn't find a single item of Tusk's among the pieces displayed. Too bad; she'd have to wait for the next live auction.

Crossing to the photo gallery, she perused the racks of pictures. It was hard to find her group among the hundreds of people. Scanning the rows, she stopped at a picture of Cliff Peters and Kent Harwood among the tour bus crowd. Deep in discussion, they appeared oblivious to the turmoil surrounding them. Cliff's posture was hunched while Kent smiled in a manner befitting a crocodile approaching its victim.

"Hey, Marla, we should buy this photo. You and Dad look great," Brianna said, tugging on her elbow. She held up one of the shots from formal night.

"Okay, let's add it to our collection. What else have you found?" Unable to resist several souvenir photos from their ports of call, more shipboard poses, plus an album bearing the cruise line's logo, Marla ended up with a stack of items.

"Ninety-nine dollars and eighty cents?" she said to the cashier. "Holy highlights, these things add up fast."

Kate ambled over and paid for a few of her own. "I always swear I'm not going to buy any more photos, but I do regardless."

"We'll enjoy them when we get home," Brianna chimed in. "Hey, it's time for me to meet my friends. I'll catch you guys later. We're going to the party on the pool deck."

"Don't be too late getting back to our cabin," Kate called.

"Why not? We're at sea tomorrow. I can sleep all morning."

Marla's brows drew together. "Your grandparents will worry if they wake up and you're not there."

"Where the heck else can I go?"

Vail glowered at her. "Don't be rude, muffin. If Grandma tells you to be back by a certain time, I expect you to obey. You're not old enough to stay out all night yet."

"You just can't accept that I'm growing up, Daddy." With a sniff, Brianna turned away and bounded toward the elevators.

With that responsibility lifted, Marla turned to the elder couple. "So Dad, what's this I hear about you being a fledgling artist? Being new to the art world myself, I have a lot to learn. It's nice that you have someone like Irene on board to offer advice."

"Marla says you've been spending time with that woman," Kate snapped. "Perhaps more so than Oliver."

"Have you noticed how they're almost never together?" John responded, his voice laced with anger. "Irene keeps company more often with a drink in her hand than with her husband. I feel sorry for her."

"Sorry?" Kate sneered. "That's just your excuse to pester her. I wonder if she really thinks you're such an art prodigy or if she's using you as a male door prize."

His complexion reddened to the extent Marla feared he'd have a stroke. "You don't like my hobby. I have talent, and you won't acknowledge it because that might make your stuff less important. Well, I'm retired now, and I'll do what I want!"

Kate drew herself upright. "Fine. Enter all the art shows across the country. See if *she'll* travel with you."

Lifting her chin, she spun and stalked away.

CHAPTER 13

"**I**'ve never seen Dad so upset, but then I haven't lived at home for a number of years." Vail stretched his tall form onto a chaise lounge by the pool deck, where they'd gone to spy on Brianna. Well, not spy exactly. They'd only wanted to make sure she had found her group of friends.

It gave Marla a thrill to watch her almost stepdaughter gyrating on the dance floor. Brianna would give them anxiety attacks when she got older. Her spirited nature wouldn't keep her at home and already she bristled at restraints.

Settling onto a lounger near a lamppost, Marla inhaled the salty night air. From their vantage point, she could see the dancers, but the steel-band music was pleasantly muted.

"Do you think Irene is using your father like your mom suggested? If Irene isn't getting enough attention from Oliver, she could hope to make him jealous by flirting with another man."

Vail scowled. He didn't look at all relaxed, his shoulders tense and his head bent forward. Silver framed his temples. "I doubt that's the case, especially if you saw them talking to an art dealer. Dad obviously hopes to gain an introduction to the art world from his connection to her."

"So? She could be preying upon his interest. You know, hang around with me, darling, and I'll set you up with the right people."

"Dad is smart enough to recognize when he's being taken for a ride. He's a retired attorney, remember?"

"Following a dream can make you desperate."

"Uh-uh, not Dad. He knows the score. Mom, on the other hand, would rather keep her eyes closed. I think his retirement has been really difficult for her."

"Well, if he starts entering art competitions and winning, she'll have to acknowledge his talent."

"I'll ask Dad about that dealer on St. Maarten. Maybe the guy wants to buy some of his work. It's possible Dad sent a sample ahead, but that would mean he's been in cahoots with Irene from the beginning. In other words, this cruise wasn't the unexpected treat we'd been led to believe."

She heard the hurt in his tone. "I'm sorry if things aren't going smoothly for your parents. Their problems will iron out eventually. The best we can do is offer your dad encouragement. He and your mother will have to find common ground themselves."

"It was a mistake to let Brianna stay in their cabin. She's caught in the middle."

"Your daughter is smarter than her years, Dalton. Don't worry about her. Look what a great time she's having."

A waiter circulated in their direction, carrying a tray of green drinks that looked like frothy seawater. "Care for an Anchors Away, one of our specialty beverages? Only eight-ninety-five, and you get to keep the glass."

"No, thanks," Vail barked.

Judging from his harsh response, changing the subject seemed a safe route. Marla didn't want him to brood about his parents the entire trip. It might make him have second thoughts about their wedding.

"I need to tell you about my conversation with the countess," she commented, brushing a tendril of hair off her face. "She said Bob Wolfson possesses land in Mexico, and her family, which is into vanilla plantations, has been trying to get him to sell. When he refused, she approached Sandy. Bob's wife didn't know anything about his real estate purchases there."

"Is that the whole megillah?" Vail asked, grinning. He'd taken to learning Yiddish words to impress her clan at their recent family reunion.

"Not quite." Marla shifted so she could see him clearer. Tiny white lights strung about the deck provided illumination, along with lamps. Relaxing with the ship's swaying motion, she heard splashes from below as the bow cut through the swells. Then the steel band swung into a rendition of "Hot Hot Hot."

"Countess Delacroix suggested it was the man who'd followed us inside the guavaberry shop who'd drugged my drink, and that he'd been hired by someone on the ship."

"No shit. Like whom? Tell me, and I'll go bust up the guy."

"She didn't know. The countess gave me some mumbo jumbo about a legendary goddess being offended by Bob's sacrilege. Apparently, he wants to build a resort in Mexico when he has enough land. He buys more property during each annual cruise."

Vail's eyebrows raised. "Where do you think Bob gets the funds to invest?"

"Good question. Countess Delacroix claimed the goddess is getting retribution for Bob's selfishness by infecting everyone from the museum with evil."

"If Bob keeps buying more property, why can't she beat him at his own game?"

"Funny, she mentioned a game, too. She said that if we knew all the answers, the game would be over, and that that was the whole point of this voyage."

"Weird."

Marla glanced up to note a conga line snaking in their direction. Grabbed from her perch by a squinty-eyed fellow in a flowered shirt, she tumbled into place between a stick-thin youth and a pimpled pre-teen.

"*Olé, olé,*" sang the crowd, bouncing along to the Caribbean beat. Trapped between a tangle of arms and legs, Marla fought to free herself until she spotted Heidi Stark bumping and grinding her body against Cliff Peters nearer to the band. Hmm, maybe she could ask him about the photo in which he stood talking to Kent.

Her view eclipsed by other dancers, she side-stepped without looking where she was going. A sudden shove thrust her toward the pool's edge. Flailing her arms, she lost her balance. Her glance took in the loose safety netting over the pool, drained for the night. She screamed, the sound drowned by a trumpet blast from the band.

A hand grasped her ankle as she tumbled backward. She grabbed at a loose piece of mesh, hoping to avoid hitting her head against the concrete wall. Strung out between the netting and her rescuer like a fish being reeled in, she closed her eyes to a wave of dizziness.

"Hold on," she heard Vail's voice slash into the background noise. More hands reached out and hauled her backward while the music ended to a chorus of shouts.

Slung onto the pool deck, she heaved in short, shallow breaths. Sweat oozed from her pores. She couldn't move, couldn't contemplate what had just nearly happened.

"Are you all right?" Kneeling by her side, Vail peered into her face. His own complexion appeared ghastly.

"I'm fine. Thanks." Tremors shook her body while she squeezed his hand in silent gratitude. It took a few moments to regain her composure. "Did anyone see who pushed me?" she asked in a shaky voice.

"It may have been that dude in a flowered shirt," said a familiar gruff voice. Marla twisted her neck to view Kent Harwood crouched beside her. "He disappeared, but I think it's the same man who yanked you out of your lounge chair."

"You were watching us?" Vail said, his steely eyes flashing.

The heavyset man plucked a toothpick from his pocket and stuck it between his teeth. "I just happened to be passing by, buddy. Don't get all uptight."

"Passing by, my ass. Who are you?"

Kent's beady eyes scanned the crowd. "This isn't the time or place. Can you stand, Marla?" His unkempt hair fell into his face, reminding her of Professor Snape in the *Harry Potter* movies. Which side did the exterminator represent, good or evil? His concerned tone indicated the former, but she wasn't ready to trust anyone from the museum.

With the men's assistance, she regained her feet. Other than being shaken and feeling her shoulders throb, she seemed okay. Dalton fussed over her like a mother hen, which touched her heart. But when Brianna suddenly flew into her arms with a cry of dismay, Marla burst into tears. Mortified, she attributed her weakness to shock and fatigue.

"Hey, I'll be all right, guys. Let's just go to our cabin, Dalton. Brie, do you want to come with us tonight? We can ask the steward to put down the extra bunk bed."

"No, thanks," Brianna said. "I told Grandma I'd be in by one. I've gotta go. Are you sure you're not hurt?" Her coffee eyes looked large and round in the moonlight.

Marla hugged her, planting a kiss on her cheek. "I need a good night's sleep, that's all. Kent, let's talk tomorrow. If you put your cards on the table, I'll put mine. Deal?" She looked him squarely in the eyes.

He gave her a steady gaze in return. "You've got it," he replied, chomping on his toothpick.

Stepping closer, he invaded Marla's personal space. He smelled like diesel fumes and stringent cleaning solution. *Do your laundry, pal*, she thought with an inner grimace.

"Anybody see Brooklyn Jones?" Kent added. "I've been looking for the fellow since dinner."

"Have you tried his cabin?" Vail suggested.

"Yep. No one answers. I'm just wondering because Brooklyn said he had something to tell me. We were gonna meet for pizza, but he didn't show."

"Maybe he forgot," Marla offered, turning toward the sliding glass doors leading inside to the bank of elevators.

Keeping pace, Kent gave her an oblique glance. "Maybe. In the meantime, watch your step, will ya? We wouldn't want you to have another accident." Breaking off from their group, he trounced down the stairway.

"That guy is nasty," Brianna remarked. "You should

offer to cut his hair, Marla. Did you smell him? He stunk like a truck."

"You're right. I wonder if he's been prowling below decks. And if so, why? He couldn't expect to find Brooklyn there."

Vowing to ask him the next day, Marla retired to their cabin. No more snooping, she promised herself, at least not until the art auction on Thursday afternoon.

Marla's plan to avoid complications succeeded during the morning, when she ate a leisurely breakfast, strode laps around the sports deck with Vail, then plunked herself down on a royal blue upholstered lounge chair in the solarium. Other than sore shoulders, she seemed none the worse for wear from her incident last evening.

A bunch of men cooking their skin in the Jacuzzi shmoozed loudly about their recent stock purchases. Marla winked open one eye to regard the woman who took the chair beside Vail. She wore a red shirt with white shorts and held a Nora Roberts novel. Another guy in bright orange swim trunks strolled by listening to his iPod, while a man with a paunch studied his *Tropical Tattler*. She heard the swish of waves over the muted popular tunes playing on the loudspeaker.

Ding dong, ding dong. "Good morning, ladies and gents. This is David, your cruise director, reminding you that at eleven o'clock, we have our Win-a-Cruise bingo game where one lucky winner will take home a certificate for a free seven-day Caribbean cruise. We're also giving away lots of cash, so we hope to see you there!"

A woman walked past carrying a coffee cup and a plate of breakfast pastries. Marla's mouth watered from the aroma of cinnamon and baked bread.

"I'm hungry again," she told Vail as she patted her stomach.

Glancing at the skin exposed by her bikini, he coughed. "If you eat much more, you won't fit into those things."

"Oh, like you should talk. Who ate an omelette and three doughnuts this morning?"

"Cops are supposed to eat doughnuts."

"Not so many. I could use another cup of coffee and maybe a yogurt. I've been eating too many carbohydrates."

He threw down the Michael Crichton novel he'd been attempting to read. "I'll get it," he said, jumping up. "I can't sit for so long. I've got *schmaltz*."

Marla repressed a chuckle. "*Schmaltz* is chicken fat. You mean, you've got *shpilkes*. You're restless."

"Right. I'll be back."

Ding dong, ding dong. "This is Eric, your auctioneer, inviting you to attend our champagne art auction this afternoon immediately following the towel-folding demonstration, puffy eye seminar, and men's belly flop competition. You won't want to miss this chance to add pieces to your collection at forty percent or more off retail prices. Whoo-hoo!"

I wonder if John brought along any of his stained-glass pieces, Marla mused. The former museum curator could evaluate their worth. Eric's validation might convince Kate to support her husband's efforts. Spying her future mother-in-law tromping through the solarium, she stood and waved. She'd saved a couple of extra seats just in case and leapt at the opportunity to talk to Kate undisturbed.

"Tell me," she said after they'd greeted each other and Kate had spread her towel on one of the empty chairs, "did John bring any of his art pieces with him? I'd love to see what he makes."

Kate pressed her lips together, then said, "They're too fragile, and we didn't have any extra space in our suitcases. I'm sure he'd be happy to show you samples when we're in Florida."

"Do you really hate his hobby that much, or is it the thought of traveling to art exhibits that bothers you?" Marla wiped a line of sweat off her forehead. Her skin felt heated, and the breeze seemed to have died. Speaking of John, where was he? She hoped for Kate's sake that he wasn't kibbitzing with Irene again. Afraid to ask, she waited for the older woman's reply while keeping one eye tuned for Vail's return.

"I don't begrudge him his interests," Kate said, twisting a strand of red hair around her finger. "And it isn't that I don't like to travel. What bothers me is that John doesn't consider my needs. I can't just up and run off to these events when I have my own schedule. It's as though my life doesn't exist."

"I get you. Dalton is like that sometimes. He'll make plans without consulting me first."

"Besides, this could just be a passing fancy. He was never into crafts until he retired and took a class at our church's senior citizen center. Then he goes out, buys all sorts of supplies, and works himself into a frenzy. I just don't understand."

Marla crossed her legs. "It could be that while he was working, he didn't have time to express himself artistically. I'd think most wives would be grateful their retired spouses found something to do. Otherwise, he might hang around the house and annoy you."

Kate winced. "I suppose you're right. On the one hand, I'm glad he's occupied so I can go about my own business. On the other hand, he's so passionate about this new hobby that he doesn't talk about anything else. We've got travel brochures lying around the house. He wants to participate in juried art shows. Why? To sell his work, or to win prizes?"

Marla sought a glimmer of comprehension. "Possibly he's looking for validation to make himself feel useful. When people retire, often they lose their source of self-esteem. It has to be a blow to the ego, so perhaps this is his way to compensate."

"If that's true, I haven't helped by putting him down." Bending forward, Kate pursed her lips, then continued, "I'll try to be more encouraging, but only if John asks me before he makes any travel plans. I might be willing to go with him, assuming we have nothing else on the calendar."

Marla heard what her future mother-in-law wasn't admitting, that she feared John would go off on his own. Retirement could lead to marital strife if a couple found themselves veering in opposite directions. She supposed they had to work at compromising all over again.

Holy highlights, marriage is hard work. Do I really want to dive into this morass? she asked herself. *It's better than diving into an empty pool with a torn safety netting and no one to catch you*, she reasoned. *Let that analogy be a lesson. If you don't want to go through life alone, you have to make sacrifices.*

She cleared her throat. "Where is John now?"

"He's playing bridge in the card room. We're meeting you for lunch. Brie should be finished with her makeover session by then. Her group is spending the morning in the spa," Kate explained. Leaning over, she patted Marla's arm. "Brie talks about you all the time. You have no idea how much she respects you. You're a wonderful role model, dear. Dalton is a lucky man to have you."

"Thanks," she said, a warm glow spreading through her.

After lunch, Marla went searching for Kent Harwood. She only had an hour before the art auction. When she didn't find him in any of the public lounges or on deck, she gave up and headed to the gallery.

Dalton had refused to accompany her, citing fatigue as his excuse. Brianna had run off with her crowd, John had headed below for a nap, and Kate had made a beeline for the Internet Café to research wedding reception sites for Marla and Vail.

Finding a seat next to Betsy, Marla scrutinized the patrons. Irene, Brooklyn, and Kent remained absent. Strange; they'd shown up for nearly every other event. Chatting idly with her friend, she kept her eye on the door but none of them entered.

The auction proceeded, with people waving their bid cards excitedly over a mystery set. It turned out to be a minor artist's work, making the museum members grumble in disappointment. Only one painting sold from Tusk's collection. Thurston won the nude woman gazing at a vase of flowers.

"Where's Irene?" Marla asked Oliver as they squeezed down the staircase after the event concluded. She held the free limited-edition seriolithograph she'd gotten for attending, a tropical scene by Pauker.

The big man ran a hand over his partly bald head. "She had an upset stomach and went to rest in our cabin."

"Betsy and I might stop by the Cargo Café. I like their Hair Raiser brand coffee." She hesitated. "Would you like to join us?"

"No, thanks, my dear. I've got things to do."

"I'm hoping to run into Kent. I was disappointed he didn't come to the auction. Neither did Brooklyn. Have you seen them around?"

"Sorry." He shook his head. "Isn't there a kitchen tour this afternoon? That's where I would go to find Brooklyn."

"Good idea. Thanks."

She and Betsy signed on for the tour, which gave them a tantalizing glimpse into the culinary department. Standing beside gleaming stainless steel stations, white-uniformed chefs demonstrated their technique, offering samples to taste. Her appetite whetted for dinner, Marla proceeded to search for Vail after the tour concluded. Brooklyn still didn't show up on her itinerary, and neither did Kent.

Her manhunt turned up Irene Smernoff having a cocktail with Eric Rand in a quiet corner of the Pirate's Grotto. *Irene recovered fast from her indisposition*, Marla thought, edging her way toward their booth while trying to remain out of sight.

Irene had one hand around her martini glass and another hand on top of Eric's wrist. Leaning inward, she offered him a view down her cleavage.

I don't understand how you're not cold wearing such a skimpy dress in this air-conditioning. Maybe that's why you keep scooting nearer, to share his body heat, Marla mused.

Irene murmured something in an imploring tone, but Marla couldn't make out her words. Stepping closer, she fumbled when the ship swayed and knocked her against a bronze statue of a grizzly bear with glowing red eyes. It didn't budge, fortunately for her. Even the smallest sound would echo in this space.

"I can't," Eric's voice carried clearly. "Do you think you're the only one? Everyone's made an offer to buy Alden's triptych. You'll have to wait until the last night, like everyone else, my love."

Holding the bear to steady herself, Marla inched around its bulk to a better vantage point. No one else sat in the dimly lit room. The pair must have obtained their drinks from the bar on the upper level then come down here to talk in private.

"He's threatening to tell Delaney about us," Irene replied.

"That's always been a risk." Marla heard the censure in Eric's radio announcer voice.

"Please. I'll even . . ."

Irene lowered her decibels and Marla had to strain her ears. No luck. Darn, she wanted to hear what they said. From the way they kept touching each other, she gathered they'd shared a more intimate relationship in the past.

Venturing forward, she didn't watch her footing and tripped over a cable taped to the floor.

"Marla!" Irene sprang from her seat, alarm crossing her features.

Eric rose more slowly, a look of anger on his face. He no longer had the boyishly cheerful mien he put on for the auctions. His mouth tight with determination, he marched toward her. His heavy footsteps resounded on the polished wood floor.

Irene scurried to reach him. "No, Eric, don't."

CHAPTER 14

"What are you doing here?" Eric demanded.

Marla backed up a step. "I was looking for Kent Harwood. Have either of you seen the man? He missed the auction and I need to talk to him." She heard dishes clanging and ice rattling into glasses from the bar upstairs.

"Haven't seen the guy."

"But you know who he is. You're acquainted with everyone from the museum."

"Evidently, so are you. Kent isn't here. Go look elsewhere."

"I will." She swung her gaze toward Irene. "Your husband said you weren't feeling well and were resting in your cabin. You should've seen that colorful beach serigraph by Fanch at today's auction. I was tempted to bid on it myself." She forced a chuckle. "Eric is such a great auctioneer that he makes me want to raise my bidding card on everything."

Eric balanced on the balls of his feet, as though he couldn't decide whether to rush her or leave her alone.

"What do you want?" he growled, seeming so different from his usual cheerful personality that her mind went momentarily blank.

"We've never properly met," she gushed, extending her hand with a bubbleheaded grin. "I'm Marla Shore." She nodded at Irene. "Irene and I are dinner companions."

Pressing his lips, Eric gave her a quick handshake. His sweaty palm told her he was unnerved by her abrupt arrival. He still wore his bow tie and sports coat from the auction. Its dark color matched his slicked-back ebony hair, tinged with gray.

"I've heard about you," he replied in a flat tone that didn't hint at his opinion. "Somebody screwed up, and you were seated at the wrong table."

"Yes, I believe my fiancé's parents were slated to sit with the Smernoffs. We should have been at the other table with his daughter. Did you arrange that ahead of time, Irene? John must have been terribly disappointed when your plans didn't work and you were seated at separate tables. You had arrangements to discuss with him, isn't that correct?"

"What's this?" Eric said, twisting to regard his companion. He didn't sound pleased from his cutting tone.

Irene plunked down her empty martini glass. "It has nothing to do with us," she reassured him in a shaky voice. Her body swayed, and she stabilized herself by grabbing a nearby column. The ship's rocking motion seemed more pronounced here, or else she'd just imbibed one drink too many.

"Tell me about this fellow," Eric ordered.

"I said, he's not a problem."

"Let me be the judge of that, my dear."

Irene stiffened. "Are you forgetting that it's my money—" She stopped when he jerked his head in Marla's direction. "Very well, I suppose you might find the information useful. But I need another drink first. Marla, would you like something from the bar?"

Wearing a scowl, Eric acquiesced to her wishes. After he returned with Irene's cocktail and a Coke for Marla, he prompted the older woman to continue. They sat around a polished wood table bolted to the floor. Marla popped the tab on her soda can.

"John Vail is a budding artist," Irene said, clutching her glass and staring at the clear liquid, while Marla noticed with fascination that her foundation makeup had pooled in her creases.

"He'd entered a competition where I was one of the judges. I liked his work and contacted him. John is fantastic in the stained-glass milieu. Not the usual variety, you know, business card holders and such." Irene's eyes fired with enthusiasm. "His designs are unique. I offered to sponsor his entry into juried art shows."

"What were you doing in Marigot?" Marla asked, not about to let the opportunity pass.

"I have contacts throughout the art world, darling. That particular shopkeeper likes unusual pieces, so I had John send him a few samples. Pierre wanted to meet the artist in person before placing an order."

Irene's altruism stunned her. "Did Oliver know you and John planned to meet on this cruise?"

"He doesn't concern himself with my activities." Her chin lifted, belying her insouciant tone.

Irene cared more than she let on about her husband's neglect, Marla thought. Could that be what had driven her into another man's arms?

"You shouldn't worry about John making a play for Irene," Marla told Eric. "He loves his wife. But you two . . . you go way back to when Eric was curator at the museum, don't you?"

Irene and Eric exchanged an intimate glance. "Not that it's any of your business, but I was in charge of the art collection," Eric explained. "Oliver and Irene attended many of our social events. I couldn't help running into her."

"Especially when Olly left me stranded," Irene interrupted.

"Yes, um, we started discussing art, you know. Both of us share that interest. And then one thing kind of led to another."

"I see." Marla tilted her head. "And I appreciate your sharing this with me. I'll keep my lips sealed."

Eric pushed himself from his chair. "If you ladies will excuse me, I'd best go check the lockers. Someone tried to break in last evening. I can't imagine why." The words tripped sarcastically off his tongue.

"Wait, I have another question," Marla called, then hustled after him as he headed toward the spiral staircase. Irene slipped out through another exit.

"I'm wondering if you have any of Alden Tusk's pictures on board that show a woman wearing a ballet outfit? I modeled for him when he lived in South Florida, and I'd really like to find one of those paintings. I had forgotten all about him until I heard his name mentioned at your auction."

Eric halted, his foot on the lower rung. "I know he did some portraits of girls in dance costumes, but we don't have any in our collection. I can check the catalogues for you, if you like."

"Thanks, I'd appreciate that. Tell me, what's so important about Alden's triptych? The museum gang is spastic about it."

He gave her a hooded glance. "There's a reason the middle piece was missing after Tusk's death. By all indications, he'd painted a portrait of his killer. And that person most likely is one of the people sitting beside you at dinner."

"Killer? I thought his fall was an accident."

"It's more likely Alden was pushed."

Like Helen? Marla mused as she climbed the atrium steps searching for her family.

Her steps invariably took her toward the art gallery. Upstairs, the door to the auction room itself stayed locked when unattended. Knowing that Eric had gone below decks to check the storage containers, she questioned the glimmer of light around the door frame.

Padding silently up the carpeted staircase, she reached a hand to try the doorknob. It twisted easily. She swung the door open and spied a familiar figure scurrying from one of the back workrooms.

"Oh, Marla, it's you," Kent Harwood breathed in relief. His florid complexion and sheen of sweat betrayed his state of nerves. Doubtless he had been afraid of being caught red-handed by the auctioneer.

"You needn't worry," she told him, leaving the door ajar behind her. "Eric is on one of the crew decks checking his lockers. What are you doing here? And how did you get in, by the way?"

He shot a glance at her from under his thick eyebrows, his glare much like that of a seagull searching for prey. Was the fish he hunted small enough to chew, or so big that it might bite back? "I have talents that aren't evident," he said, rolling the words in his mouth as though choosing them carefully.

"Along with an education that you hide. You're no bug man, Kent. What do you really do for a living?"

He shrugged. "I suppose if I tell you, it might help keep you out of trouble. I'm investigating theft at the museum."

"What kind of theft?" She thought of Bob Wolfson's

real estate purchases. Was the business manager dipping into funds belonging to the museum?

"Reproductions are being substituted for original works of art. Eric Rand tipped off the insurance company after he left and arranged for Brooklyn Jones to claim they had a pest problem in the kitchen. I came in under the guise of being an exterminator, which I'm actually licensed to do. I studied entomology in college," he explained, "but ended up going into investigative work because it paid better."

Good disguise, Marla thought, *and you just lost your gruff manner of speech. I hope your awful haircut and loud shirts are part of your camouflage, too.*

"So did you find the triptych?" she asked, peering around his bulk.

"Nah, Eric must have it squirreled away somewhere." Jabbing his thumb, he indicated they should move out. After they'd each passed beyond the door, he jiggled a tool in the keyhole to set the lock.

"Did you ever see the side panels?"

"I got a peek after the accident. Everything had been roped off for the fund-raiser, and by the time the commotion had died down, someone had removed the center triptych piece from the exhibit."

"What did the outer panels show?" Exiting the gallery, Marla waited for him to join her.

Kent halted to remove a toothpick from his pocket and stick it in his mouth. "Both scenes show a room with traditional furnishings. One side holds a piano, and the other has an ornate fireplace. Each panel contains a portrait of a lady. The two ladies are wearing long gowns and are staring at each other from opposite ends of the room, although it's clear their eyes actually focus on the center."

"So? What's the big deal?"

He glanced at her. "You have to see it to understand the emotional impact. They look horrified, as though they're watching some atrocity."

She strolled beside him down the corridor toward the nearest staircase. "What do you think it means?"

"That something bad happened to Alden, and this was his way of relating the experience. Mind you, it may have been a past event, but nonetheless, you get a creeped-out feeling from seeing the pictures."

"Maybe Alden painted himself committing an inappropriate act, and his guilt compelled him to capture the scene on canvas. He could've done it as a means of atonement."

Kent's lips shifted the toothpick. "Possibly, but then why would someone remove it?"

"To protect him?"

"Could be, but I have another theory," Kent replied. "What if the central panel implies a crime? Surely the guilty party would want to bury it."

They descended to deck three, where the photo gallery was crowded with passengers. No sign of any family members or museum people. Thank goodness. She wanted to continue their discussion uninterrupted. Music from Mariner's Martini Bar drifted in their direction, along with the smell of cigarette smoke.

"That makes sense," Marla said, wrinkling her nose. "It could account for Alden's 'accident' and the missing piece if this other person didn't want the scene revealed." Then she added, returning to her original idea, "Or if Alden was guilty, he could have decided at the last minute that he couldn't give himself away. Alden could have hidden the panel before leaping from the balcony and taking his own life."

"What about the music Martha said she heard from the gift shop just before Alden screamed?"

"You know about that?"

"I make it my job to learn about everything."

A shank of hair tumbled across his forehead. Noting the greasy strands, Marla bit her lip to keep herself from commenting aloud. *When did you last wash your hair, pal? I don't care if it's part of your disguise. Make an appointment at the ship's salon.*

"Do you know who's substituting fake works of art at the museum?" she asked, scratching an itch on her arm.

"I've got some clues, but I'm not ready to point the finger at anyone just yet. You hear anything relevant? I understand you and your boyfriend have been asking some sharp questions."

"Well, it's not Betsy, because she noticed a painting in St. Maarten that she said was an exact duplicate of one back in the museum. She wouldn't have mentioned that if she's involved."

Pausing at the foot of the atrium staircase, Kent tilted his head. "Oh yeah? Brooklyn said he had news about her. I haven't been able to hook up with him since." His gaze darkening, he chewed on his toothpick.

"I hope he's okay."

"Me, too. I'd better go look for him. And if I were you, I'd keep my mouth shut about our conversation."

She wondered if she ought to mention the incident in Philipsburg. Her probes must have hit a nerve, because someone wanted her out of the way. Probably she could scratch Kent Harwood off the list, but it bothered her what Brooklyn Jones might know about Betsy.

* * *

When Brooklyn didn't show up for breakfast on Friday morning, Marla's alarm escalated. He didn't make it to the dining room, nor did she spot him upstairs at the buffet. Aware that time was short and she had to get ready for their shore excursion on Grand Cayman Island, she phoned Brooklyn's cabin number. Getting no response, she tried Kent's stateroom.

"I haven't seen him," Kent's gruff voice replied on the telephone. "I'm waiting for a call back from ship's security. They've checked his room. He's not there, but his passport is on top of his nightstand. If he doesn't turn up, they'll page him. Hey, can you do me a favor on shore?"

"Sure, what is it?" She gestured at Vail, who was pacing by the door. *Just a few more minutes*, she mouthed.

"Keep an eye on Wolfson."

What happened to minding my own business? Now you want me to spy for you? "Why?"

A pause. "Brooklyn told me that Bob Wolfson asked him to sign off on some invoices at work that included kitchen items he never ordered. I don't care to think Bob had anything to do with Brooklyn's absence, but I'd like to know what he does in town today. I may be late getting off the ship."

"I don't know how much help I'll be." Marla shrugged. "We're going on the stingray snorkeling adventure."

"Oh. Well, never mind then. We'll just have to hope Brooklyn turns up."

Marla kept her concerns to herself while she stuffed various advertising flyers and brochures into her bag. From here on, she intended to give Vail her undivided attention.

Slated to meet his parents and Brianna before descending to the gangplank, she hustled alongside him down the corridor with closed cabin doors on either side. She could swear this hallway got longer each time they strode its length. During the wait for the elevator, she filled Vail in on the conversation she'd had with Kent Harwood.

"I'm glad you told him we're off duty," Vail said in a dry tone. His fingers made figure eights along her spine.

Her mouth curled in pleasure. "That feels good," she murmured, edging closer.

He rubbed his hip against her. "Not as good as I'll make you feel later."

"Then stop that, or we'll be heading back to the stateroom instead of the exit."

Grasping her shoulder, he turned her to face him. "There's nothing I'd like better," he answered, giving her a fierce kiss.

The elevator's arrival along with his teasing banter took her mind off the museum gang. Soon they found themselves in the Sailaway Lounge, where his parents had already obtained tickets for the tender. When their number was called, they descended to the gangplank deck. The small boat bobbed on the swells as crew members assisted passengers in boarding. Squeezed together on rows of benches, they jostled elbows while the engine revved prior to launch. Wind whipped the passengers' hair as they got under way.

Waves splashed against the bow, the water an incredible shade of turquoise that made her impatient to dive into the bath-warm ocean. Sparkles of sunlight glinted off the crests as they neared the shoreline.

Kate shaded her eyes even though she wore a wide-brimmed hat. "Look, there's a Royal Caribbean vessel anchored farther out. Their passengers are also coming in by tender."

"Crap, that means the shops in town will be crowded," Brianna griped.

"Brie, we didn't come on this cruise just to shop. And please watch your language," Vail remonstrated.

"Listen to your father." Marla squinted behind her sunglasses. Even though they sat under cover, the sun's reflected glare hurt her eyes. "Ladies don't use bad words."

"And you don't? Give me a break. I've heard you say—"

"Brianna!" Vail's authoritative tone brooked no arguments.

Giving him a disgusted glance, the teen shut her mouth. Nobody spoke, occupied with private thoughts. Marla, busy sorting the flyers she'd grabbed from their cabin, decided she didn't need the one advertising facials in the ship's spa. She gave Brianna the jewelry shop ads to browse while she studied the port guide and map. Vail, working on the ship's daily trivia quiz, muttered to himself.

"Peachtree Street is in Atlanta, isn't it? What about Via Veneto? It's about famous streets," he told Marla.

"That's in Venice," Kate contributed, applying sunscreen to her arms. She and John planned to take a taxi to the turtle farm. They'd been to Grand Cayman before.

Once on the pier, they separated. "We need to find our tour group," Marla said to Vail and Brianna. "Do you see the van anywhere?" Their excursion included transportation to a marina, from which they would sail to the stingray sandbar. It had cost them forty-five dollars each for three hours. Finished by one o'clock, they'd have plenty of time for shopping later.

"Folks, can you stand together for a shot, please?" hollered the ship's photographer, cornering them for a Welcome to Grand Cayman pose that would cost a mere ten dollars to purchase. *Buy enough photos, and you could pay for another cruise*, Marla thought, grinning at the camera. She almost felt sorry for the guy sweating in the heat while trying to snap photos of the milling passengers.

They located their van and boarded quickly. Inside, Marla tapped Brianna's shoulder. "Head for the rear. I see a few empty seats back there."

Sinking into an empty space next to the teen, Marla swung her large beach bag onto her lap. She'd brought enough supplies for a weekend, and it was a relief to get the weight off her arm.

"Have you noticed how cruises advertise their all-inclusive rates?" she said to Vail, who sat across the aisle. "You get room and board, port visits, and activities, but then you end up paying twice as much for drinks, tours, photos, shopping, and gambling. Your money goes down while your weight goes up."

"Some would claim that's a fair trade-off for a week of fun in the sun," he answered in a mild tone. "Say, there go the Wolfsons. Isn't that the bus for the botanical garden group?"

She twisted her neck. "Oh, yeah. We won't have to worry about where Bob's going, then. At least not until later." She watched the other passengers board, squinting as she caught sight of another familiar face. The elegant blond woman wore a snappy red outfit with a matching hat. Accompanying her was a white-haired man sporting a naval cap, dress shirt, and dark trousers.

"It's Countess Delacroix and her gentleman friend," Marla stated. "I wonder if she's going along to put the screws on Bob to sell his property in Mexico. He isn't aware that Sandy knows what's going on, so that should be an interesting ride."

Vail leaned toward her and said in a low voice, "Didn't someone other than Kent Harwood say to watch him in Grand Cayman?"

"Bless my bones, you're right. Martha said the same thing to Oliver. Damn, we're on the wrong tour. We should have gone on theirs."

Her ponytail swishing, Brianna rapped on Marla's wrist. "Listen to yourself, Marla. You just cursed. How can you tell me not to use bad words when you do it?"

Chiding herself, Marla rolled her eyes. "Some occasions call for them, honey, but you have to be careful which ones you choose."

CHAPTER 15

A motorized snorkel boat shuttled them to the sand-bar two miles offshore. Marla sat with Brianna on an open bench in the rear but Vail preferred the shaded area up front. Since the rumbling engine made hearing difficult, Marla relaxed and enjoyed the ride. Closing her eyes, she took a deep breath of the fresh sea air and savored the sensation of skipping over the waves. The wind beat salt spray onto her skin, warmed by the sun.

I could get used to this. We'll have to take a longer cruise next time.

She snapped open her eyelids to regard the gleaming water, a lighter shade of jade in the shallow depths. Sweating under the tropical sun, she yearned to dive in, especially when the ocean turned a brilliant aqua as they got farther from shore.

When the boat reached their destination, certified guide masters distributed yellow life vests and gave an instructive briefing before cutting them loose.

Clutching her snorkeling mask and tube, Brianna brushed past her toward the swim steps prior to entering the water.

"Brie, don't forget to inflate your life vest," Marla called. They wouldn't need it on the sandbar, three or four feet deep, but where they entered from the boat, the depth could reach over six feet.

Swimming came second nature to Marla. Her mother had given her lessons at a country club in New York, where she'd grown up. They'd joined the club every summer, and she'd been forced to participate in day-camp activities while her mother played Mah-Jongg and her father sat reading the *Wall Street Journal*. Up north, people didn't have private pools like residents in South Florida. Child drownings were not a common cause of death for children aged four and younger there, either.

For a moment, she hesitated with her foot on the ladder while tiny waves splashed against the hull. Memories of a past tragedy surfaced to haunt her. If only she hadn't answered the telephone call she'd been told to expect by Tammy's parents when she'd baby-sat for the toddler. In those few seconds, the child had climbed from her playpen and fallen into the backyard pool.

"Marla, get a move on," Brianna yelled from the water.

Gathering her courage, she plunged into the warm sea. The submersion sloughed off her guilt like a cleansing *mikveh*. "Be careful," she hollered back, wary of stingrays after the Crocodile Hunter's accident.

Several other boats bobbed nearby in the water. Small stingrays congregated by the sandbar as though knowing they'd get fed. Tiny fish squiggled past as Marla's feet found the sandy bottom. She stood waist deep in the water and watched shadowy shapes glide in the current.

"Get some squid, Marla," Brianna advised, sticking her hand into the bucket their driver held out.

Her ponytail hung sopping wet, but the teen's face radiated such joy that Marla's own anticipation rose.

"Hold the bait like our guide said, or the stingray will suck your hand," Marla warned. "Oh, yuck."

Nearly dropping the slimy chunk of squid, she offered it as instructed. With her other hand, she tentatively touched the top of a stingray that swam close. Its skin felt like sandpaper. The creature allowed her to pick it up in her arms like a baby, but she held it out from her body, afraid it might suck on her flesh or sting her with its barb. Her fingers brushed its smooth underside before she gently released it.

Suddenly Vail was behind her, breathing on her neck. "You'll have good luck for seven years if you kiss the thing between its eyes, fourteen years if it's a male."

She turned into his arms. "No, thanks, I'd rather kiss you." Buoyed by the water, she did just that until Brianna tagged her.

"Stop it, you guys. We're here to see the stingrays."

"This feels so great. I could stay here forever." Marla ducked down, dipping her shoulders in the warm water. Her companions mimicked her, and they joined hands and danced in a circle, laughing in a sea of contentment.

A holler from their guide brought them back on board their craft. After toweling herself dry, Marla bought rum punches for herself and Dalton and a water bottle for Brianna, plus bags of chips. Feeling sticky, she sat on a bench in the shade and sipped her drink. The boat rocked back and forth, making her queasy. Or maybe she just needed salt replenishment after their exertion. After eating a few potato chips, she addressed the others.

"We could go back to the ship to shower."

"Don't be such a wimp, Marla." Brianna, munching on a Dorito, shot her a glance. "We still have a few hours for shopping."

"Yeah, but we're missing lunch," Vail griped between them.

"You would think about food!" Afraid she'd get too sunburned, Marla put down her plastic cup and wrestled her T-shirt over her head.

"I could meet you back at the ship," he said, with a hopeful grin. The engine kicked in, and their vessel turned into the wind. They picked up speed and soon bounced over the waves.

"No way, Daddy," Brianna cried over the ensuing noise. "You promised me a pair of Gucci sunglasses."

Marla glanced at him in surprise. Usually he tried to restrict his daughter's spending. "Where do they sell those?" she asked, digging into her bag for the port guide. "Hey, here's a place where we can grab a quick meal," she told Dalton, pointing to the map. "It's just off Harbour Drive. That's the main drag, so we can wander into the shops from there."

"Sounds good to me," Vail said, patting her knee.

Two hours later, Marla stood on the corner of Edward Street near the post office, burdened by several packages and stuffed from eating a grilled burger. She'd spent nearly an hour in the Tortuga rum shop, where she, Brianna, and Dalton had agreed to meet his parents. Spying an opportunity to get gifts for people at home, she'd bought a selection of rum cakes, tropical coffees, jerk sauce, rum fudge, and liquors.

"Dad and I will meet you down the street," Vail said, his face pinching in a look of impatience. He hadn't bought much, just a couple of books on plant life and island history, a souvenir mug, and a pack of hot sauces. "We'll be inside the artifact store. Dad wants to see the antique treasure coins."

"Marla," Kate said, drawing her attention before she could comment, "there's the duty-free center on the next corner. Didn't you want to look at their Sorelli jewelry and Swarovski collection?"

"I wanna go in Toucan Tango first," Brianna said, tugging on Marla's elbow. "It has some cool souvenir stuff, and I'd like to get a beach towel. I could use another pair of flip-flops, too."

"Okay, but the duty-free store might have the Guess watch that you want."

They hustled from store to store, adding purchases, which the men dutifully carried as they shuffled along until John called it quits.

"I'm going back to the ship," he announced, his shoulders sagging with fatigue. "It's getting late, and I thought I'd join the virtual reality golf tournament." His eyes scrunched behind his spectacles, as though he were already imagining himself swinging the club.

"Aren't there any art places here where you could solicit customers for your stained-glass work, dear?" Kate asked him in a tentative tone.

Marla exchanged a glance with Vail. Well, this was new. She watched John for his response.

The older man coughed. "Irene recommended only one gallery, and I didn't bring samples along."

"You could mail them from home."

"Nah, this place designs pieces in black coral, and

the other art galleries in town sell name-brand china and crystal. Believe me, it's not worth the effort." He waved a hand in dismissal.

"If you say so." Kate's meek tone was so unlike her that Marla gave her a sharp look.

John must have known his wife was trying to please him because he smiled and thrust an arm over her shoulder. "We can get a sundae at the ice cream bar if you come back with me," he offered.

"Sure thing. I'd like that. Brie, have you finished shopping yet?"

Brianna gave Marla an imploring glance. "I still haven't found a place that sells the new Britney Spears perfume."

Marla had in mind a gift she wanted to get for Vail, but she needed to lose him beforehand. "And I'm not done either. We missed the Treasure Chest and Hot Tropics."

Vail groaned. "Don't you have enough souvenirs?"

"Look, why don't you catch the tender with your parents? I promise we'll be on the next one."

"I'm not leaving you alone."

"She won't be alone, Daddy. I'll be with her. Can I use my credit card?" Under Marla's urging, he'd broken down and added his daughter to his credit card account.

He scrutinized Marla's face, while she plastered on a loopy grin. She was careful not to betray her thoughts with any tells, a term she'd learned from Vail. She didn't show a single twitch, lose eye contact, or move her hands.

"Understand that I'll come back for you if you're not on board by four o'clock."

"Then we don't have much time. Let's go, honey."

She'd satisfied Brianna's needs and was on her

way to buy the crystal stingray she'd seen in one of the gallery windows, thinking it to be the perfect remembrance for Vail of their first cruise together, when she nearly collided with Bob Wolfson, emerging from a bank building.

"Marla, what are you doing here?" He sprang back and grabbed his midsection, a panicked look on his face. Was it her imagination, or had he gained a few pounds in the waistline? Then again, it might just be his wide belt that added the illusion of weight. Or maybe she'd only seen him in loose-fitting shirts before that covered his waistband.

"We're shopping. Where is Sandy?"

He held his abdomen until he realized she was staring; then he dropped his arm. "We've been here before, so Sandy went back on board the ship after our tour. Now, if you don't mind, I'll be on my way before this heat gets to me." Sweat beaded his brow.

Marla stood in his way. "Is it true that you cruise here every year?"

He gave her a startled glance. "Who told you that?"

"Countess Delacroix, or was it Helen? Sorry, I can't remember." She winked at Brianna, hoping the girl would play along. "I'm just so fascinated that the countess owns vanilla plantations," she babbled. "The land in Mexico has been in her family for generations. I can understand why she wants to buy the adjacent piece of property to expand their operations."

"What's your point?"

Where are you getting the money to buy territory in a foreign country? Is the IRS aware of your purchases? Do your visits to Grand Cayman have anything to do with their offshore banking business?

As she sought a tactful way to pose her questions, she was grateful when Brianna cut the silence.

"Marla spotted the countess talking to your wife in the casino," Brianna said, her expression giving nothing away. Vail's face also froze into a mask when he questioned suspects, Marla realized. His daughter was becoming a chip off the old block. "Like, it's so cool that you shmooze with royalty."

"Madame Delacroix isn't royalty, kid. She's a nuisance who won't take no for an answer. She wants a piece of my nest egg, and I'm not giving her any part of it."

"Is there anything I can do to help convince her in your favor?" Marla offered, hoping Bob would elaborate his angle.

"Nope." Scratching his jaw, he regarded her with a puzzled frown. "At least you try to understand. Nobody else gives me that respect. No one."

"I could understand the game a lot better if you'd tell me the rules."

He grabbed Marla's arm. "What you don't know won't hurt you, Marla. You too, kid. I may be playing with a curveball, but other folks out there are playing for blood. Stay with your family, and you won't get in the way."

"What the hell does that mean?" Brianna said after Bob left them standing in front of the bank.

"Brie, I don't like your language. Who are you hanging out with that's using those words?"

The girl shrugged, her ponytail swinging. "It's no big deal. Everyone my age uses them."

"Is that so? Well, I don't want to hear bad words from your mouth, understand? It upsets me, and if you hope to earn respect in the work world someday, you'll keep your speech clean. As for what's going on with Bob Wolfson, I wish I knew."

She dropped the subject during their foray into the nearby Colombian Emeralds store, where Marla bought the crystal stingray. Cruise passengers bustled in the last-minute rush to buy souvenirs before the day's end. Back outside after making their purchase, Marla and Brianna watched a seagull squawk overhead, soaring beyond the traffic, tourists, and construction.

Marla's clothes stuck to her back, and she was grateful for the ocean breeze as they trudged toward the harbor. They hopped onto the last tender heading for the *Tropical Sun*. She had just enough energy left to escort Brianna to her grandparents' cabin before seeking Dalton and a hot shower.

He bounced up from their bed when she burst into the stateroom. "Thank God," he cried, reaching her in two quick strides. Grasping her shoulders, he gave her a kiss that was both fierce and passionate. She sniffed his fear for her and sidestepped momentarily to plop her bags onto the couch.

Wrapping her arms around him, she melted into his strong embrace and savored the feeling of having someone care for her.

"I saw Brie safely to your parents' cabin," she said after they broke apart. She slipped her T-shirt off her sweaty body and grimaced. "Yuck, I need to get washed. Then I'd like to grab a snack. Did you eat already?" Her stomach rumbled, and she felt weak from dehydration. No way would she make it until dinner two hours from now.

Vail gave her a sheepish grin. "I already ate chicken wings and fries out on deck."

"Figures. I just want something light, like fruit. Oh, we ran into Bob Wolfson," she said, wriggling out of her bikini after removing her shorts. "He was coming out of some bank building. The guy wasn't too happy to see us."

"Why not?" Vail regarded her from beneath his thick eyebrows. His gaze intensified as he perused her nudity.

"I don't know what he was doing inside, but he seemed to have gained a few pounds. His belt was buckled on its last hole."

Vail snickered. "Mine will be too, after a few more meals aboard ship."

"Has anyone found Brooklyn?"

"Not to my knowledge. I thought we'd ask around together."

"Okay." She shivered in an air-conditioned draft. "I'd better get in the shower before I freeze my *tuckus* off."

Holding her wet clothing by the thumb and forefinger, she headed for the bathroom. After shaking the sand out over the sink, she rinsed her swimwear, squeezed it dry, and piled it on the counter. Inside the shower was a pullout string that attached to the opposite wall. She'd hang the items on there after cleaning herself.

Washing her hair and shaving her legs required her to maneuver between the sink and the shower. At least the ship hadn't started moving yet. It was much easier to wash without the rolling motion.

When she emerged from the shower, a towel wrapped around her head, she saw an empty stateroom. Where had Dalton gone? Ah, she saw a note propped on the nightstand.

Brie called. She wants company to get a snack. We'll meet you at the Outrigger.

Blow-drying her hair, getting dressed, and applying makeup took another half hour. By the time Marla snatched her purse and entered the corridor, only forty-five minutes remained before dinner. The ship had gotten under way, as evidenced by the seesaw movement that made her stagger from side to side like a duck on drugs. Glancing outside, she noted the sky had clouded and rain threatened.

Heading aft, she stopped by the purser's desk to pick up an extra copy of the daily newsletter. After sticking the paper in her purse, she meandered around to get her bearings and ended up on deck four.

"Marla!" she heard Betsy's voice call from inside the Nautilus Lounge.

Pausing by a wooden ship's wheel in a glass display case, Marla searched for her table companion. Rope-lined round cocktail tables receded toward a wall where drapes were drawn over the windows. They didn't block the slivers of light that illuminated the brunette waving to her.

"Hi, Betsy," Marla said, sauntering over. Her observant eye took in the girl's slumped posture, glassy expression, and empty wine goblet. "How was your tour?"

"Great." Betsy gestured with a limp hand. "I went on the kayaking safari. Met a cute guy, too."

"So why do you seem so down?" Marla said, torn between wanting to join her family and cheer her friend up.

"Please sit. Do you have a minute?"

She planted a hand on her stomach. "I'm supposed to hook up with Dalton and his daughter on deck eleven, plus I'm so hungry I could pass out."

"My treat. I'll order some nachos. What do you want to drink?"

"A Coke would be great, thanks. What's up?" Sinking into a chair, she winced inwardly at the thought of Vail's annoyed reaction when she'd fail to show upstairs. She'd catch him at dinner. Helping a friend in need was more important right now.

"I was browsing in the shops after our excursion." Betsy cracked her knuckles, while Marla surreptitiously admired the way she'd scrunched her hair. "I saw a Rolex just like my father used to own."

She paused when the waitress arrived. Marla gave her order, and Betsy requested another glass of Australian Shiraz.

"Don't tell anyone else about this, please, including your fiancé. I'm just so ashamed." Twisting her napkin, Betsy glanced toward her feet.

"Go on," Marla said, with an encouraging smile.

"As I said, the Rolex was like my Dad's. I needed money, you see, and I didn't have any other means of getting it. My job sounds fancy, but it doesn't pay all my bills, and Gloria's medical expenses came to several thousand dollars. What else could I do?"

"Whoa, you're going too fast. Who's Gloria?"

"My baby sister." Betsy's gaze lifted, her expression pain filled. "She wanted an abortion, but our parents are religious. We're Catholic," she explained, "and Gloria didn't want them to know. She was right to believe they'd cut off her allowance if they found out."

"So your sister got pregnant and came to you for money?" Marla struggled to comprehend.

"You got it. I mean, Gloria is still in school. She's got another year left in college. I couldn't turn her away, but I didn't have the cash either."

"And so . . . ?"

Betsy hung her head. "Dad hardly ever wears his Rolex. He keeps it locked up until he has some fancy affair to attend, and I didn't see anything listed on Mom's calendar. So I pawned his watch intending to buy it back before he even noticed it was missing. But when I returned to the shop, the watch was gone. Someone else had bought it."

"Like you didn't need that kind of *tzures*."

"Sorry?"

"*Tzures*. It's a Yiddish word meaning woes or troubles."

"No kidding. When I got the note on my cabin door, I got kinda scared and hopeful at the same time."

"Huh?"

"You know, the message that read 'I know what you did and I have what you want.'"

"Oh, that note." Had everyone in the museum group gotten that same message? "I don't understand the connection."

"Don't you see? It can only mean one thing." Betsy leaned forward. "The person who bought Dad's watch from the pawn shop may be on board the ship, and he's offering to give it back to me."

CHAPTER 16

"How can anyone know what you did with your father's watch?" Marla asked Betsy after the waitress delivered their order. Too hungry to wait, she dipped a nacho into the bowl of melted cheese and crunched it in her mouth. "And wouldn't it be the wildest coincidence that this same person is on the cruise?"

Betsy shrugged. "I can't imagine what else that note could mean. It's creepy, Marla. Like, somebody's been watching us. Someone who knows our secrets and enticed us on board with free tickets. But why?"

Marla tapped her finger on the table. "There's one item that everyone in your group would like to possess: Alden Tusk's triptych."

"Holy mackerel, you're right." Nodding thoughtfully, Betsy cracked her knuckles. "Poor Alden. He had so much angst in his life. Now he's haunting us, so we're forced to examine the past." Casting her eyes downward, she fell silent.

Raising her Coke glass, Marla offered a toast. Liquor always loosened people's tongues. "To Alden, a talented artist who was taken from the world too soon."

"Hear, hear." Betsy downed her Shiraz.

"Look, if I can keep your secret, you can keep

mine." Marla leaned forward. "I've only told Dalton, but I modeled for Alden in his early days as an artist, before he made a name for himself. I posed in my ballet outfit for several of his paintings. I'd forgotten all about him until this cruise."

"How could you not mention it before?" Betsy said, reproof in her eyes.

"I didn't think it mattered."

"Hello, have you considered that your being here may not be a coincidence? And that you've been seated at our table for a reason, not a mistake?"

"Impossible. Dalton's parents bought our tickets." *And John has a link to Irene*, she reminded herself. Irene, who had had an illicit relationship with Eric Rand.

"How much contact did you have with Alden in your role as publicity manager?" Marla asked. "Did you ever go to his studio, see his work? I'd love to find one of the paintings he did of me. Do you remember any portraits of a woman in a leotard?"

Betsy's brow creased. "Not really, but then he'd already been established when we met."

"How did that happen?"

"I fell in love with his work at an outdoor art show, and, well . . . we clicked."

Marla sat upright. "You and Alden?"

"Yeah, we were an item." Betsy gave a tight smile. "He wasn't an easy person to care about. The guy had hang-ups. Alden wouldn't talk about it but you could see it in his paintings. The children he portrayed were always unhappy. When I asked him why, he closed me out. And I noticed he was very skittish about orchestral music. He'd only listen to rock stations."

"How did you get along with him if he was so difficult?"

"By being gentle and not making demands. I helped Alden in the studio, fed him, and let him make the first move in terms of any further intimacy. I know it did him good, Marla." She cocked her head, while Marla munched on cheese-dribbled chips. "After he painted the triptych, Alden acted like a new person. Somehow it redeemed him. But that wasn't enough. He suggested that I apply for a position at the museum. I'm responsible for getting him the gig at the fund-raiser."

"I've gathered that much." Marla sipped her Coke, enjoying the syrupy taste and the bubbles sizzling down her throat. "So it was important to Alden to show his work at your art museum. Didn't you wonder why? Was it just recognition he craved, or something more?"

Betsy gave her a shrewd glance. "In retrospect, I'd say he wanted to send a message to one of my colleagues via the middle triptych panel."

Marla shook her head. "I still don't understand."

"Look at it this way. Alden felt traumatized by something. He felt better after painting this picture. He meant to show it at the museum. The center piece disappeared on the same day he died. That panel must explain what we're missing."

"Likely it's meaningful to someone from the museum gang."

"Don't omit Eric Rand. He might hang out with the crew on board the ship, but he had belonged to our museum staff."

"Eric told me he suspects the center panel reveals Alden's killer."

"What?" Betsy stiffened. "Alden's fall was an accident."

"That's what I thought, but Eric believes otherwise. Kent Harwood saw the outer pictures. He said each piece contains a woman looking toward the center with an expression of horror."

Betsy's eyes widened. "Holy mackerel."

"His triptych must point the finger at someone in your group. You said Alden couldn't talk about his past, so he painted it instead. What could possibly have disturbed him so profoundly?"

Betsy clutched her glass with a white-knuckled grip. "From the way he depicted children in his work, I'd always suspected he'd been abused as a child. That would explain why he had such trouble getting close to me. We were finally moving forward when he . . ." Her voice trailing off, she blinked rapidly.

"If that's true, perhaps the painting shows his abuser, but it still doesn't explain who brought you all on board and why."

"Alden's completed set is here," Betsy replied in an earnest tone. "Someone might be seeking justice by exposing the missing panel. I can't imagine who would have gone to all this trouble and expense. You can eliminate some of us just by cost. I could never afford to buy cruise tickets for the entire gang."

So you say, but what if one of your group members has financial backing? Then money would not be an eliminating factor.

That would put two people in partnership, though. And it again drove home the thing that puzzled her the most—why? Who cared enough about Alden, besides Betsy, to seek justice for a possible murder that was never proven?

"Did Brooklyn know about your relationship with Alden? I gather you kept it under wraps. Brooklyn meant to tell Kent Harwood something about you, but now no one can find him."

Betsy arched her eyebrows. "Find whom, Kent? That man is strange. He doesn't act like any exterminators I've known."

You've got that right. "If you promise not to tell, I'll share another secret with you."

"Go ahead; my lips are sealed."

"Kent is an insurance investigator. He's looking into theft at the museum. But Brooklyn is the person who's missing."

"Brooklyn knew about me and Alden, but why would he tell Kent? What kind of theft?" Betsy's voice rose an octave.

"Substituting fakes for original paintings. Brooklyn may have hoped Alden had confided in you. If Alden had discovered who was stealing paintings at the museum, the guilty party may have bumped him off to ensure his silence."

"By shoving him over the railing? From the position of his body, the police said it appeared he had leaned his back against the railing before toppling over."

"So he could have been facing someone."

"I suppose. Most of us were outside setting up for the dinner party, but just about everyone slipped away at some point for various errands."

"Not Martha. She was in the gift shop and fancied she heard flute music right before Alden screamed."

Betsy waved a dismissive hand. "The sound system was off, but the gift shop sells chimes, so it could have been one of those making noise."

"Didn't you say Alden had an aversion to classical music?"

"Right. What does that have to do with anything?"

"It's odd that Martha heard someone playing an instrument just before Alden died."

"Marla, for God's sake, I've been looking all over for you," Dalton interrupted, charging in their direction like a Rottweiler sniffing fresh meat. "You could at least have let me know where you were." With a curt nod, he said to her companion, "Hi, Betsy."

"Sorry," Marla replied with a flush of guilt. "I ran into Betsy and lost track of time." Truly, she'd acquired John's habit of wandering off alone. Or maybe she wasn't used to the idea that Dalton expected her to account for her movements. At first, his protectiveness had been a challenge, but now that she knew it sprang from his concern, she found it endearing.

"We need to go in to dinner," he said. "It's almost six."

"Okay." Collecting her purse, she signaled for the waitress.

Betsy snatched the check before Marla could grab it. "This is my treat. You were good enough to listen to my problems."

"*Our* problems," Marla corrected. "Everyone at our table is involved, one way or another. I hope Brooklyn shows up. I'm worried about him."

"Me, too."

When Marla and Vail stopped to greet his parents and Brianna in the dining room before finding their own seats, Marla noticed the empty chair right away. Brooklyn's absence didn't seem to faze Cliff Peters. The buff young man was already stuffing down a buttered roll.

"Has anyone seen Brooklyn?" Marla asked.

Kate gave her a troubled frown. "I know you were anxious about him. Have you checked the infirmary? Maybe he got sick."

"I'll ask Kent. He was looking for Brooklyn earlier." She let her face soften. "Sorry I didn't make it upstairs. I got sidetracked by Betsy."

That caught Cliff's attention. He raised his head, eyes partially hidden by a shank of ebony hair. "What's she been telling you?"

"Nothing that relates to your private affairs," Marla said pointedly.

Tossing his napkin down, he half rose. "You're not even part of our group," Cliff snarled. "Why don't you mind your own business?"

"Because when someone goes missing, I wonder what happened to them. You don't seem to care."

"Maybe I do care, but there ain't nothing I can do about it. Maybe I figure one of us might be next unless we keep our nose to the ground."

"Then you'll be certain to stay out of harm's path." Marla's lips twisted in a cynical smile. "Martha missed the ship's sailing. Helen fell down the stairs. Someone tried to waylay me in St. Maarten, and now it's Brooklyn's turn. You *should* be worried, but if we work together, we might find out who's pulling the strings."

John, digging into his salad, glanced up. "Helen hasn't made it back to dinner. Is she discharged from sick bay?"

Marla had noted the other empty chair. "I don't know. I haven't heard anything from her since my visit there."

Kate wagged a finger. "Marla, can we discuss these topics later? Brie should have a peaceful meal," she said with a kindly smile.

"Absolutely. Come on, Dalton, let's go."

They wound through the cavernous room to their assigned seats. Kent Harwood, chewing on a celery stick, regarded them over his menu. "Brooklyn Jones is nowhere on board the ship," he blurted. "The crew filed a missing person report and notified the Coast Guard."

Marla glanced at him with dismay. "What do you think happened?"

Kent tilted his head. "People fall overboard. Remember the news reports about a Connecticut man who disappeared on his honeymoon to the Mediterranean, a Canadian lady whose husband reported her missing, and a fifteen-year-old girl lost at sea?"

"That last one really bothered me when I read about it," Vail commented, leaning back while the busboy filled his water glass. "I understand congressional subcommittees are conducting hearings on cruise ship crimes. The cruise lines don't like to publicize sexual assaults, robberies, and disappearances, but they happen."

"What do you expect?" Kent responded. "A cruise ship is like a contained city involving different nationalities. You can't control everyone. At least now there's an agreement to report serious incidents to the FBI. They can't sweep their dirt under the rug anymore."

"True, but I doubt Brooklyn's vanishing act has anything to do with crimes perpetrated by the crew," Marla put in.

"How do you know?" Irene spoke up, looking as though she'd ingested a lemon pit. "Somebody booked our tickets and assigned us these tables. That person also knows our cabin numbers. If I'm not mistaken, that's insider information."

"Someone from the crew must be involved, perhaps in collusion with one of us," Kent muttered, glancing at each of them in turn.

If you're correct, pal, and that person is sitting right here, you've just put yourself in their target sight. "Has anyone checked on Helen?" Marla inserted to distract the others. "I'm wondering if she's out of the infirmary yet." With a bright smile, she plucked an olive from the relish bowl.

Kent pushed a greasy lock of hair off his forehead. "Helen was gone from sick bay when I checked to see if Brooklyn had been admitted. I presume she's staying close to her cabin."

"Or she went to the buffet." Vail bristled impatiently. "Which brings to mind, what are you having to eat?"

They segued into small talk over the meal and discussions of the upcoming art auction.

"I hope you don't mind when I go to the auctions," Marla said under her breath to Vail. "We could be taking a salsa lesson or listening to music in one of the lounges."

"You don't have to go," he said, forking a bite of smoked trout into his mouth.

Marla had ordered gazpacho for an appetizer. "I'm still hoping one of Alden's pictures with my ballet poses might turn up, plus I'm learning a lot about different artists. It's quite interesting," she replied, dipping her spoon into the cold tomato-based soup. Her toughest decision of the day had been what to select for an entrée. Lobster thermidor, salmon fillet, roast duckling, veal loin, or prime rib. All of her favorites! If she didn't gain at least five pounds on this trip, it would be a miracle.

The miracle came when Eric Rand announced at the auction that he was giving them a sneak preview of an item for sale on the last night of the cruise. He'd start it off as a mystery piece tonight, with any interested parties holding up their bidding cards so their numbers could be recorded. Then when they returned on the final evening, the heavy bidding would begin.

Marla's pulse accelerated when the assistant set up three easels. Eric, wearing his earpiece microphone, along with a pale-lemon shirt, black pants, and trademark bow tie, paraded in front of the audience like a leopard showing his spots.

Betsy, in the adjacent chair, elbowed her. "Do you think it's Alden's set? Holy mackerel, I wish we'd sat closer."

They'd taken seats off to the side, where Marla could watch the proceedings while sipping her free champagne. She could barely feel the ship moving; they might just as well have been at a theater Stateside. Crossing her legs, she held her bidding card lightly between her fingers. Would Eric really tease them with a glimpse of Alden's triptych? Sitting upright, she listened for his introductory spiel.

"This is the opportunity of a lifetime, folks. A one-of-a-kind set by a talented young artist. This guy was slated to be one of the movers and shakers in the art world before his untimely demise. I don't need to tell you how much the value of his work has gone up since then. Get a piece of the action by owning this fabulous suite. I'll give you a quick look now, but return for our final blowout auction, and you'll have the chance to win this wonderful addition for your home gallery."

The audience took in a collective breath when Eric paused. "Retail price: fifty-five-thousand dollars. This is hand signed, folks. You can have the complete set for the bargain price of twenty-nine-thousand five-hundred dollars. Who wants it? Two, seven, twelve . . ."

Each time he read off a bidding card from the audience, he banged his gavel on the podium. A girl wearing a black shirt with the ship's logo rapidly scribbled the numbers onto a slate.

Marla's hand had shot up despite the price and so did everyone else's from the museum crowd. Thurston Stark looked about to burst a blood vessel, while Oliver Smernoff's eyes bugged out. Kent Harwood bent forward, focusing intently. Beside him, the Wolfsons jostled with each other, Bob waving his card in the air while Sandy tugged on his arm. From her disapproving expression, Marla guessed she didn't want him to bid. But who could resist the call? This had to be Alden's set.

As he called out the last number, Eric pumped his fist in the air. "All right, ladies and gents, this is what you've been waiting for. It's Alden Tusk's famed triptych. Whoo-hoo!"

He reached over and flipped the first canvas around, then did the same with the flanking painting. Squinting, Marla observed two ladies in long gowns, each gazing toward the center of a traditional drawing room. They almost appeared to be looking at each other, but their focus actually aimed at some point in between. Abhorrence showed on their faces.

Then Eric flashed the critical central portrait. A boy, maybe eight or nine, sat on a stool wielding a brush. He was painting strokes on a canvas. A man hovered nearby, touching the child in an inappropriate manner. She had no trouble discerning the boy's reaction. His large, dark eyes held a troubling mixture of self-loathing and empty resignation.

"Oh my."

Betsy's words were barely out of her mouth when Eric whipped the pictures away.

Marla cursed under her breath. She wanted to get a closer look. From this distance, she couldn't see details.

"That little boy . . . it's Alden," Betsy whispered, meeting her questioning gaze. "I'd seen pictures of him when he was younger. But the other . . . I can't tell."

"Me neither, but you could guess what the man is doing. It goes along with your suspicion that Alden might have been a victim of child abuse. The evidence is right there in his middle painting."

"Poor fellow couldn't talk about it, so he painted what happened to him." Betsy's face sagged. "Just the act of portraying this scene must have been incredibly painful."

Marla scratched her forearm. Was it possible to get mosquito bites on a ship? "You'd said he felt better after painting this picture, so it probably served as a catharsis for him. Why then did he offer the piece to the museum for its fund-raiser? To expose whoever had abused him as a child?"

"Hello . . . why else?" Betsy said.

"That means someone among us is a closet pedophile."

As the auction drew to a close, they stood to get in line for their free picture. Maybe Kent knew what the other museum members were hiding, she thought, glancing at his hairy neck from behind. He had been investigating the museum gang in search of a thief, but maybe instead he'd uncovered other buried secrets.

CHAPTER 17

Marla missed the chance to confer with Kent Harwood about his investigation into the backgrounds of the museum members. Momentarily distracted when she spotted Countess Delacroix in the line for a free work of art, she whipped her head forward in time to see Kent scurry off.

"Drat, I was hoping to catch him," she told Betsy.

"What for? Do you think he'll share anything he learns? He's investigating theft at the museum, not a possible murder."

"They may be related."

Betsy poked her elbow. "Give it a rest for now. Wanna take a walk? I need to build an appetite for the chocolate buffet."

"No, thanks. I think I'll have a word with the countess. Did you see her arrive at the auction? She must have been sitting behind us."

"Sorry." Betsy's eyes lit as though torched. "Holy mackerel, there's that Texan I met at the singles party. His company has made gobs of money in construction barricades."

Marla caught a glimpse of a tall, broad-shouldered guy with a trim beard before he ascended a nearby staircase. Nice butt.

"Here, get in line ahead of me. Then you can chase after him. He seems to be alone."

After Betsy departed, Marla accepted her free picture at the checkout desk and handed in her bid card until the next auction. She didn't bother to look inside the envelope to see what painting she'd received. Instead, she spun on her heel and marched back to where the noblewoman waited with her gentleman friend, ever dapper in a white dinner jacket.

"Madame Delacroix, what a surprise," Marla droned.

"Indeed." The countess's face crinkled into a smile, her make-up glowing like grease paint. Or maybe Marla made the connection in her mind because the countess's lips curved upward but her eyes chilled. No actress worth her salt would emit such contradictory signals. Marla admired the classic lines of her outfit, a royal blue ensemble with silver threads. She'd blend in perfectly with the décor in the Starlight Lounge.

"How are you this evening?" the countess asked politely.

"Curious. How did you make out with the Wolfsons on your shore excursion?" Marla shifted her position so the glint from the crystal chandelier wouldn't hit her in the eye. Stumbling when the ship rocked, she steadied herself.

Countess Delacroix pursed her lips. "How very gauche of you to inquire about my personal business, but then my sources tell me you possess plenty of—what is the word?—chutzpah." Holding onto her companion's arm, she shuffled forward in line.

Marla wouldn't have thought the countess needed any free pictures, but who knew? "So did your offer to buy his property still meet with resistance? Vanilla is such an important commodity. You'd think Bob would cash in on its worth. I mean, Mexico being the heart of the industry and all."

She needn't worry about being overheard. Bob and Sandy had already moved on. By mentioning the countess's passion, Marla hoped to encourage her to talk.

"That only makes his land more valuable," the countess replied. "However, I used a lever that will help him see the light." Lifting her chin, she raised her voice. "*Mon dieu*, why can they not go faster? I shall be late for black box bingo."

Sensing a dismissal, Marla tried another tack. "I'm looking forward to the chocolate buffet tonight. What's the chance they've used vanilla from your company to make the sweets?"

Countess Delacroix arched a penciled eyebrow. Actually, if she drew it outward any farther, it would end up looking like a question mark.

Bad Marla. Stop being so critical.

"I am unaware of who supplies the ship's kitchen ingredients. If I saw the vanilla beans, I could tell."

"Really. How so?"

"We brand our beans when they are green, and the markings remain after they dry. Vanilla rustling has always been a concern to growers because it is such a valuable crop."

Marla's brow folded in thought. She couldn't deny the topic intrigued her. "Haven't synthetics consumed much of the market?"

The countess and her escort reached the checkout desk, where they exchanged their bidding cards for a complimentary work of art. "*Vraiment.* Ninety-seven percent of the vanilla used today is synthetic.

Still, the current demand is for twenty-two-hundred tons of natural vanilla annually."

"That's a lot," Marla agreed.

The older woman paused just outside the exit. "You seem sincerely interested, *cherie*. So let me share with you some more particulars. Besides playing a role in the food industry and in perfume making, did you know vanilla has industrial applications? It is utilized to make medicines taste better and to cover the strong smell of tires, paint, and household products."

"Is that right? I had no idea. So how do the synthetics compare to the real stuff? Wouldn't they be just as good in these industries?"

Countess Delacroix grimaced, while her gentleman friend turned away with a bored expression. "Vanillin is the organic component mimicked in synthetics, but natural beans contain additional elements that cannot be duplicated. Thus, natural vanilla has a much richer smell and taste." She glanced at her watch. "Pardon," she said in her French accent, "I have to go."

"Wait. What's French vanilla?"

"It is a custard base for ice cream, not a type of vanilla."

Marla kept pace as the countess climbed the staircase. "Is it true that vanilla is good for an upset stomach?"

"*Oui.* That is why people drink sodas like cola when they feel ill. These contain vanilla, which calms the digestion."

"So growing vanilla is really a contribution to mankind. Is this what you told Bob to convince him to sell his property?"

The countess stopped, one foot on an upper step. "Oh, no, I said I knew where he is getting the money for his real estate purchases." She clapped a hand to her mouth. "*Mon dieu*, I should not have said that, should I?"

Marla's eyes widened. So if Bob didn't want the countess to blow the whistle on his activities, he'd have to accept her offer. "How did he react?" she asked.

Countess Delacroix frowned. "Bob understands that he could buy land elsewhere to build his resort, but he is afraid."

"Afraid of whom? And where *is* he getting the money from?" *Could he be blackmailing someone who's threatened him in turn?*

"What you do not know cannot hurt you," the gentleman said, startling her. He cleared his throat. "Come, *mon amour*, your bingo money is burning a hole in your pocket." While firmly tugging on his lady friend's hand, he said to Marla, "*Au revoir.*"

Wishing she'd had the opportunity to learn more, Marla met her group at the late show and related her findings after the curtain fell. Dalton didn't want to talk about Bob Wolfson, the countess, or Alden Tusk's hang-ups. He brushed off her report with a shrug.

"Let's go dancing," he suggested as they filed out of the theater. "I need the exercise." Regarding her, his eyes smouldered. Clearly the man had another type of exercise in mind.

"Bor-ring," Brianna chimed, her ponytail swishing. "Let's get in line for the midnight buffet. We can preview the food and take pictures. It's already eleven-thirty."

Marla gave the teen's shoulder an affectionate

squeeze. "How can you eat again? I'm still full from dinner."

Kate and John, along for the company but not necessarily the food, urged Marla to check out the array of sweets.

"How can you pass up all the chocolate?" Kate queried. "Even if you don't eat, it's a feast for the eyes."

"You'll miss night owl bingo," Marla commented, noting that John's face seemed more relaxed. He no longer had that constant frown on his forehead.

Kate snuggled close to her husband. "We should stick together tonight," she said, smiling meaningfully. "Besides, I'm kind of hoping they'll have éclairs. They're my favorite."

Not only were éclairs on the menu, but so were Black Forest cake, chocolate peach cake, chocolate cream puffs, chocolate lemon cake, chocolate tart topped with pistachios, candied pineapple slices dipped in dark chocolate, and more.

Salivating, Marla snapped photos to show people back home what they'd missed. *Diet be damned. I can't wait until they open the doors for real.*

Grabbing a plate thirty minutes later, she didn't know where to start. White chocolate–dipped strawberries, cocoa layer cake decorated with fresh kiwi, chocolate mousse, and an edible display of chocolate sushi tempted her. All were laid out artistically on amber satin drapes and intermingled with butter and ice carvings depicting the Eiffel Tower, dolphins, sea horses, and myriad fantasy creatures.

"Oh gosh, I'm so stuffed," she moaned, clutching her stomach when she and Vail finally entered their cabin past one o'clock. "I shouldn't have eaten that last truffle. I'm gonna barf."

"Me, too." Vail threw aside the towel on his bed that the cabin steward had shaped like an elephant. "We'd better walk up and down the steps a few extra times tomorrow."

Marla tucked her purse into a drawer. "The ship arrives in Roatan at nine. We'll have to get ready early. Hey, the message light on the phone is flashing."

"Hi, Marla," said Helen's voice when she hit the playback key. "I wanted to thank y'all for visiting me in the infirmary and let you know that I've been released. I'm taking it easy in my stateroom for a couple of days, so don't worry about me."

"What did she say?" Vail asked as he yanked his shirt over his head, revealing a muscled chest sprinkled with dark hairs.

Intent on listening, Marla gestured for him to wait. "And Marla," Helen's voice continued, "don't worry about anyone else either. We're all okay. Just watch your own back, huh? I'll see you at the farewell dinner on Monday night."

"Strange, I wonder what she meant," Marla said to Vail after she'd related the message. Why did Helen tell her not to worry about anyone else? Because she should be concerned about herself? What did Helen know that Marla didn't?

Her gaze trailed down Vail's torso to his waist, where he was unfastening his pants. *Oh heck, who cares?* She glided closer, her senses heightening. His spice cologne filled the air.

"You have that look," he said, grinning down at her. With deliberate slowness, he slid his zipper south.

"Damn right I do." Warmth pooled in her female zones. The ship's gentle rolling motion served as an aphrodisiac while she studied the planes and angles of his face, memorizing each craggy prominence.

Unable to resist touching him, she stroked his jaw, already bristling with stubble.

A growl rose from his throat. His eyes fired, and his head descended. Pulling her close, he claimed her mouth, his lips crushing hers.

Marla's mind swirled, succumbed to a carnal mist.

The world receded until it consisted of nothing but the two of them. When his hands caressed her, she yielded to his sublime skill. Her cares fell away. Her clothing soon followed, and she forgot that anything else existed.

Ding dong, ding dong.

"Good morning, ladies and gents," came the captain's voice over the loudspeaker on Saturday morning. "We hope you're ready for a pleasant day in Roatan. The skies are clear, the temperature is a delightful seventy-six. We've cleared Customs, and you're free to proceed to the gangway on deck one."

"That's our signal," Marla said to her gang. She and Vail had met up with Kate, John, and Brianna in the Outrigger Café for breakfast. They'd brought their beach bags so they could go directly to the exit.

She'd watched their arrival into port from the pool deck earlier. Her first glimpse had noted mountain ranges, villages terraced up hillsides, and occasional cars on a coastal road. Greenery graced the island, which had a rocky shore on the harbor side. Concrete-block houses in muted pastels looked substantial, not like shacks. The water, uniformly deep blue, was skinny-dipping calm.

In contrast, the scene on the pier blindsided her with chaos. A costumed dance troupe entertained the throng. Wearing red and white shirts, blouses, and

turbans, eight men and women gyrated to a drum-
beat and waved people to a box labeled TIPS promi-
nently displayed on a stool. Behind them rose the
behemoth ship, painted white, portholes on a lower
deck beneath the deluxe wide-windowed cabins.

Marla could barely hear the island music. People
chattered, engines idled, and guides yelled out tour
names. Passengers milled about, seeking the appro-
priate transport for their excursions. Beyond the parking area was a security gate manned by uniformed
guards. Natives hawked at them from the other side,
pressing forward like a mass of humanity, eager for
tourist dollars. She gripped her purse close to her
chest.

Locating the van for Tabyana Beach, Marla's group
hustled over. It promised to be a hot day, with the air
already warm and sticky. Grateful for the air-
conditioned interior, the five of them climbed inside. The vehicle sat four across on each side of a center aisle, with latecomers crammed beside the driver.
Marla spotted some of their museum mates out the
window.

"There's Sandy," she mentioned to Vail. "She and
Bob are going to Carambola Gardens, and then
they're planning to take a taxi to the butterfly farm.
Betsy passed on the snorkeling this trip to do the
canopy tour at Gumbalimba Nature Park."

"What about Kent Harwood? Is he tailing anyone?"

"Kent told me he's joining the dolphin encounter.
The Smernoffs and Starks are heading for Las Pal-
mas Beach Resort. Oliver wants to look in their shops
for quality native art."

If it hadn't been for Brianna, she thought regret-
fully, they might have chosen a different excursion.

The teen had wanted to lie out on the beach, not explore nature parks or swing from the rain forest canopy. And she wasn't old enough that Marla would condone her going off alone with friends.

Hoping she'd be able to relax for a day, she settled back in her seat. The driver revved the motor and they crawled forward, past the gate with barbed wire on top. Outside the barrier, wares beckoned at an open-air market. That appeared to be the extent of the local shops.

At least she wouldn't have to worry about extending her credit card debt.

"Forget the designer mall," Marla advised Brianna, sitting on her right. "Looks like they have mainly wood carvings, Honduran coffee, T-shirts, and pottery."

Squeezed between Vail and his daughter, she peered out the window at a cluster of ramshackle buildings, many of them on stilts, before they headed into the lush hills behind a Nissan pickup truck. Horses grazed on a pasture as they chugged up an incline. Wildflowers growing on a grassy patch by the roadside provided splashes of color.

"Isn't this beautiful?" Kate gushed, pointing to a vista of jungle vegetation when they reached the summit of one mountain. She wore a straw hat, shorts, and a wraparound tunic over her one-piece swimsuit.

Marla, not in the mood to talk, nodded. She focused on a town terraced up a hillside where stray dogs roamed. Laundry on a line flapped in the breeze, while slatted windows on the dwellings meant natural air-conditioning. They rounded a curve with a wooded slope on the right and a white car passing on the left. An electric wire crossed the road overhead. The other side of the range boasted wealthier homes and a glimpse of the jeweled sea far below.

From the tour guide, she learned there were 60,000 people living on the island, which at forty-nine square miles was the largest of the Bay Islands. Surrounded by the world's second-largest reef, Roatan had a rich underwater environment that drew scuba divers, snorkelers, and fishermen.

"Roatan has a one percent crime rate because the jail cell is ten by ten and holds up to thirty people," the attractive young woman told her captive audience from the front of the van. Marla's lip curled. Vail had straightened at the mention of a jail. "It has no toilets, no air-conditioning, and someone must share food with you or you'll starve."

Holding a microphone, the guide staved off questions. "Artifacts that we call *yabba-ding-dings* are still found throughout the island. The Paya Indians were the first residents. They were a smaller and less advanced group than the Mayans. When one of them died, the survivors broke and buried their clay pottery along with the body. Pieces of pottery, shells, and other ceremonial relics tell the island's history."

Marla returned her attention to the view out the window, not caring that Columbus arrived in 1502. The slave trade, pirates, and battles with British troops didn't excite her either. When she heard mention of treasure chests, however, she perked up. Having recently discovered Grandfather Andrew's hidden gemstones at Sugar Crest Plantation Resort, she could relate to the topic.

Roatan had been a pirate stronghold for Captain Henry Morgan, who plundered Spanish ships carrying gold from mainland Honduras. In the 1920s, British archaeologist Mitchell-Hedges explored the ruins of a pirate fortress at Old Port Royal. He discovered four wooden chests filled with gold doubloons.

Back in New York, he sold off his loot for $6 million and bought himself a castle in England.

But that wasn't his most noted discovery. Mitchell-Hedges also uncovered a crystal skull in Belize said to have supernatural properties, and ancient artifacts in limestone caves at the far end of Roatan. He believed these mysterious relics to be remnants from the lost civilization of Atlantis.

Other explorers, Howard Jennings and his friend Robin Moore, came in the 1960s. They unearthed chests containing silver bars and gold coins. Much more could remain hidden on the island, a lost legacy from the thousands of pirates who'd lived there.

Marla's ears closed, and she began dreaming of a different type of treasure: the liquid kind. She couldn't wait to claim a lounge chair on the beach, sip an icy rum drink, and sink her feet into the powdery white sand.

Tabyana Beach turned out to be everything she'd hoped for in a tropical paradise. As they entered the grounds, she let her eyes feast on the twisting vines, almond trees, coconut palms, pink bougainvillea, and sea grapes. Buildings sprinkled among the shrubs held changing rooms and showers, a barbecue pit, and the ever-present gift shop.

Emerging from the van into the bright sunshine, she heard a steel band playing "La Bamba." Waves swished in the distance, where sparkles of light glinted on the sea.

"Take my picture," Brianna said, thrusting her digital camera into Marla's hand. She posed in front of a painted wood sign that read: TABYANA, THE LOST CARIBBEAN. Tropical foliage and red flowers framed the shot.

Marla took a turn next, adjusting her malleable

turquoise hat—purchased from the ship's boutique—
to shadow her face. She wore flowered capris and a
solid top over her two-piece swimsuit. Turquoise appeared to be a popular island choice; many of the ce-
ment-block houses with tin roofs they'd passed were
the same color, reflecting the sea.

"I'm hungry," Vail said, pointing his nose in the
direction of the lunch hut. He'd stuck a baseball cap
on his head to shade his face.

Marla adjusted her sunglasses. "What do you want
to do first, honey?" she asked Brianna.

"Let's reserve our chairs," Brianna said, bouncing
with excitement. She'd slung a beach towel over her
shoulder. "Hey, look, there's a parrot." She pointed
to a green bird sitting on a branch. Tropical trees
and palms shaded a lush expanse of sand before the
beach proper. Marla and Brianna snapped more photos of each other beside the colorful bird, who eyed
them as though they were intruders.

"I'm going to the bathroom," Kate announced.
"Anyone else need to go?"

"We'll meet you, Grandma." Brianna strode away,
her legs long and slim. She'd be a stunner when she
grew up, Marla thought, hustling to keep pace.

"I'll check out the food," Vail called, veering toward the mouth-watering barbecue smell.

John trudged along in Marla's wake. She paused
to let him catch up. "Do you like the beach?" she
queried, hoping to draw him out.

"It's okay," he said in a noncommittal tone, "but I
can't stay too long in the sun." His lack of swim trunks
gave truth to his words. Knobby knees showed beneath a pair of Bermuda shorts, partially covered by
a loose-fitting Tommy Bahama silk shirt.

She pointed to a pair of lounge chairs under a thatched-roof cover. "Why don't you take that spot? It's shady but you won't be far from the rest of us."

He nodded, a floppy canvas hat bobbing on his head. Tromping over, he claimed both spaces, in case Kate decided to join him.

"Oh, Brie, look," Marla cried.

"What?" Brianna halted.

"You can get your hair braided. See?" Red lettering on a white board read: PROFESSIONAL HAIR BRAIDING, WELCOME TO ROATAN, INSTRUCTION GIVEN ON HOW TO CARE AND REMOVE YOUR BRAIDS. The board stood next to a poster displaying customers' photos. An empty white chair leaned against a palm trunk, fronds shading the ground. The lady must be on break, Marla figured.

"Why should I get that done here?" Brianna said with the incredulous tone of a teen who felt her elders lacked a few mental marbles. "I can go to your salon at home."

"I don't use colored beads, nor am I good at ethnic styles. You'd have to ask Nicole." Nicole, salon manager in her stead, was their specialist on ethnic hair design.

"Never mind. Let's claim our spot before it gets crowded."

Slatted beach chairs formed rows along a sandy stretch interspersed with graceful palms. Overhead, fluffy clouds drifted in an azure sky. Hills rose to the left, where the land curved around the lagoon. On their right was some kind of dock with small boats, and a sign attached under a coconut palm: PLEASE DO NOT TOUCH OR STAND ON THE CORAL.

"I'll go test the water," Marla said to Brianna,

who'd laid their towels and beach bags over several chairs. "Do you want to come?" She couldn't wait to dip into the ocean.

"I'll wait for Daddy. You go on ahead." With a blissful sigh, Brianna sank onto a chaise and stretched out, tilting her head to catch the sun.

Marla waded into the water, letting the foam swoosh around her ankles. She couldn't believe the clarity, nor the mixture of colors: turquoise, aqua, jade, and farther out, cobalt blue. Salt spray mixed with coconut scent in the air. Water lapped at her calves, rose to her knees as she ventured farther. Its warm silky feel seduced her into dunking herself. The sea embraced her, soothed her skin with its gentle current as she crouched neck deep.

Squinting behind her sunglasses, her hat left on shore, she saw a middle-aged man stand in the shallow depths and wipe water from his eyes. Heads bobbed all around from swimmers who'd submerged their bodies, and their laughter reached her ears.

A brief moment of fear slashed through her as she thought of a tsunami. The flat surface could change in an instant into a broiling mass of water. No warning, and they'd all be dead, drowned.

Her gaze lifted to the horizon, where dark sea met lighter sky. The tableaux looked so tranquil, but looks could deceive. So could people.

First Martha, and then Brooklyn. Gone. Like the tsunami victims.

Or maybe not.

Helen's message . . . Could she have been referring to them?

CHAPTER 18

"**W**here are we going? This isn't the way to the port," Dalton said to the driver transporting them to their ship. He'd ushered them into his vehicle as soon as they'd appeared at the pickup point on Tabyana Beach. Without waiting for other passengers, the native had screeched off in a cloud of dust before they'd even been seated.

On their left, the ocean stretched to the far horizon. "We take da scenic route, mon. I show you da place where dey found pirate treasure."

"Do you mean Coxen's Cave?" Brianna asked excitedly. "Cool, I'd love to see it."

Marla unfolded a map from her purse. "Isn't that inside Gumbalimba Park? We'd have to pay to get in, and according to this map, the park is near West Bay. We're going in the opposite direction."

"This be a private spot, lady, where Captain Morgan buried his chests full of gold doubloons. Mebbe you dig and get lucky."

"Surely you can't be taking us to Old Port Royal. I've read my island history. That's forty miles away on the east end."

They left the paved roadway and bumped along a

dirt road. Reddish clay soil spewed from the tires. Their van continued to follow the coastal route.

"I take shortcut inland to ship. You'll see."

True to his promise, the driver cut onto another paved road about twenty minutes up the coast. Engine revving, the van climbed into the hills. Greenery met Marla's eyes on either side, with electric poles at periodic intervals. Overhead wires presented an incongruous sign of civilization amid the forest.

Studying her map, she saw a couple of roads that cut across the island toward the town of Coxen's Hole, although these were situated at a considerable distance from their original route. Nonetheless, they had plenty of time before the ship sailed.

Feeling gritty from sand and sweat, she took out her water bottle and gulped a few sips. The sun had sapped her energy.

She let her eyes drift shut until a jolt aroused her.

"All right, ladies and gents, we get off here," said their driver, shutting off the ignition. "I show you overlook to pirate cave. Den we go to ship."

"I'll stay put," Kate said, her face flushed from the heat and fatigue. Wisps of hair had escaped from her hat and were sticking to her moist forehead.

"Sorry, I check oil while you have look-see. Everyone out." After hustling them off the van, he led them on a winding trail through a jungle thicket to a ridge. "Limestone cliffs are riddled with caves. Look closely, and you can see ruins of old fortress. You wanna visit, dat path take you downhill."

"I don't see anything," Brianna whined, flinging her backpack onto a rock. "Let's go back to the van."

"Listen up," Vail said to the guide's retreating back, "something doesn't seem kosher here. We didn't pay for any extra stops, and this seems out of the way.

Don't waste our time—" He stopped when the driver spun around, gun in hand. "Shit. I should have seen that coming."

"Don't blame yourself; you're on vacation." Marla winced as she considered her own lack of foresight. "I imagine someone paid him to delay us." *Like the fellow in St. Maarten who'd drugged her drink?*

"I not want to hurt anyone," the skinny man said, waving his weapon. His eyes glimmered with fear, not malice. Noting how his hand shook, Marla didn't move. "You wait until I leave. Then you walk to nearest village. Fisherman can take you to airport."

Vail's hands curled into fists, but he didn't budge. His eyes trained on their driver. "Airport? We have to get back to our ship. Who hired you? We'll pay you more."

"No deal, mon. I got reputation to maintain." With those words, he flipped about and hoofed it to the van. They heard the engine catch, roar into action, and diminish as the vehicle tore down the road.

"At least we didn't leave our bags on the van," Marla said with an air of dejection. Just what they needed. A hike through the jungle. Were Dalton's parents capable of strenuous activity? How far would they have to go before finding help?

"Thank goodness for small things," John replied in a cheery tone. "Let's go, people. We have a long walk ahead of us." Putting his foot forward, he started back along the trail.

"You sound like you're enjoying this," Kate accused, stumbling along in her sandals.

"Consider it an adventure, dear. God knows we have little excitement in our life these days."

"What's that supposed to mean? That I bore you?"

"You like to play it safe. I'm ready to take risks,

enjoy life to its fullest. Who knows how much time we have left."

"Not much, if we don't make it to civilization before dark," Kate griped. She tripped on a tree root and yelped. As she recovered her balance she dropped her beach towel. "Oh yuck, now it's full of this awful clay." Shaking it out, she wrinkled her nose.

"Anybody got bug spray?" Brianna asked, stomping along. She'd flung her backpack across her shoulders and stuck a sun visor on her head.

"I wish." Kate swiped her forehead. "God, it's hot."

"This is nothing compared to Florida in the summer. Right, kids?" John marched along, undaunted by their situation.

Kate, inhaling deeply, grumbled, "I'm already out of breath."

"Did anybody tell you that you have a flair for the dramatic?" John snapped. "Come on, we'll never make it if you go at a snail's pace."

"Mom and Dad, stop a minute. We have to figure out which way to go," Vail said. "Marla, let me see your map."

"We're on the north side of the island." Pointing, she showed him their approximate location. "We have to get across the hills to the other side. If we can reach French Harbour, we could hire a fishing boat, like the driver said."

She didn't share her thoughts. They'd never make it to the ship on time.

Vail's glowering expression told her he had reached the same assessment. "We'd better get going then. Mom, are you okay?" He regarded Kate with consternation.

His mother squared her shoulders. "I'll be fine.

Take the lead, Dalton. We'll follow. Come, Brie, walk beside me."

Following the road didn't turn out to be such a good idea. It curved east, heading up the island instead of crossing the ranges. Faced with this obstacle, they halted.

"We have three choices," Marla said, consulting her map. "I think we're right over here. If we keep on this road, it will take us to a paved section running to the south side, but much farther to the east. We can backtrack to the coastal strip until we get to a major intersection. Or we can cut through the woods and try to reach this little road heading to French Harbour. There aren't any direct routes."

"I hear water," Vail said, cocking his head. "If it's running downstream, we might be able to follow it toward the ocean. That may be quicker."

Breaking off from their path, he crashed through the underbrush for the source of the noise. The others, not wishing to be left behind, staggered after him. He paused by a brook where water trickled down a series of rocks into a small pool.

"It doesn't go anywhere," he said disappointedly. Stooping, he splashed his face. "Feels good, though."

Marla stepped to the bank, kicked off her sandals, and stuck her feet into the cool water. Ah, what relief. Wiggling her toes to clean off any remaining sand from the beach, she bent over to rinse her hands.

After they'd refreshed themselves, they set off through a clearing in a direction Vail deemed south. He used his watch as a compass, reassuring the others that they couldn't get too lost on an island where they'd eventually end up at the ocean.

Dubious about his advice, Marla followed him

through the jungle. Vail took the lead, swishing the air in front of him with his towel to demolish spiderwebs.

"Stamp your feet and make noise," Brianna said from Marla's rear. They walked single file, with John at the end. "It scares away snakes."

"Snakes!" Marla squeaked. Brushing away a branch that swiped her face, she grimaced. Spiders were bad enough, but snakes? Bird cries echoed through the jungle along with a strange chittering. Leaves rustled overhead. Glancing up, she squinted behind her sunglasses. Was that a monkey she saw swinging on a vine?

Shuddering despite the heat, she watched her footing. Rocks, gnarled roots, and fallen coconuts made for slower going than she would have liked. Sunlight filtered through the canopy, glistening on cobwebs and fluttering butterflies. Ephiphytes vied for space with strangler figs and wild banana plants.

"Here's a bunch that looks ready for picking," Brianna cried, rushing ahead. She threw a banana to each of them and they consumed their snack, finishing the fruit off with a sip from their water bottles.

Marla tore off a couple of extra bananas, brushed away any clinging dirt, and stuffed them into her sack. "I'd suggest you all take a few. We may need them later."

"I have to go to the bathroom," Kate stated.

"Not again." John glared at her. "You just went before we caught the van."

"So? I have a small bladder."

"You have a funnel. It goes from your mouth straight to your pee-pee."

"Pick a tree, Mom," Vail said with resignation. "We won't look."

"Fine. I have tissues if anyone else needs them. Brie?"

The teenager shook her head, swinging her ponytail. "Something might bite me on the tush. I'll wait."

Minutes later, Kate came streaking toward them. "There's a giant creature in there! It looks like a dinosaur."

"Nonsense," Vail scoffed. "Let me see." He loped toward the site. "It's only an iguana," he called, his tall form barely visible behind the foliage.

A screeching noise made them all jump.

"What's that?" John rasped.

"Probably a howler monkey," Vail replied, returning to their clearing. "Come on, we're wasting time." Forging a path past a large fern, he signaled for the rest of them to follow.

Under other circumstances, Marla might have enjoyed the beauty of their surroundings, but not when they had a schedule to keep. If they got lost, they'd roam for hours in the forest. She wouldn't care to be there after sunset. Swatting at an insect, she kept pace, skirting a cashew tree, a cluster of crotons, and a red-tipped ginger plant.

A parrot squawked from a nearby tree beyond a stand of bamboo. Distracted, Marla almost tripped into what looked like an anthill, out of which spilled a posse of slimy beetles. Grimacing, she scratched her arm, feeling as though bugs crawled along her skin.

"Hey, here's shelter," Vail yelled, speeding forward.

Marla hastened to catch up, viewing the ramshackle shed with doubt. Perhaps it had been erected for travelers, but from the looks of the jagged hole in its roof, the structure hadn't survived the latest tempest. A scraping noise came from the shed's rear, accompanied by a man's grunt and the sound of gravel hitting stone.

When they rounded the corner, two men glanced up. They wore sweat-stained clothing, floppy canvas hats, and boots. One of them held a shovel and the other stretched a measuring device between a forked tree and a large boulder. From the mounds of earth piled beside a trench, it appeared they'd been digging.

Their faces scrunched in a manner that meant they were none too happy to have visitors. Marla got a whiff of their unwashed bodies and hung back.

"Oh, are we glad to see you," Kate cried, rushing ahead before Marla could warn her. "Do you have a phone? Or a car?"

"Who are you?" the taller white man groused, swirling saliva in his mouth before spitting. His leathery skin bore the ravages of too much sun. Gripping the shovel, he spread his legs in a challenging stance.

Marla could feel Vail tense. His fingers wagged at his waistline, as though reaching for a weapon that wasn't there.

"We've been stranded," Kate said, smiling and fluttering her hands in the air. She looked as innocent to danger as a baby bird cast from its nest. "Can you help us? Our ship is due to sail, and we have to reach the port."

An avaricious gleam entered the man's eyes. "Oh yeah? If you're on one of them fancy big ships, maybe you're worth somethin'. You people from the States?"

"Are you nuts?" countered his pasty-faced companion. "These folks will tell where they seen us, Eddie."

"Keep your trap shut."

"But we gotta—"

"You're right." Eddie lifted his shovel and addressed the newcomers. "Get into the shed," he told them.

Marla wasn't about to be locked up in a dark hidey-hole again. She exchanged glances with Vail, who then gestured to Kate to move back. When the older woman returned a bewildered stare, Marla gritted her teeth. Really, how could Kate be so naive? *Get out of the way*, she silently urged.

At her side, Brianna stooped to fix her sandal but grabbed a handful of dirt instead and threw it at their assailants.

Vail sprung into a dive and tackled Eddie at the legs. Toppling backward, the tall man took Vail with him and tried to clobber him with the blunt end of the shovel. The two men rolled on the ground struggling while Shorty flew at Kate.

John grabbed his wife's hand and yanked her out of the way. Shorty stumbled into Marla's path, reassessed his prey, and drew a knife. He swung at her stomach.

Marla blocked the thrust with her beach bag, then smashed her knee into his groin before he could react with the blade.

Howling, he doubled over. Using a move Vail had taught her, she elbowed him on the jaw, resulting in the satisfactory sound of crunching bone. He went down like laundry in a chute.

Breathing hard, she bent to steady herself.

"We've got to help Daddy!" Brianna cried, clutching her arm.

The men tossed on the packed earth, a flurry of battling arms and legs. Eddie had dropped his shovel, but he rained a series of punches at Vail, his leaner frame proving more agile.

Kate and John stood off to the side watching in horror.

Marla felt a wave of helplessness, afraid she'd hurt her fiancé instead of Eddie if she attempted to interfere.

"Look out!" she hollered when Eddie, on the top, scrabbled for a rock and aimed it at Vail's head.

Vail turned his neck but still received a glancing blow. Stunned, he let his arms fall to his side.

Eddie circled his hands around Vail's throat.

Marla stood petrified. How could she help him?

She needn't have worried. Vail reached up and thrust his thumbs at the man's eyes. Cursing, Eddie jerked back.

Vail swung his legs up, clamped them around Eddie's torso, and used the momentum to toss the man over his head.

Leaping to his feet, he stomped his heel onto Eddie's face.

"Let's go" he yelled after Eddie went limp.

Blood dripping from the wound on his temple, he weaved toward a slope that headed downhill. They half slid, half stumbled down the steep, slick trail. A muddy depression at its base showed large paw prints that made Marla gulp nervously, especially when the stench of something dead fouled the air.

"Now what?" she said when they halted beside a tree scarred with claw marks. It must have rained recently in this section, because the leaves were dripping wet. She'd forgotten they were in a rain forest, where downpours were frequent events.

"You're bleeding, Dalton," Kate said, a look of concern on her face. She seemed none the worse for their adventure, though. Ignoring her own discomfort, she dabbed at her son's face with her towel.

"That doesn't matter now." He brushed her off.

"I'll get cleaned up later. We have to find a way out of here."

"Y-you didn't kill that man, did you?" Kate asked in a shaky voice.

"I doubt it. No good son of a bitch."

"I wish they'd had a car," Brianna added, taking a long swallow from her water bottle.

"How do you think they got there?" John's eyeglasses had fogged, and he employed his shirt to clear them.

"I've been wondering the same thing." Wiping sweat from her brow, Marla regarded him. "They may have parked a vehicle out of sight of the shed. We can't go back to look for it, though. It's not worth the risk of them coming after us." She paused. "Do you hear gushing water? We must be near a waterfall."

Surrounded by dense foliage, she listened to the muted whooshing and the wind creaking through a stand of bamboo. A flash of bright green caught her eye, and she glimpsed a macaw high in the canopy, where sunlight filtered through the branches in swathes of mist.

"Is this the sort of thing you do all the time?" John asked his son. They trudged along in a line.

"Only since I met Marla."

"Marla is real good at solving crimes, Grandpa," Brianna proclaimed. "She's helped Daddy with lots of cases."

"So have you, muffin. You've both earned your deputy badges." Vail beamed at them proudly.

"Hot dog! I need to get on the ball with Irene. We're missing all the excitement," John said to Kate.

"Irene? What does she have to do with anything?" Kate shot back. Her sharp tone could have felled a tree squirrel.

"She's a real estate agent. I've been talking to her about finding a condo in Fort Lauderdale."

"Oh yes, Marla mentioned that she's seen you together. I thought you were acquainted through the art world."

"That, too. If you ever listen to me, you would know these things. We've talked about getting a place in Florida."

Here we go again. Marla trotted ahead, finding the source of water to be a stream and following it. The others marched behind. Hunger gnawed at her stomach. Their exertion had put her fuel gauge on empty.

"Look, there's the ocean!" Pushing aside the spiny leaves of a cycad, she peered below at the sparkling sea. Off to the right was a fishing village.

Eager to reach civilization, she led the way down another slope, skidding down the grassy mound in her haste.

Marla worried about Kate, whose breathing had become more labored. John seemed to be in better shape, although his florid complexion indicated the heat and stress were getting to him. Perhaps they should be checked out at the infirmary when they made it back to the ship.

If they made it back to the ship. Glancing at her watch, she pressed her lips together. Less than thirty minutes to go.

Coated with sand, sweat, and flecks of mud, they approached a whiskered fellow shooing away chickens in his yard at the base of the hill.

"Excuse me," Vail said with an earnest expression. "We need a quick ride to the port. Is there anyone with a boat we can hire?"

The man grinned, showing gaps in his teeth. "The

fishing boats, they be out already, mon. But I can take you in my truck. What you be willing to pay?"

After a brief negotiation, the man chugged around a corner and returned in a rattling pickup truck with peeling paint.

His customers climbed in, and they started off along the bumpy clay road. It was slow going at first, with pools of water from recent rain in low-lying sections. They skirted potholes but continued to bounce ahead while Marla gripped the sides of the truck to maintain her balance. Good thing they hadn't eaten in a while. They were more likely to get motion sickness here than on the ship at sea.

They passed dwellings painted turquoise, coral, or sand and built on stilts. Stairs led to main floors, open to ocean breezes, with balconies in front. Sloping tin roofs capped the structures and provided protection from heavy rainfall.

A man pedaled by on a bicycle, while to their left, boys played on a makeshift raft offshore in shallow water. Mountain ranges rose in the distance. Leaving town, they sped past a church, an above-ground cemetery, and a coastal stretch of mangroves before the harbor came into sight.

Their driver screeched to a halt in front of the marketplace and across from the port security gate. No more time. The ship was due to raise the gangplank any minute.

Kate and John showed their ID to the guard and charged through the gate. While Vail paid off their savior, Marla followed Brianna into a covered stall.

"We can't go without buying something," Brianna said, eyeing a selection of pottery, mugs, magnets, and native art.

"Come on, it's too late." Marla's fingers curled with urgency.

"Just one more minute. *Please*."

Aware of the seconds ticking by, Marla snatched a painted wood carving of palm trees with *Honduras* scrawled beneath and several bags of roasted coffee beans. Who could resist?

"Okay, I'm ready." Brianna held a mahogany box and a beaded necklace.

Looking frantic as he caught up with them, Vail cried, "For God's sake, the ship is about to depart, and you two are shopping?"

"Look at these salad bowls," Marla told him. "Aren't they beautiful?"

He growled. "Let's go."

"How about a walking stick for our next jungle adventure?"

"Marla . . ."

Time's up.

She paid for their purchases and ran.

CHAPTER 19

The next morning, Marla and Vail decided to leave the ship after all the tour groups for Cozumel had departed. Since it was Sunday, she didn't want to get into town too early. After eating at the buffet, where she'd consumed a waffle with cherry sauce and whipped cream, they strolled the promenade deck to wear off the calories.

"I'm glad we're not going on any tours today," she told her fiancé, striding beside her. "You know how Bob Wolfson owns property in Mexico? And how he and Sandy cruise here every year? I wonder what he does when they're in town. Sandy seemed to indicate that she went shopping on her own."

Vail, stiff from his battle the day before, rolled his shoulders. "Let it rest, Marla. We could use a day off from interfering in everyone else's business."

"Wouldn't you like to know who was responsible for our problems yesterday? Bob acted funny when I ran into him on Grand Cayman. He must be covering up something that he doesn't want us to learn. I'd like to follow him if we catch up to him today."

"Good for you. Maybe I should have gone along with Mom and Dad to Tulum. I hope Brie likes the Mayan ruins. It's a long bus ride."

"I thought they'd be exhausted after trekking through the jungle on Roatan."

"They paid a hundred and nine dollars apiece for their excursion. Dad wouldn't cancel."

Marla's eyebrows lifted. "That price includes lunch."

"Yeah, in a box."

She paused by the railing. "I gave your Dad my Bonine tablets in case they need it for the ferry ride. A smaller boat is bound to be rockier than this big ship."

As their vessel approached land, she noticed a beacon flashing from a lighthouse. Soon a view of houses popped up along the coast. Although the sun had just risen, cars snaked along a road toward town. Wind whipped her hair, while she noted a Carnival cruise ship sailing a parallel course.

"I told security to report our driver to the Honduran authorities," Vail said, "but they took that as a joke. We didn't get any license plate number, and his description fits dozens of men. Besides, we made it back to the ship intact."

"Barely in time. We're lucky they waited to raise the gangplank. We could have missed the ship same as Martha did in San Juan. It almost happened to me in St. Maarten."

"These were not random acts. Someone we know was behind them. Someone who wants us out of the way."

Drawing in a deep breath, Marla watched as buildings came into sharper view along the shoreline. "Has the FBI been notified about Brooklyn's disappearance?"

Vail's mouth firmed. "Who knows? Until the laws change, jurisdiction over cruise ship crimes remains a problem. It's common for ship's personnel to call local authorities to deal with serious events. As for murders, forget it. You can't get forensics people in here before the steward cleans the cabin."

"I guess the sad lesson is to be as cautious as you are at home." Her gaze focused. "Look, I see a McDonald's arch."

The *Tropical Sun* aimed for a concrete pier where signs faced the waterfront: BIENVENUTO PUNTA LANGOSTA, SEÑOR FROG'S, and DIAMONDS INTERNATIONAL.

She patted her hair in place. As the ship docked, the breeze lessened. Crystal-blue water stretched out to sea, deepening from royal blue to navy. Warmed by the sun, she thought about changing into shorts but decided to keep on her capris and turquoise top.

They descended to their cabin to freshen up, pack their belongings, and check the *Tropical Tattler* for a departure time.

"Look what this says," Marla said, reading from the newsletter. "Tropical Cruise Lines has received reports of passengers becoming ill after drinking alcoholic beverages ashore. Please be aware that the contents of drinks in port may be unknown and may be much stronger or contain different ingredients than expected. Tropical Cruise Lines disclaims any responsibility for resulting illnesses or intoxication." She glanced at Vail. "Great, now they tell us this. I should have known before I sampled that liquor in St. Maarten."

"Their warning should apply to tap water also, including ice cubes. You don't want to get Montezuma's revenge."

"Is that worse than norovirus?" Marla waved her bottle of hand sanitizer. "Don't leave home without it."

Ding dong, ding dong. "Good morning, ladies and

gentlemen. We have a glorious day ahead of us in Cozumel. Those of you departing on tours may descend to the gangplank. May I remind you that the Mexican Agriculture Department forbids you to bring ashore any fresh fruit, vegetables, or dairy products."

"Hey, I could have used this yesterday," Marla said, still reading her newsletter. "Twenty minutes of aromatherapy foot massage for forty-five dollars. Maybe I should sign up for one later this afternoon."

"Unnecessary. My services come a lot cheaper." Giving her a sexy grin, he waggled his eyebrows.

"Right, like we have time." She stuffed the newsletter into her bag. They had a busy schedule that evening, too. Chili burgers and Corona beer on deck for a buccaneer fest, followed by a comedy and juggling act in the Meridian Showroom, then their choice of a newlywed game show or 80s Ladies Night before a champagne waterfall in the atrium lobby at midnight.

But she couldn't think of that now. Setting her shopping goals took precedence.

"Are you ready?" Vail asked, donning his sunglasses.

She grinned. "Ready and armed with my credit cards," she replied, shouldering her handbag. "Let's go."

Trudging along the pier in the blazing morning sun, they passed the Carnival ship and someone's private yacht before reaching an escalator. Marla searched for quicker access to the street but she didn't see any. The escalator led upstairs to an outdoor shopping center, Punta Langosta Mall.

"Figures we'd have to stroll by a collection of shops in order to get anywhere," Vail commented wryly.

"Is that Heidi wearing a coral tank top by Los Cinco Soles?" Marla said, raising on her tiptoes. If so, the blonde had just disappeared inside the souvenir store. Scanning the throng for other familiar faces, she felt a wave of disappointment. Oh well, her table-mates were bound to have taken advantage of the other activities on the island, like snorkeling, which is what Betsy had decided on.

Stores beckoned, tempting her with duty-free liquors, Mexican blankets, onyx chess sets, silver jewelry, and Kahlúa-filled chocolates, but she didn't linger. This might be good for last-minute shopping, but they'd have a bigger selection in town.

Winding their way around, they found a staircase to the lower level. It took them to Avenue Rafael E. Melgar.

"Island tour, lady?" said a fellow on the street tagging after them. Other hustlers tried to run them down, offering driving services.

Vail kept a brisk pace as they passed the Hotel Vista Del Mar on their right. To their left stretched the aqua water, rippling in a light breeze. Radio music blasted from a jewelry store where the door was propped open. A truck rumbled past, competing with the rat-a-tat from a jackhammer and the rapid-fire Spanish spit out from all directions.

Strolling along the smooth pavement, they passed the Habana Cigar Company, advertising HABANOS, UNIQUE SINCE 1492. No need to stop there, but D'Arce Jewelers Internazionale showcased museum-quality silver figurines. Fascinated, Marla glanced at the horse and lion but hastened on when the greeter caught her eye.

Fotomega came next, along with camera supplies

and a sign reading CALL HOME, INTERNET PHONE SER-
VICE. Pizza Hut, Sunglass Island, and Caribbean Diamonds didn't interest her either.

Crossing an intersection, she skirted a mound of
concrete debris piled in the road. Down the side street,
a man hauled water bottles from a truck labeled AQUA
PURIFICADA CRISTAL, while a sweeper worked his way
along the curb with a broom and dustpan.

"Do you see Bob Wolfson anywhere?" Marla asked
Vail as they paused by a plaza sporting a fountain
with dancing waters and with palm trees ringed by
red clay borders. A lady stood outside the open door
of El Guerrillero, a souvenir shop where mannequin
heads graced the top of a poster advertising hair braids.

"Nope. He may have slept in this morning or gone
on a tour. Maybe he'll show up after lunch."

She wrinkled her nose, sniffing garbage. "I'd love
to find out what he does here."

"Come inside! Maybe you see something you like!"
yelled a store hawker as they resumed their pace. A
hot breeze blew off the ocean, ruffling the hairs on
their arms.

At the corner with an Aqua Safari store on one
side and Goodmark Jeweler on the other, a seven-
piece mariachi band played while onlookers gawked.
The musicians wore white long-sleeved shirts and
black pants with rows of shiny metal studs down the
edges. They played beside a utility pole from which
hung a blue and yellow sign: GOTTA GO TO GOODMARK
JEWELERS. A middle-aged guy stood by filming with
his camcorder. His wife watched, her shopping bag
bulging more than her belly.

"Isn't this where the alexandrite stones are?" Vail
asked.

Marla studied her port map. "No, that's Goodmark

Gallery at the opposite end. What do I need to see them for?"

He shrugged. "I just thought you might like to learn what they're worth."

"Why? I know the gems that I found at Sugar Crest Resort were valuable, but my brother needed them more than me. I can do without seeing them change from red to green in different kinds of light. These are probably from Brazil anyway, not the rare Russian stones."

"How about this place? You haven't bought anything yet." He pointed to D. Montero's Silver Shop, its front door open to the air, like all the other places.

"Let's keep going. I want to find a store that sells vanilla. According to what I looked up on the Internet, if it's really pure extract, the label should say it contains thirty-five percent alcohol. Otherwise it could be the synthetic variety with potentially harmful ingredients."

After yielding to temptation and visiting Mi Casa for Mexican crafts, Viva Mexico for tequila souvenirs, and Pama Duty Free for brand-name cosmetics and perfume, Marla headed for the Silver Emporium and Diamonds International. She spent more than her budget on a tanzanite necklace, white gold earrings, and silver bracelets for her salon staff. Then she dodged into a huge emporium selling everything from hot sauces, coffee, and vanilla to papier-mâché, pottery, and pewter.

Bewildered by so many choices, she sauntered toward the food section to examine a brown bottle labeled Natural Vanilla. Contents listed were vanilla beans extracted in water, alcohol, and corn syrup. It also said, THIS PRODUCT DOES NOT CONTAIN COUMARIN.

"So is it real or not?" Vail asked, examining a selection of tequila. He seemed fascinated by the worms inside some of the bottles. Holding one bottle upside down, he shook it.

"If I had to guess, I'd say no, but I could be wrong. I wish the countess was here. I'd ask her."

Her wish came true, although it wasn't until later, after they'd shopped their way down the avenue. Her arm muscles ached from hauling so many bundles. They took a break for lunch at Palmeras restaurant in a plaza opposite the tender pier and then resumed their trek. The sun warmed her back, making beads of sweat glisten on her forehead. She filled her lungs with the salty sea air.

Opposite the main street, a seawall separated the avenue from the shoreline. Colorfully painted mannequin heads like porcelain carnival figures adorned posts at regular intervals. They reminded her of Mardi Gras masks. In the background, a masted ship sailed by, flags flapping against a sky dotted with cumuli.

"Did I tell you how lucky I am to be with you?" Marla said, turning to Vail. He'd learned to tolerate shopping because it made her happy. In return, she had acquired an enjoyment of parks where he liked to identify the different trees. Next time they took a cruise, she hoped they'd have the opportunity to do more nature excursions. Brianna liked parks too, but she preferred the beach more.

His face crinkled into a smile. "I'm the lucky one to have you. Look at all these fellas giving you the eye as we walk past. They're envious of me."

"Truthfully, I'm trying to ignore them." Their blatant stares made her uncomfortable. Maybe it was because she imagined one of them trying to lure her and Vail down a side street.

Reaching an intersection, she stepped off the curb and glanced to her right. Parked cars lined one shaded side of the crossroad while motor scooters claimed space at the opposite curb. Electric wires draped the overhead space. An ice truck approached, bumping along the uneven pavement.

"Hey, is that the countess coming out of that building over there?" Marla squinted, wondering if she needed prescription sunglasses. She could just make out the woman's swirl of blond hair, but the way the lady moved gracefully in her heels and the skirt ensemble she wore with a wide-brimmed hat told Marla she'd hit the mark. Even a shopkeeper wouldn't wear an outfit so formal.

"You're right," Vail said as the countess strode in their direction. She appeared to be alone, which struck Marla as odd. Where had her gentleman companion gone? Instead of a small handbag, she carried a large portfolio case snugly under her arm.

"Marla," the countess said with little enthusiasm when they encountered each other. "I see you and your fiancé have been generously contributing your money to the people of Cozumel."

"Yeah, it's a good thing this is our last port. I'll have to extend my working hours to pay off the bills."

The elder woman flicked her gaze toward Vail. "*Vraiment?* Then you need to marry, so your amour can buy baubles to circle your neck and clothes to adorn your body."

"Where is your friend? Did he stay on the ship?"

"*Non*, Claude went on the submarine expedition. I had business in town and did not require him to accompany me."

Require? Undoubtedly, the countess pulled the strings in their relationship. Interesting how she expected Vail to be the dominant partner in marriage. *So what does that make me, an accessory? Maybe you're an accessory as well, only to crime.*

The countess glanced over her shoulder and narrowed her eyes almost imperceptibly. "I have calls to make. We will not see each other again. *Au revoir, mes amies.*"

Vail raised his eyebrow in a questioning slant. "Aren't you continuing the cruise?"

Countess Delacroix gave a theatrical shrug. "My mission is accomplished, and I must follow through on the mainland. But you need to beware, *cherie*," she told Marla. "Certain parties aboard are poised to erupt. You do not want to be caught in their crossfire."

Sensing the woman was about to leave, Marla clutched her bony arm. "Wait. Do you know who's been plotting against us? We almost didn't make it back from Roatan. Someone paid our driver to take us on a detour so we'd miss the sailing."

The countess peered down her nose. "I know who it is *not*, but he, too, still searches for answers. You may consider him a friend. And that is all I can say." Turning away, she left.

"Whom do you suppose she means?" Marla asked Vail.

"Kent Harwood? We know he's investigating the museum gang."

"How would the countess possibly be acquainted with him? From what I've gathered, she's never been to the museum, plus he only works there part-time."

Vail pointed down the street. "What about that guy?"

Twisting, she let her jaw drop in surprise. Bob Wolfson was emerging from the same door as the countess had exited. "Bless my bones, we found him! Let's go see what he's been up to."

Waving, she attempted to catch his attention, but he hurried off in the opposite direction. Feeling as though her shopping bags had accumulated weight during her brief conversation with the countess, she scurried after him, Dalton by her side.

Her steps faltered when she regarded the office from which he'd appeared. "Real estate? Do you suppose he was buying more property? And where's his wife? How did he ditch Sandy when she must be suspicious about his investments?"

Clearly enjoying the puzzle, Vail gave her a lopsided grin. "Maybe Sandy convinced him to make a deal with the countess."

Marla shifted her burdens, ignoring a painful twinge in her shoulder. "You could be right. If I were his wife, and he pulled something like this behind my back, I wouldn't be too happy. She's entitled to share in his nest egg."

"So she might've demanded that he sell his property. Bob can't take the money back to the States, because he'd have a big tax liability. Speaking of which, where did he get the cash in the first place to make his land purchases?"

They exchanged stunned glances. "The bank on Grand Cayman Island," they said in unison.

"Typical route for money laundering," Vail cracked.

"Holy highlights, that could be what Helen meant. Somehow the head docent figured out Bob was siphoning funds from the museum. She's hot to trot for the guy and doesn't mind taking risks, meaning she'd flee to Mexico with him to enjoy his bounty. She must be figuring he's eager to leave his staid wife."

Glancing around to make sure they weren't being overheard, she stepped closer to an overhang to benefit from the shade. "And Brooklyn knew. Brooklyn told Kent that Bob had charged for kitchen items he'd never ordered."

"That's three people. But we're guessing. Let's go inside the office here and ask some questions."

Posing as a wealthy couple interested in investing in Mexico, they mentioned their association with Bob Wolfson to the dark-haired woman in a red suit who greeted them in Spanish, and then flawlessly switched to English after Marla spoke.

"Señor Wolfson is one of our regular customers," the lady said, while Marla stared at a mole on the woman's nose. "We count on his business every year at this time. What can I do for you? Are you interested in a villa, perhaps, in Guadalajara or Lake Chapala? More than fifty thousand Americans live there now, so you'd feel right at home."

"That's not quite what we had in mind." Marla offered a conspiratorial smile. She plopped her packages on an empty chair and felt her shoulders sag from relief. Rubbing her neck, she continued, "We understand Bob bought property in the mountains." Surely vanilla grew on fertile hillsides? Her guess relied on the countess's claim that she owned adjacent territory.

While the saleslady maintained a polite expression, her eyes chilled. "I'm so sorry; you must be misinformed."

"Countess Delacroix is our friend," Vail cut in, his tone hard-edged. "She claims her family owns estates in the area, and they were seeking to expand their vanilla-growing operation. Did Bob Wolfson accept her offer to sell?"

A lightbulb popped in Marla's head. "I told Bob he should give up his idea to build a resort and settle for a more intimate bed-and-breakfast instead. That would appeal much more to the tourist trade. It wouldn't require as much capital either. We're sort of interested in doing the same thing."

"Oh, I see. Then you might be interested in this plot of land over here." The woman walked to a display of terrain in a glass case. "Señor Wolfson just purchased this section with the proceeds from his sale to the countess. It is a prime location for a hacienda, as you see. And more than one lodging facility will bring in tourist dollars."

"It looks great. We'll have to think about it." Vail jerked his head, signaling they should go. They'd gotten the information they needed.

Marla hesitated. "If we should decide to buy, what kind of currency do you accept? I doubt that Señor Wolfson pays in traveler's checks." She chuckled as though that were a joke they shared.

The real estate agent folded her arms across her chest. "He brings cash, but you may do a wire transfer. Or you can speak to our investment department."

"That won't be necessary, thanks. We'll let you know." Vail shuffled Marla outside after the lady gave them a brochure.

"Hold on," Marla said as they reentered the world of traffic congestion, construction noise, and Spanish dialect. She veered toward the main avenue. "So you think Bob was embezzling money in his job as business manager? If so, what did that have to do with Alden Tusk's death?"

"The artist may have discovered Bob's crimes. Don't forget, Kent Harwood is on the case because somebody is substituting fake paintings for original artworks. Maybe Bob has been doing more than cooking the books. Maybe he's responsible for the museum thefts as well."

CHAPTER 20

"I can't believe how late it is," Marla said as they hurried back toward the ship.

"Time flies when you're having fun," Vail replied in a sardonic tone. He compressed his lips as though doing so would keep the fatigue dragging on his eyelids from spreading.

The crowd in downtown Cozumel had increased threefold as the day's tour excursions had emptied their occupants into the main shopping district. Marla wove her way through the throng, feeling as though her arms were being pulled from their sockets. Her bundles weighed heavier with each step. Vail carried his share with a stoic expression, but Marla could tell from the set of his shoulders that he was pushing it.

"Maybe we can still make afternoon tea on the ship," she said brightly. Food would revive them both, especially a cup of coffee with cookies and fruit.

"Look, there's Betsy," Vail said as they approached the street corner near Goodmark Jewelers.

The museum's public relations director stood watching the mariachi band. Betsy couldn't have been in town too long, because she hadn't bought anything. Straps from her swimsuit peeked out from under her scoop-necked shirt. Shorts and sandals completed her sporty attire.

"Hi, how's it going?" Marla greeted her. "How was the snorkeling expedition?"

Betsy's face became animated as she poked Marla in the ribs. "Hey, guys. You wouldn't believe the water here. It's so clear you can see straight to the bottom, and the fish are fantastic. I hated to leave." Her gaze focused on their packages. "Holy mackerel, you've been busy."

Marla grinned, ignoring Vail who stood by with his eyes narrowed as though alert for pickpockets. "Man, I am *way* over my budget. But who cares? I may never get here again."

"Never say never," Vail muttered.

She rounded on him. "Why? Would you go on another cruise?"

He shrugged, jostling the bags in his arms. "I suppose so. The ships leave right from our backyard, so it's no big deal to hop on one, and the food beats eating donuts every day. I'd hope for a more restful trip, though."

"*You*, rest? That'll be the day."

He raised an eyebrow. "I meant that I'd prefer to spend a week where no one is out to kill us."

"Oh . . . yeah."

Betsy mouthed something, but Marla couldn't hear her over a sudden blast of trumpets. "I'd like to pick up a CD of this music!" the brunette shouted, her eyes gleaming. "It makes me want to dance."

"Too bad you can't ask Oliver Smernoff. He's bought a disc of native music in every port."

"You're right. I thought he downloaded most of his tunes and went around with those iPod things in his ears so he wouldn't have to listen to Irene. Or maybe Olly listens to the CDs at home when he paints."

Marla's heart skipped a beat. "Oliver paints? I didn't realize he had artistic talent."

"Oh no? He used to be quite good and even taught art classes in the past. I don't know why he stopped, but obviously his interest in art led him to the museum." After stepping aside so a family of four could pass, Betsy leaned closer. "I'm just grateful Olly never had any contact with Alden when he practiced his instrument. Poor Alden couldn't stand to listen to anything orchestral, especially flute music."

Marla and Vail exchanged glances. "Oliver plays an instrument, *and* he paints?" Marla said slowly.

Betsy froze. "You don't think . . . ?"

"We have some questions to ask people," Vail stated. "Let's get back to the ship."

"I just got here," Betsy pointed out, "and I want to shop. You guys go ahead."

"Are you nuts? You shouldn't be here alone."

"I'm not a *shlemiel*, Marla. Thurston and Heidi are inside that jewelry shop. I'll tag along with them."

Relief washed over her. She wouldn't want anything to happen to Betsy this close to the end of their cruise.

"Okay, then we'll see you at dinner. Happy hunting!"

An hour later, Marla felt refreshed after dumping her bundles in the cabin, showering, and changing into black slacks and an amethyst knit top. Pleading fatigue, she remained in the cabin while Vail went topside for a snack.

He must have turned their radio on, because as

she laid down on the bed, closing her eyes, she heard soft music playing in the background. Her eyelids popped open. What had Vail meant when he'd said they had more questions to ask people? Was he thinking the same thing as her?

A sudden obsession to find the museum director gripped her mind. Leaving Vail a note that she'd gone to locate Oliver, she decided to try his stateroom first. Remembering the tale of a honeymooner who'd vanished from his balcony cabin, with bloodstains left behind, she vowed not to enter unless Oliver's wife was present. It was too easy to toss a body overboard with no one the wiser.

When no response came to her knock on the Smernoffs' door, she trod down the hallway toward the midship elevators. She'd look for Dalton, and they could proceed together.

The elevators were held up by people returning from Cozu-mel, so she forced herself to climb to deck eleven. Every couple of landings, she stopped to catch her breath. Her legs didn't ache as much as at the beginning of the cruise, but she seemed to get winded easier. Or maybe she was just tired after walking in port all day.

Admiring a Burmese sandstone carving of an eleventh-century deity in a glass case, Marla waited until her respiration slowed before gripping the banister again. A Cambodian bronze warrior kept her company at the next rest stop.

Unfortunately, her climb brought nothing but frustration, because she couldn't find Vail when she searched the throng at the buffet. Pushing her way outside, she propped her sunglasses on her nose while scanning the bodies at the pool area.

Her gaze zeroed in on Kent Harwood, who squatted on the edge of a chaise lounge facing Cliff Peters. Cliff lay back sunning himself, his muscular body greased like a wrestler's. He didn't seem in the least concerned about whatever Kent was saying, despite the angry expression on the inspector's face.

Deciding not to bother them, Marla passed through to the solarium and spa. Where had Dalton gone? Inspiration hit, and she hastened toward the teen center. He might be looking for Brianna.

Her search proved fruitless, even when she tried his parents' cabin, the promenade deck, and various lounges. Since they hadn't left port, the shops and casino were still closed. Thinking of all the hideaways on board, she detoured by the Pirate's Grotto, but her spirits fell when she found the disco deserted. Nor was her fiancé skulking about the photographer's gallery.

Don't tell me Dalton is missing now. Her heart pounding, she figured he'd have to turn up by dinnertime. Contemplating the other possibilities made her vision blur.

"Marla, come have a drink with me."

Whirling at the sound of Irene's voice, she caught sight of the elegant blonde in a quiet alcove by Mariner's Martini Bar, on the other side of the stairway.

"Have you seen Dalton?" she asked, approaching. Having a drink wasn't a bad idea. It might quell the panic blooming inside her. "I can't find him anywhere. I've looked all over the ship."

"That can be a good thing, darling. Sometimes we have more fun without the men." Irene's words were slightly slurred, undoubtedly due to the two empty glasses in front of her.

As Marla took a seat opposite the round table,

Irene waved at the waiter. Bracelets clinked on her arm, six white-gold chains sharing wrist space with her diamond watch. Although casual dress was the mode for that evening, Irene wore a pair of silver silk trousers and a beaded black top.

"What did you and Oliver do today?" Marla asked after the waiter took their orders. She wondered if they still served drinks when passengers got too tipsy. "We went into town for shopping. I bought these earrings." Lifting her hair, Marla showed off her new purchase.

"You can never lose with jewelry." Irene tried to smile, but with her frozen facial muscles, she only managed a grimace. "Olly and I went to the Mexican folkloric performance. It was colorful albeit rather standard."

"Was that your choice, or his?"

Irene switched her gaze to the floor-to-ceiling window. "You know how Olly likes his music."

"That's true. Did he ever play an instrument, Irene?"

Irene didn't answer until the waiter delivered their beverages. She'd ordered her third martini while Marla got a Caribbean Cooler. Taking a sip, she smacked her lips. She needed the energy from the fruit juice.

"Olly is obsessed with the arts in general," Irene said, swirling the liquid in her glass. "If he'd been a better instrumentalist, he might have joined an orchestra. As for painting, he got as far as teaching novices but was never good enough for the galleries. Mediocre, that's his middle name." From her sour expression, she meant that across the board.

"What does he play?" Marla asked in a conversational tone. "Maybe he'd like to join the passenger talent show."

"Hell no." Irene gulped down a large swallow. Her

hand shook as she replaced the glass on the tabletop. "He plays his flute in private."

Marla couldn't help the gasp that escaped her lips.

"Oops," Irene hiccuped. "I'm not supposed to tell anyone."

"Why is that, Irene? Is he shy about it?"

Irene gave her a searing look that could boil water. "I don't believe so, darling. He has other reasons. But why in heaven shouldn't I tell you? You're not one of us."

While she waited for Irene to continue, Marla's mind raced with possibilities. According to Betsy, Alden Tusk had an aversion to hearing the flute. Martha, the gift shop manager, claimed she heard flute music immediately before Alden plunged over the balcony railing to his death. Just how were those facts related?

"Olly threatened to reveal our secret," Irene said in an increasingly slurred tone. "You won't rat on me, will you?"

"Of course not," Marla replied, wondering why Irene hadn't come forward during the police investigation. But how could she if her husband was involved? "I'm sorry, what secret is that?"

Ice rattled from the direction of the bar, and Marla glanced around to make sure they weren't being overheard. The lounge was beginning to fill with predinner passengers. She caught a whiff of lady's perfume, similar to her favorite, Obsession. Resisting the urge to crane her neck to search for Dalton's familiar face, she focused on Irene.

"Our daughter . . . she isn't his," Irene's voice grated. "Delaney is the result of my affair with Eric Rand."

Marla's brow wrinkled. "Your daughter? I wasn't aware you had a child."

"She's grown now and living on her own. The sad

truth, darling, is that my passion for Eric has never abated. Especially when Olly isn't . . . he doesn't . . . he's never been very attentive in our sex life."

Marla nearly jumped from her seat. "If you'll forgive me for asking, then why are you still together?"

"Olly needs my money. And I fear he'd break Delaney's heart if he told her. She adores her daddy and might turn against me. My baby is the only good thing in my life, Marla."

Marla, seeing the distress on Irene's face, reached across the table to pat the older woman's hand. "When the truth comes out, she might be glad Oliver isn't her father."

They locked gazes, and Marla saw that Irene understood what she meant. "Here, I'll show you some pictures," Irene said, with a misty smile. "I took these of Delaney when she visited us for Mother's Day."

After Marla made appreciative comments and Irene packed away the photos, Marla said, "I appreciate what you're doing for Dalton's dad. John said you're introducing him to the art world, and he's excited about participating in the various shows."

Irene gulped down the remnants of her drink. "His wife is holding him back."

"Kate may have a change of heart. Aren't you also helping them find a condo in Florida? I remember you said you worked in real estate."

"I like to keep my hand in it." Her expression sobered. "It's not that I need the income, but working gives me a sense of independence. Know what I mean?"

"Sure do." Marla pulled her key card from her purse.

Irene gestured. "Put that away, darling. It's my treat. You've made me feel a whole lot better."

"I'm glad," she said, half rising. "Now if you'll excuse me, I have to find my fiancé. And don't worry, Irene. Things will work out for you."

She headed for the staircase, deciding to check their cabin first to see if Vail had stopped by.

Vacancy met her disappointed glance. The efficient steward had already turned down their bed, leaving a towel twisted into a penguin shape, and chocolate mints on each pillow. She'd miss this service when she got home.

Sick to her stomach with worry, Marla wound her way through the ship's maze to John and Kate's stateroom. Hearing Brianna's excited voice from within, she felt a whoosh of relief. At least they'd returned to the ship safely.

Her ease didn't last long. Kate said they hadn't seen Vail either, but then they'd only just made it back after lingering in the shops outside by the pier.

"Do you want to come in, Marla? We're getting ready for dinner, but you can wait with us," Kate said in a kind tone. "I'd love to hear all about your day."

"Likewise, but I have to find Dalton. I thought he'd be in the Outrigger Café but I didn't see him." She bit her lower lip. When she did catch up to her betrothed, she hoped he would have answers to some of the questions that plagued them.

An increase in vibration told her the ship was getting under way. While people were occupied, she might be able to slip into the art gallery unnoticed. A burning desire to see Alden Tusk's center painting took hold of her; it might confirm her theories.

On the seventh deck, she slipped past the polished wooden door into the ornate foyer. Overhead, the crystal chandelier gleamed brightly, sparks of light flashing off its facets like the jewels she'd seen in town. The place was empty, so she tiptoed past paintings propped on easels and up the red carpeted stairway toward the gallery beyond.

Oddly enough, the upper doors weren't locked, which would have inhibited her progress but proved to be a lucky break instead. Why they weren't secured became evident soon after she entered the auction house. Someone had ripped paintings off walls, toppled easels, and left a side door ajar. She hadn't really studied the workrooms before, but now she saw they were set up for repairs, framing, and packing in preparation for shipping. She bet the auctioneer had an office there too.

Likely, the center triptych painting, if not locked away in the bowels of the ship, was inside one of those warrens.

A low moan drew her attention as she picked her way through the chairs and trashed canvases. Behind the podium, a floor-to-ceiling curtain provided a backdrop that wavered in the air-conditioning. Or else its motion was a result of the ship picking up speed. The vessel's rocking had increased, making her steps unsteady. Lurching from side to side, she berated herself for drinking the rum concoction too fast.

Shadows lurked in the depths beyond the lighting, but the moaning had come from the opposite side.

Hey, why are the lights on?

Because the miscreant who'd wrecked the place had been searching for something. Probably the same thing she wanted to see before it was exposed to the public in full detail.

The moaning repeated.

Her palms sweaty and her heart pounding, Marla called out in a soft voice, "Hello, who's there?"

"Help me," a man's voice croaked.

She stepped through the portal into the first workroom, but it wasn't until she wound her way past a floor strewn with tools, broken frames, glass shards, and nails that she saw the man stretched beyond. Eric Rand lay halfway into his office, blood oozing from a wound on his head. Bruises darkened his face, but he didn't appear to be mortally hurt.

"Where's your phone? I'll call Security," she said, stooping beside him.

"No." The word barely escaped his parched lips. "Take the painting. Hide it."

"But you're hurt. You need assistance." Gripping his cool hand, she scanned the room for a clean cloth. The gash on his temple still oozed and might need stitches.

His palm squeezed hers. "Do as I say. It's my only proof. B-behind the pickle . . ."

"What?" Was he hallucinating? His injury must be worse than it appeared.

She tried to yank her hand from his grip, but he held on. "Look behind the pickle . . . brightly colored scene, musicians playing." His expression, a pained grimace, suddenly brightened. "*Le Sacre du Printemps*. Should be labeled." And then his grasp went slack and his eyes clouded.

Feeling her throat constrict, Marla slid her fingers to his wrist, where his pulse, rapid but steady, reassured her that life still flowed through his veins. However, she knew from past experience that a concussion was nothing to dismiss.

The man needed a medic, but curiosity drove her to ponder what he'd meant. He'd mentioned a scene with musicians. Very well, then. This seemed important.

She rose from her stooped position. Obviously, she

wouldn't find the item in this room, which contained a standard desk and accoutrements. Nor did she see such a painting in any of the workrooms through which she strode. Aware that each minute was critical to Eric's need for medical treatment, she began a methodical search through the auction room.

She almost missed it, hanging on the wall. A colorful panorama of a dozen musicians playing various instruments. *Picot, the artist's name, you idiot, not pickle.*

Scraping a chair over to the spot, she stood on the seat cushion and removed the picture with a small measure of difficulty. Wasn't this a larger version of one of their free seriolithographs? Perhaps. She ventured a guess that Eric had purposefully enlarged one, then mounted and framed it to disguise what lay underneath.

Leaping from the chair, she carted the heavy picture to the first workroom. Using a box cutter from an open drawer, she slashed a line across the top and down one side of the brown paper sealing the rear. Gently peeling back the layer, she peered inside. Nothing lay hidden there. The reproduction appeared to be fastened to the frame.

But what if it wasn't the right picture?

Obtaining a different tool, she pried the nails loose and freed the Picot from its prison.

Behind it, a painting fell away, into her hands.

She recognized the parlor setting, muted tones, and artist's style without a doubt. Tusk's center portrait, the one she'd seen before only in a flash. Eric must have removed it from the original frame to hide it here until the final auction. A firefly in her stomach fluttered and sank.

Beside the figure of the small boy who sat on a stool painting a canvas was the man whose blurry features remained indistinguishable, but whose actions couldn't be denied.

But that wasn't the damning clue.

Marla's gaze drew inexorably to the shiny metal flute lying on a nearby table.

CHAPTER 21

"I'll take that, if you don't mind."

Marla spun at the sound of Oliver Smernoff's deep voice.

"I don't think so." Hoping she wouldn't damage the precious artwork, she cleared a space on the counter and carefully laid down the canvas.

"Give me the painting." Reaching toward her, the museum director took a step forward. His hulking figure filled the space like a grizzly bear, blocking her exit.

"In a minute," she said, stalling. "Tell me, are you responsible for hurting Eric?"

"He wouldn't tell me where he'd hidden Tusk's piece. I'm glad I waited around. You finished the job very nicely."

"I know why you want this painting so badly," she said in a taunting tone. "You're the man hovering over Alden." She'd left the box cutter in its drawer. If she could distract him, she might be able to grab the sharp implement and use it as a weapon.

His lip curled. "People couldn't tell it was me in the center panel unless they knew the significance of that flute. Martha heard me playing right before

Alden toppled over the balcony rail. That's why I paid someone to delay her in San Juan."

"Huh?"

His lip curled. "I figured if Martha missed the ship's sailing, she'd fly home. Then she couldn't clue in whoever had brought us on board."

"Everyone knew she'd reported hearing music that night."

"Yeah, but they discounted her statement. I didn't want her harping on it. Someone might add two and two together."

"So you paid some fellas on the island . . ."

"To make sure she didn't surface until the ship left port."

A surge of hope swept through Marla. "You mean Martha isn't dead? Where is she?"

"Who knows? I'll worry about her later." An unnatural gleam entered his eyes. "You're my concern right now. Too bad I couldn't lose you and your companions on Roatan. That driver was eager to take my money."

She edged sideways. "Why did you want to get rid of us? For the same reason?"

"That's right." He nodded, advancing another step. "You'd been asking too many questions, and who knew what Martha had told you. I tried to put you out of action in St. Maarten, but that plan backfired."

"How did you know I'd go inside the guavaberry emporium?"

"I paid a native fellow to tail you. How he disposed of you was up to him. He didn't look to be the reputable sort; that's why I approached the guy. I told him not to cause you any permanent damage, just to temporarily detain you."

"Oh joy. Thanks for that much." She supposed the

director possessed some scruples; otherwise, he wouldn't have cared about the outcome. Under the circumstances, she might never know if the proprietress at the bar had been involved. "Did you eliminate Brooklyn, too? He's been missing."

"That isn't my doing. Come on, Marla, quit rambling. Give me the painting so I don't have to hurt you."

"Brooklyn noticed how Bob Wolfson ordered kitchen supplies that he hadn't requested," she said quickly. "Your business manager doesn't have the best interests of the museum at heart. You might want to examine the books when you get home." *Assuming you keep your job and aren't in jail.*

"Tell me something I don't know," Oliver sneered, taking another step forward. "It just so happens that I'm fully aware of Bob's financial transactions."

She gaped at him. "So why haven't you said anything? I'd think it would take the heat off you."

"Bob saw the flute in my office. If I expose him, he'd rat on me. We're covering for each other."

Feeling the counter nudge her spine, Marla slid toward the drawer. "Bob's not the only one who knows you play the flute."

"Irene?" He gave a harsh laugh. "She won't talk, or I'll tell Delaney she isn't my daughter."

"Is that why you've done all this? You're jealous of Eric Rand? Has he always come between you and your wife?"

He gave her a look of pity. "You don't get it, do you? Alden's painting tells the story. He used to be my pupil when I taught art. I enjoyed music even then, and I'd play my flute for him before we began. Our sessions included more than just art lessons, Marla."

Horror gnawed at her stomach lining. "You abused

him, an innocent little boy? No wonder he hated hearing the flute. He associated it with your vile acts."

"Poor Alden developed a true phobia. Years went by, and he couldn't face his past. But the day came when he could express himself in his painting. And when he heard that I was about to initiate a children's art program at the museum, he feared that I might resume my previous tendencies."

"So he intended to use the fund-raiser to expose you?"

"Presumably. Alden had painted the figure blurry enough so my features wouldn't be distinguishable, but anyone who knew our history together and that I play the flute would question me. My reputation would be ruined. So I sent Alden a note. I offered to resign my position if he withdrew his triptych from the fund-raiser. We set a meeting to discuss it."

Comprehension dawned. "You met him upstairs at the museum while everyone else was outside setting up for the event."

"Correct. I maneuvered him close to the railing and then withdrew my flute from where I'd hidden it. Hearing the music caused him to back up in a fit of panic."

"To where you'd already loosened the railing supports?"

"Exactly. He tried to come at me when he realized I had no intention of keeping my end of the bargain. We struggled. He leaned against the rail, lost his balance. The screws gave way."

"And you tipped him over for the final touch."

His bared teeth gave her the affirmative answer. Noting his muscles tense, she offered one last attempt to delay him. "What about Helen? Why did you push her down the stairs?"

"I didn't hurt Helen. You won't be so lucky. Fortunately, disappearances on cruise ships happen all the time these days."

Marla saw movement from the corner of her eye. Eric Rand, conscious, was crawling in their direction.

She twisted and snatched the blade from the drawer. Before she could turn, Oliver grabbed her wrist in a painful vise. He squeezed hard, making her gasp in agony. Just as her fingers loosened, something smashed into Oliver's knees from behind.

Eric had lifted a broken chair and rammed the legs into her assailant. The effort exhausted his strength, and the auctioneer collapsed like a sand castle in a wave.

Oliver bent over, howling. Her respite didn't last long. With a triumphant cry, he scooped a hammer from the floor and straightened to his full height.

An evil leer on his face, he raised his hand for a killing blow. As his arm came down, she parried his thrust with her elbow. They wrestled while he pinned her against the counter with his body. If he got a good swing at her head with that hammer, it would be over.

"Marla," she heard Eric's voice rasp, "Alden's painting."

"What?" Did he mean for her to secure the artist's painting for safekeeping? He must be really out of it. Didn't the guy see what was going on?

It struck her what he meant at the same time as Oliver's palm hit a glancing blow to her temple.

She saw stars, and her pulse throbbed. Losing ground against Oliver's strength, she faltered. He lifted the hammer with another triumphant cry.

Damn you, I refuse to suffer another concussion. Once in my life was enough.

Twisting, she seized the wooden frame that she'd left on the counter and twirled around. *Crack*. A corner connected with Oliver's jaw, producing a satisfactory crunch.

Their eyes locked.

Oliver's gaze widened, and then he slid to the floor like a blob of paint.

Marla stood frozen, her breath coming in pants. Eventually, she had enough presence of mind to kick him to see if he responded. Thankfully, he didn't budge.

They all needed medical attention. And if she was quick enough, she could just make dinner.

Dalton's face showed a mixture of consternation and relief when she arrived at their dining table. He leapt from his seat, confronting her. "Where the hell have you been? I've been searching the ship high and low for you. If Mom hadn't said she'd seen you earlier, I would've called the FBI myself."

"I ran into our killer." Lifting her hair, she showed him the bruise on her temple.

"By God, who did that to you?"

"Holy mackerel, are you all right?" Betsy said, shoving her chair back and rising.

The Wolfsons and Starks stared at her in shock while Marla noted two empty seats at the table. Kent Harwood didn't react at all, swiping another roll when no one was looking.

"If I'd met you earlier," Vail said, "you wouldn't have had to face the brute alone. Who was it?"

"I wasn't alone. Eric Rand helped me."

"Against whom?" His face reddened, as though steam were about to shoot from his ears.

"Oliver. He's responsible for everything. Well, almost everything."

Betsy glanced at his empty seat. "Where is he?"

"In custody. I imagine Irene was too embarrassed to join us, although I have her to thank for clueing me in. She might be better off once she clears the air with her daughter."

"What daughter? Never mind, you'll tell me later," Vail said. "Meanwhile, Brie is worried about you. Go tell her you're okay. And I need to make a phone call. Be right back."

Marla wound her way through the crush of bustling waiters to his parents' table. Upon spotting her, Brianna knocked back her chair and rushed over.

"Marla!" the teen cried, hugging her.

"I'm fine," Marla said in a reassuring tone, patting the girl's shoulder. Moisture tipped her lashes. Before meeting Vail and his family, she hadn't been used to anyone except her own mother caring about her.

"We've all been so concerned," Kate remarked, plopping her napkin on the tablecloth. John gave a solemn nod in agreement.

"I discovered that Oliver was responsible for our problems in Roatan, among other things," Marla replied. "Let's meet after dinner, and I'll tell you all about it. I want to hear about Tulum also. In the meantime, please enjoy your meal. It's been a long day, and you're probably starved."

Back at her table, she regarded Dalton after placing her order. "So where were you this afternoon?"

Smiling, he winked at her. "You'll see in a minute or so. Pass the butter, please."

Too hungry to argue, she complied. Halfway through her salad course, she looked up to note two newcomers claiming the empty seats at their table.

"Brooklyn!" Marla exclaimed, catching sight of his familiar face. He grinned at her, a white slash in his dark complexion. Helen sat next to him in Irene's chair. Aside from her wrist in a removable cast, she looked comfortable in a pair of capris, sandals, and a knit top.

"Dalton called and said it was safe to come down," Helen said. "He'd come to my stateroom earlier when you were looking for him," she told Marla. "And he found Brooklyn there. We insisted that he fill us in on things, so he stayed a while to chat. Holy macaroni, I'd never have suspected Olly."

"Sorry to worry everyone," the café manager said, settling his bulk and flipping a napkin open onto his lap. "I've been hiding out in Helen's cabin." He gave Bob Wolfson a sheepish glance. "I thought it was you, man. Didn't want to take no chances and end up like Martha."

"Except Martha's all right," Helen babbled. "I received an e-mail from her that she'd made it home. Someone pulled the same trick on her as they did to you in St. Maarten," she told Marla. "Eventually she got free and found her way to the airport in San Juan."

"That's a relief." Thurston Stark had recovered his voice, although he sounded hoarser than normal. "We'll be looking for a new museum director now, even if Olly is only charged with assault and not murder."

"That's questionable," Marla said. She then shared Oliver's confession about how he'd abused Alden Tusk as a youth and how Alden had intended to prevent him from resuming his perversion via a proposed children's art program. She also told them that Oliver had lured Alden to his death at the fund-raiser, hoping to abscond with his triptych, but that someone else had beat him to it by stealing the critical center panel.

"I can't believe we had a pedophile on our staff," Thurston muttered.

"Is there actually such a thing as a phobia to flutes?" Heidi said in her girlish voice. Her neckline showed off a sparkling emerald necklace that matched the green in her dress.

"Yes, it's called aulophobia," Marla answered, leaning back so the busboy could remove her empty salad plate. "I asked the doctor in the medical center. Presumably Alden developed this fear because Oliver played the instrument prior to his abusive sessions. Flute music acted like a trigger for Alden's self-loathing and feelings of dread."

Falling silent to examine her food that had just arrived, she sniffed the sautéed onions and garlic accompanying the red snapper, pimiento rice, and baked plantains. A trio of musicians serenaded diners with Mexican music while the ship's photographer hopped from table to table plopping a large sombrero onto people's heads and snapping pictures.

Marla cringed when he approached their group, but waving him off had no effect. The guy was as persistent as a life-insurance salesman.

Kent Harwood, who'd been silent until then, finally spoke up after swallowing a mouthful. "Looks like the museum staff will have more than one vacancy."

The others glanced at him, startled. Without waiting for any further explanation, Bob Wolfson blurted out a confession. "You've got no proof that I'm responsible for the bookkeeping problems," he said, eyes narrowed behind his spectacles. "I've kept careful records."

"Ah, but you can count on Countess Delacroix to take up the slack in that regard," Kent said, his lips broadening in a slow smile.

"I don't understand," Kate commented to Marla the following night. "Where does the countess come into the story?" They sat outside on the aft terrace, overlooking the ship's wake that frothed in the moonlight. "By the way, Marla, I love what you did with my hair. My bridge pals at home will be envious."

Marla smiled proudly. That morning, she'd trimmed the layers on Kate's auburn hair, which had given it more lift. A balmy breeze teased wisps of bangs onto Kate's face. Marla felt a surge of affection for the older woman, whose generosity seemed boundless. They'd already packed for debarkation and left their suitcases out in the hall for pickup. Aside from a quick breakfast the next morning, they wouldn't see each other again for some time.

"I talked to the museum gang today to set things straight," she told Kate, along with Dalton and John, who occupied the other seats at their round table. Brianna had gone to a farewell party with her new friends. "Too bad Eric didn't make it to the final art auction this afternoon. He would have been proud to see Irene win the bid on Alden's triptych. Oliver's wife plans to donate the set to the museum for its permanent collection."

"You didn't answer Mom's question about the countess," Vail remarked. He leaned back, arms folded across his chest, legs spread wide. A sexy grin curved his sensuous mouth.

Marla's skin tingled. She knew what he wanted to do in their cabin on the last night of their cruise.

"Eric Rand engineered bringing everyone from the museum aboard," she explained, starting from the beginning. "He'd been convinced Alden's death wasn't an accident and felt he had been wrongly fired from his curator position. He spent the past few months collecting information on each person present in the museum on the day Alden died.

"He's the one who swiped the center triptych painting after the artist's death, having realized its significance. However, Eric couldn't identify the person molesting Alden, nor did he know who played the flute, even after Martha mentioned hearing the music. So he devised this scheme to flush out the killer. Using his connections at the cruise line, he bought the tickets and sent one to each person involved."

"Wait a minute," John said, drumming his fingers on his chair arm. "Where did he get the money?"

"From Irene. She wanted to learn the truth, even fearing her husband might be involved. Eric hired investigators to find out all he could about the people at the museum that day. He unearthed quite a few secrets."

"So Eric Rand wrote those notes found on everyone's door?" Kate said, wearing a puzzled frown.

"That's right. He hoped his message, 'I know what you did and I have what you want,' might spook the guilty person. Kent Harwood was aboard, not because of his role as an exterminator, but because he's an insurance investigator. He'd been sent to learn who was pilfering paintings at the museum and substituting fakes in their place."

"Thurston Stark," Vail contributed in a wry tone.

"Right." Marla nodded. "The foundation chair didn't want his wife to find out he was living above his means. He worked in collusion with Cliff Peters, the security guard, but what Thurston didn't know was that Heidi was having an affair with Cliff in order to assist him. She was just as interested in maintaining their status quo, so she seduced the guard to secure his cooperation."

"Kent told you this?" Vail raised an eyebrow.

She nodded. "Cliff confessed to Kent after the investigator put the heat on him. Both Thurston and Cliff will be met by the authorities tomorrow morning, same as Oliver and Bob Wolfson."

Kate sat up straight. "Yeah, what's Bob's role? And you still didn't explain where the countess fits in."

"Bob, the museum's business manager, has been embezzling funds for years. He wired the money to his bank in the Cayman Islands, withdrew cash during his yearly cruise, and bought property in Mexico. Helen Bryce caught on to his scheme and offered to run away with him. Sandy, who couldn't help noticing Helen's attentiveness toward her husband, got jealous and 'accidentally' shoved Helen down the stairs."

"Oh my," Kate exclaimed, clamping a hand to her mouth.

"Countess Delacroix met Eric Rand when he was curator at the museum. He used to go on European trips to meet art collectors and donors. Or maybe she made it her purpose to meet him to get at Bob Wolfson," Marla continued with a weary sigh.

"The countess wanted to buy Bob's property," Vail elaborated. He rolled his eyes at Marla, as though imploring her to finish. Now that the crisis was over, he wanted to enjoy their remaining free time.

I'm trying, she mouthed back. "Anyway, the countess encouraged Eric to seek the truth about Alden's death. If he implicated Bob, she'd offer to buy Bob's real estate in exchange for attorney fees. As it turned out, Bob was guilty of embezzlement, not murder. He and the countess reached a deal in Cozumel, and she left."

"What about the rest of the people in Eric's message?" John inquired with a note of mild curiosity.

"He'd bought Helen's life insurance policy. He'll give it back, along with the watch owned by Betsy's father that he picked up at a pawn shop. Eric just needed leverage to use on people if necessary."

The auctioneer had gotten what he'd wanted: justice for Alden Tusk and restoration of his honor as curator.

Marla had never found any of Tusk's ballet portraits on board, but she intended to track them down from her home computer. No matter—she'd gotten several free pictures that would look good on the walls of their new home, as well as remind them of their first cruise together as a family.

"Here comes Brie," Vail called, then stood to greet his daughter. "How was the party?"

Brianna glanced at him with doleful eyes that glistened in reflected light from the globes situated around the deck.

"It's hard to say good-bye to people. Some of them live across the country."

"You got everyone's e-mail address, right?" Marla said, rising to give her an affectionate hug.

"Yeah, but I'll miss my friends. What's going on with you guys?"

"Have a seat." Vail yanked a chair over for her. "We've been saving the best news for last." He nodded at Marla. "You tell them."

Three pairs of eyes swung in her direction.

"Dalton and I have decided on a wedding date," she announced.

"Awesome," Brianna yelled.

"At last," John droned. "Now Kate can stop nagging."

"I'm so excited," Kate said, beaming. "when is the joyous event?"

Marla watched sparkles of moonlight gleam on the waves like the diamond on her hand. "The eighth of December. The weather is usually good in South Florida that month. We don't want to get too close to the holidays, though."

"That's marvelous. John and I definitely have to rent a place so we can help you make plans."

Marla smiled at her. "I must say that I am eager to join your family. You've made me feel so welcome. I love you all."

Vail reached over and squeezed her hand, while her heart swelled with affection. This trip has served its purpose. She'd grown closer to her soon-to-be family, and now she had many happy experiences ahead: marriage, a new house and expanded salon.

Their cruise might be over, but her next voyage had just begun.

AUTHOR'S NOTE

Ever have a bad hair day? Trade your blow-dryer and comb for a spatula and spoon, and try these recipes to lift your mood. Light a coconut-scented candle, play a Caribbean music CD, and imagine yourself sailing to the tropics with Marla in *Killer Knots*.

I love to hear from readers. Please write to me at: P.O. Box 17756, Plantation, FL 33318 and enclose a self-addressed stamped business-size envelope for a personal reply and bookmark.

E-mail: nancy.j.cohen@comcast.net
Web site: www.nancyjcohen.com
Web log: http://mysterygal.bravejournal.com

If you want to learn more about Hair Raiser coffee, visit www.hairraisercoffee.com.

Caribbean Rice with Pigeon Peas

   2 cups long-grain rice
   13 ½ oz can coconut milk
   15 ½ oz can pigeon peas
   1 cup chopped green onion
   2 tbsp butter or margarine

Cook rice as directed in 4 cups liquid: coconut milk, juice from peas, and water as needed. When liquid is

absorbed, mix in green onion, pigeon peas, and butter or margarine. Add salt to taste.
Serves 8.

Island Turkey Thighs

1 cup each chopped onions, celery, carrots
⅓ cup ketchup
½ tsp paprika
1 tsp salt
4 lbs turkey thighs
1 large oven bag
1 tbsp flour
⅓ cup dry white wine
½ cup low-sodium chicken broth
2 bay leaves

In bowl, combine vegetables, ketchup, salt, and paprika. Place flour in oven bag; shake to coat. Rinse and pat dry turkey thighs; then place in bag. Put in 13 x 9 baking dish. Sprinkle vegetable mixture over turkey in bag; then pour in wine and broth. Add bay leaves and seal bag. Cut slits in top. Bake at 350° for 1 ½ hours. Serves 8.

Apple Ginger Cake

⅔ cup light brown sugar

⅓ cup applesauce

1 large egg

3 tbsp molasses

1 ½ cups all-purpose flour

½ cup low-fat vanilla yogurt

1 Gala apple, peeled, cored
   and chopped

1 tsp baking powder

1 tsp baking soda

1 tsp cinnamon

2 tsp ground ginger

¼ tsp nutmeg

⅛ tsp allspice

Coat 8-inch baking pan with cooking spray. In bowl, combine brown sugar, applesauce, egg, and molasses. In separate bowl, mix flour, baking powder, baking soda, and spices. Add dry ingredients to molasses mixture alternately with yogurt, beating until well blended. Fold in apples. Bake at 350° for 30 minutes. Cut into squares when cool. For extra zing, sprinkle 1 tsp of light rum onto individual portions and top with Cool Whip.